A BLOOD BET

Black Jack Hollis had been killed as Elizabeth Cornish watched. Recklessly, joyously, his black hair flying, Jack had ridden into town to see his infant son. Then a shotgun, fired from a window, had blasted him from his horse and flung him to his death in the street.

"I want his baby. Go out and get that baby for me, Vance," the spinster Elizabeth ordered.

"My dear," her brother Vance declared, "before that baby is twenty-five—that was his father's age—he'll have shot a man. . . . Blood will out, like murder, sis. . . . Bet you on it!"

Books by Max Brand

Published by POCKET BOOKS

MAX BRAND

BLACK JACK

PUBLISHED BY POCKET BOOKS NEW YORK

POCKET BOOKS, a division of Simon & Schuster, Inc.
1230 Avenue of the Americas, New York, N.Y. 10020

Copyright 1921, 1922 by Popular Publications, Inc.;
copyright renewed 1949, 1950 by Dorothy Faust

Published by arrangement with Dodd, Mead & Company, Inc.
Library of Congress Catalog Card Number: 77-123498

ISBN: 0-671-41575-1

First Pocket Books printing July, 1972

10 9 8 7 6 5 4

POCKET and colophon are registered trademarks
of Simon & Schuster, Inc.

Printed in the U.S.A.

BLACK JACK

CHAPTER 1

IT WAS characteristic of the two that when the uproar broke out Vance Cornish raised his eyes, but went on lighting his pipe. Then his sister Elizabeth ran to the window with a swish of skirts around her long legs. After the first shot there was a lull. The little cattle town was as peaceful as ever with its storm-shaken houses staggering away down the street.

A boy was stirring up the dust of the street, enjoying its heat with his bare toes, and the same old man was bunched in his chair in front of the store. During the two days Elizabeth had been in town on her cattle-buying trip, she had never see him alter his position. But she was accustomed to the West, and this advent of sleep in the town did not satisfy her. A drowsy town, like a drowsy-looking cow-puncher, might be capable of unexpected things.

"Vance," she said, "there's trouble starting."

"Somebody shooting at a target," he answered.

As if to mock him, he had no sooner spoken than a dozen voices yelled down the street in a wailing chorus cut short by the rapid chattering of revolvers. Vance ran to the window. Just below the hotel the street made an elbow-turn for no particular reason except that the original cattle-trail had made exactly the same turn before Garrison City was built. Toward the corner ran the hubbub at the pace of a running horse. Shouts, shrill, trailing curses, and the muffled beat of hoofs in the dust. A rider plunged into view now, his horse leaning far in to take the sharp angle, and the dust skidding out and away from his sliding hoofs. The rider gave easily and gracefully to the wrench of his mount.

And he seemed to have a perfect trust in his horse, for he rode with the reins hanging over the horns of his saddle. His hands were occupied by a pair of revolvers, and he was turned in the saddle.

The head of the pursuing crowd lurched around the elbow-

1

turn; fire spat twice from the mouth of each gun. Two men dropped, one rolling over and over in the dust, and the other sitting down and clasping his leg in a ludicrous fashion. But the crowd was checked and fell back.

By this time the racing horse of the fugitive had carried him close to the hotel, and now he faced the front, a handsome fellow with long black hair blowing about his face. He wore a black silk shirt which accentuated the pallor of his face and the flaring crimson of his bandanna. And he laughed joyously, and the watchers from the hotel window heard him call: "Got it, Mary. Feed 'em dust, girl!"

The pursuers had apparently realized that it was useless to chase. Another gust of revolver shots barked from the turning of the street, and among them a different and more sinister sound like the striking of two great hammers face on face, so that there was a cold ring of metal after the explosion— at least one man had brought a rifle to bear. Now, as the wild rider darted past the hotel, his hat was jerked from his head by an invisible hand. He whirled again in the saddle and his guns raised. As he turned, Elizabeth Cornish saw something glint across the street. It was the gleam of light on the barrel of a rifle that was thrust out through the window of the store.

That long line of light wobbled, steadied, and fire jetted from the mouth of the gun. The black-haired rider spilled sidewise out of the saddle; his feet came clear of the stirrups, and his right leg caught on the cantle. He was flung rolling in the dust, his arms flying weirdly. The rifle disappeared from the window and a boy's set face looked out. But before the limp body of the fugitive had stopped rolling, Elizabeth Cornish dropped into a chair, sick of face. Her brother turned his back on the mob that closed over the dead man and looked at Elizabeth in alarm.

It was not the first time he had seen the result of a gun-play, and for that matter it was not the first time for Elizabeth. Her emotion upset him more than the roar of a hundred guns. He managed to bring her a glass of water, but she brushed it away so that half of the contents spilled on the red carpet of the room.

"He isn't dead, Vance. He isn't dead!" she kept saying.

"Dead before he left the saddle," replied Vance, with his usual calm. "And if the bullet hadn't finished him, the fall would have broken his neck. But—what in the world! Did you know the fellow?"

He blinked at her, his amazement growing. The capable hands of Elizabeth were pressed to her breast, and out of the thirty-five years of spinsterhood which had starved her face he became aware of eyes young and dark, and full of spirit; by no means the keen, quiet eyes of Elizabeth Cornish.

"Do something," she cried. "Go down, and—if they've murdered him—"

He literally fled from the room.

All the time she was seeing nothing, but she would never forget what she had seen, no matter how long she lived. Subconsciously she was fighting to keep the street voices out of her mind. They were saying things she did not wish to hear, things she would not hear. Finally, she recovered enough to stand up and shut the window. That brought her a terrible temptation to look down into the mass of men in the street—and women, too!

But she resisted and looked up. The forms of the street remained obscurely in the bottom of her vision, and made her think of something she had seen in the woods—a colony of ants around a dead beetle. Presently the door opened and Vance came back. He still seemed very worried, but she forced herself to smile at him, and at once his concern disappeared; it was plain that he had been troubled about her and not in the slightest by the fate of the strange rider. She kept on smiling, but for the first time in her life she really looked at Vance without sisterly prejudice in his favor. She saw a good-natured face, handsome, with the cheeks growing a bit blocky, though Vance was only twenty-five. He had a glorious forehead and fine eyes, but one would never look twice at Vance in a crowd. She knew suddenly that her brother was simply a well-mannered mediocrity.

"Thank the Lord you're yourself again, Elizabeth," her brother said first of all. "I thought for a moment—I don't know what!"

"Just the shock, Vance," she said. Ordinarily she was well-nigh brutally frank. Now she found it easy to lie and keep on smiling. "It was such a horrible thing to see!"

"I suppose so. Caught you off balance. But I never knew you to lose your grip so easily. Well, do you know what you've seen?"

"He's dead, then?"

He looked sharply at her. It seemed to him that a tremor of unevenness had come into her voice.

"Oh, dead as a doornail, Elizabeth. Very neat shot. Youngster that dropped him; boy named Joe Minter. Six thousand dollars for Joe. Nice little nest egg to build a fortune on, eh?"

"Six thousand dollars! What do you mean, Vance?"

"The price on the head of Jack Hollis. That was Hollis, sis. The celebrated Black Jack."

"But—this is only a boy, Vance. He couldn't have been more than twenty-five years old."

"That's all."

"But I've heard of him for ten years, very nearly. And always as a man-killer. It can't be Black Jack."

"I said the same thing, but it's Black Jack, well enough. He started out when he was sixteen, they say, and he's been raising the devil ever since. You should have seen them pick him up—as if he were asleep, and not dead. What a body! Lithe as a panther. No larger than I am, but they say he was a giant with his hands."

He was lighting his cigarette as he said this, and consequently he did not see her eyes close tightly. A moment later she was able to make her expression as calm as ever.

"Came into town to see his baby," went on Vance through the smoke. "Little year-old beggar!"

"Think of the mother," murmured Elizabeth Cornish. "I want to do something for her."

"You can't," replied her brother, with unnecessary brutality. "Because she's dead. A little after the youngster was born. I believe Black Jack broke her heart, and a very pleasant sort of girl she was, they tell me."

"What will become of the baby?"

"It will live and grow up," he said carelessly. "They always do, somehow. Make another like his father, I suppose. A few years of fame in the mountain saloons, and then a knife in the back."

The meager body of Elizabeth stiffened. She was finding it less easy to maintain her nonchalant smile.

"Why?"

"Why? Blood will out, like murder, sis."

"Nonsense! All a matter of environment."

"Have you ever read the story of the Jukes family?"

"An accident. Take a son out of the best family in the world and raise him like a thief—he'll be a thief. And the thief's son can be raised to an honest manhood. I know it!"

She was seeing Black Jack, as he had raced down the street with the black hair blowing about his face. Of such stuff, she felt, the knights of another age had been made. Vance was raising a forefinger in an authoritative way he had.

"My dear, before that baby is twenty-five—that was his father's age—he'll have shot a man. Bet you on it!"

"I'll take your bet!"

The retort came with such a ring of her voice that he was startled. Before he could recover, she went on: "Go out and get that baby for me, Vance. I want it."

He tossed his cigarette out of the window.

"Don't drop into one of your headstrong moods, sis. This is nonsense."

"That's why I want to do it. I'm tired of playing the man. I've had enough to fill my mind. I want something to fill my arms and my heart."

She drew up her hands with a peculiar gesture toward her shallow, barren bosom, and then her brother found himself silenced. At the same time he was a little irritated, for there was an imputation in her speech that she had been carrying the burden which his own shoulders should have supported. Which was so true that he could not answer, and therefore he cast about for some way of stinging her.

"I thought you were going to escape the sentimental period, Elizabeth. But sooner or later I suppose a woman has to pass through it."

A spot of color came in her sallow cheek.

"That's sufficiently disagreeable, Vance."

A sense of his cowardice made him rise to conceal his confusion.

"I'm going to take you at your word, sis. I'm going out to get that baby. I suppose it can be bought—like a calf!"

He went deliberately to the door and laid his hand on the knob. He had a rather vicious pleasure in calling her bluff, but to his amazement she did not call him back. He opened the door slowly. Still she did not speak. He slammed it behind him and stepped into the hall.

CHAPTER 2

TWENTY-FOUR YEARS made the face of Vance Cornish a little better-fed, a little more blocky of cheek, but he remained astonishingly young. At forty-nine the lumpish promise of his youth was quite gone. He was in a trim and solid middle age. His hair was thinned above the forehead, but it gave him more dignity. On the whole, he left an impression of a man who has done things and who will do more before he is through.

He shifted his feet from the top of the porch railing and shrugged himself deeper into his chair. It was marvelous how comfortable Vance could make himself. He had one great power—the ability to sit still through any given interval. Now he let his eye drift quietly over the Cornish ranch. It lay entirely within one grasp of the vision, spilling across the valley from Sleep Mountain, on the lower bosom of which the house stood, to Mount Discovery on the north. Not that the glance of Vance Cornish lurched across this bold distance. His gaze wandered as slowly as a bee buzzes across a clover field, not knowing on which blossom to settle.

Below him, generously looped, Bear Creek tumbled out of the southeast, and roved between noble borders of silver spruce into the shadows of the Blue Mountains of the north and west. Here the valley shouldered out on either side into Sleep Mountain on the south and the Blue Mountains on the north, half a dozen miles across and ten long of grazing and farm land, rich, loamy bottom land scattered with aspens.

Beyond, covering the gentle roll of the foothills, was grazing land. Scattering lodgepole pine began in the hills, and thickened into dense yellow-green thickets on the upper mountain slopes. And so north and north the eye of Vance Cornish wandered and climbed until it rested on the bald summit of Mount Discovery. It had its name out of its character, standing boldly to the south out of the jumble of the Blue Mountains.

It was a solid unit, this Cornish ranch, fenced away with mountains, watered by a river, pleasantly forested, and obviously predestined for the ownership of one man. Vance Cornish, on the porch of the house, felt like an enthroned king overlooking his dominions. As a matter of fact, his holdings were hardly more than nominal.

In the beginning his father had left the ranch equally to Vance and Elizabeth, thickly plastered with debts. The son would have sold the place for what they could clear. He went East to hunt for education and pleasure; his sister remained and fought the great battle by herself. She consecrated herself to the work, which implied that the work was sacred. And to her, indeed, it was.

She was twenty-two and her brother twelve when their father died. Had she been a tithe younger and her brother a mature man, it would have been different. As it was, she felt herself placed in a maternal position with Vance. She sent him away to school, rolled up her sleeves and started to order chaos. In place of husband, children—love and the fruits of love—she accepted the ranch. The dam between the rapids and the waterfall was the child of her brain; the plowed fields of the central part of the valley were her reward.

In ten years of constant struggle she cleared away the debts. And then, since Vance gave her nothing but bills to pay, she began to buy out his interest. He chose to learn his business lessons on Wall Street. Elizabeth paid the bills, but she checked the sums against his interest in the ranch. And so it went on. Vance would come out to the ranch at intervals and show a brief, feverish interest, plan a new set of irrigation canals, or a sawmill, or a better road out over the Blue Mountains. But he dropped such work half-done and went away.

Elizabeth said nothing. She kept on paying his bills, and she kept on cutting down his interest in the old Cornish ranch, until at the present time he had only a finger-tip hold. Root and branch, the valley and all that was in it belonged to Elizabeth Cornish. She was proud of her possession, though she seldom talked of her pride. Nevertheless, Vance knew, and smiled. It was amusing, because, after all, what she had done and, all her work, would revert to him at her death. Until that time, why should he care in whose name the ranch remained so long as his bills were paid? He had not worked, but in recompense he had remained young. Elizabeth had labored all her youth away. At forty-nine he was ready to begin the most important part of his career. At sixty his sister was a withered old ghost of a woman.

He fell into a pleasant reverie. When Elizabeth died, he would set in some tennis courts beside the house, buy some blooded horses, cut the road wide and deep to let the world come up Bear Creek Valley, and retire to the life of a country gentleman.

His sister's voice cut into his musing. She had two tones. One might be called her social register. It was smooth, gentle —the low-pitched and controlled voice of a gentlewoman. The other voice was hard and sharp. It could drive hard and cold across a desk, and bring businessmen to an understanding that here was a mind, not a woman.

At present she used her latter tone. Vance Cornish came into a shivering consciousness that she was sitting beside him. He turned his head slowly. It was always a shock to come out of one of his pleasant dreams and see that worn, hollow-eyed, impatient face.

"Are you forty-nine, Vance?"

"I'm not fifty, at least," he countered.

She remained imperturbable, looking him over. He had come to notice that in the past half-dozen years his best smiles often failed to mellow her expression. He felt that something disagreeable was coming.

"Why did Cornwall run away this morning? I hoped to take him on a trip."

"He had business to do."

His diversion had been a distinct failure, and had been turned against him. For she went on: "Which leads to what I have to say. You're going back to New York in a few days, I suppose?"

"No, my dear. I haven't been across the water for two years."

"Paris?"

"Brussels. A little less grace; a little more spirit."

"Which means money."

"A few thousand only. I'll be back by fall."

"Do you know that you'll have to mortgage your future for that money, Vance?"

He blinked at her, but maintained his smile under fire courageously.

"Come, come! Things are booming. You told me yesterday what you'd clean up on the last bunch of Herefords."

When she folded her hands, she was most dangerous, he knew. And now the bony fingers linked and she shrugged the shawl more closely around her shoulders.

"We're partners, aren't we?" smiled Vance.

"Partners, yes. You have one share and I have a thousand. But—you don't want to sell out your final claim, I suppose?"

His smile froze. "Eh?"

"If you want to get those few thousands, Vance, you have nothing to put up for them except your last shreds of property. That's why I say you'll have to mortgage your future for money from now on."

"But—how does it all come about?"

"I've warned you. I've been warning you for twenty-five years, Vance."

Once again he attempted to turn her. He always had the impression that if he became serious, deadly serious for ten consecutive minutes with his sister, he would be ruined. He kept on with his semi-jovial tone.

"There are two arts, Elizabeth. One is making money and the other is spending it. You've mastered one and I've mastered the other. Which balances things, don't you think?"

She did not melt; he waved down to the farm land.

"Watch that wave of wind, Elizabeth."

A gust struck the scattering of aspens, and turned up the silver of the dark green leaves. The breeze rolled across the trees in a long, rippling flash of light. But Elizabeth did not look down. Her glance was fixed on the changeless snow of Mount Discovery's summit.

"As long as you have something to spend, spending is a very important art, Vance. But when the purse is empty, it's a bit useless, it seems to me."

"Well, then, I'll have to mortgage my future. As a matter of fact, I suppose I could borrow what I want on my prospects."

A veritable Indian yell, instantly taken up and prolonged by a chorus of similar shouts, cut off the last of his words.

Round the corner of the house shot a blood-bay stallion, red as the red of iron under the blacksmith's hammer, with a long, black tail snapping and flaunting behind him, his ears flattened, his beautiful vicious head outstretched in an effort to tug the reins out of the hands of the rider. Failing in that effort, he leaped into the air like a steeplechaser and pitched down upon stiffened forelegs.

The shock rippled through the body of the rider and came to his head with a snap that jerked his chin down against his breast. The stallion rocked back on his hind legs, whirled, and then flung himself deliberately on his back. A sufficiently cunning maneuver—first stunning the enemy with a blow and then crushing him before his senses returned. But he landed on nothing save hard gravel. The rider had whipped out of the saddle and stood poised, strong as the trunk of a silver spruce.

The fighting horse, a little shaken by the impact of his fall, nevertheless whirled with catlike agility to his feet—a beautiful thing to watch. As he brought his forequarters off the earth, he lunged at the rider with open mouth. A sidestep that would have done credit to a pugilist sent the youngster swerving past that danger. He leaped to the saddle at the same time that the blood-bay came to his four feet.

The chorus in full cry was around the horse, four or five excited cow-punchers waving their sombreros and yelling for horse or rider, according to the gallantry of the fight.

The bay was in the air more than he was on the ground, eleven or twelve hundred pounds of might, writhing, snapping, bolting, halting, sunfishing with devilish cunning, dropping out of the air on one stiff foreleg with an accompanying sway to one side that gave the rider the effect of a cudgel blow at the back of the head and then a whip-snap to part the vertebrae. Whirling on his hind legs, and again flinging himself desperately on the ground, only to fail, come to his feet with the clinging burden once more maddeningly in place, and go again through a maze of fence-rowing and sunfishing until suddenly he straightened out and bolted down the slope like a runaway locomotive on a downgrade. A terrifying spectacle, but the rider sat erect, with one arm raised high above his head in triumph, and his yell trailing off behind him. From a running gait the stallion fell into a smooth pace—a true wild pacer, his hoofs beating the ground with the force and speed of pistons and hurling himself forward with incredible strides. Horse and rider lurched out of sight among the silver spruce.

"By the Lord, wonderful!" cried Vance Cornish.

He heard a stifled cry beside him, a cry of infinite pain. "Is—is it over?"

And there sat Elizabeth the Indomitable with her face buried in her hands like a girl of sixteen!

"Of course it's over," said Vance, wondering profoundly. She seemed to dread to look up. "And—Terence?"

"He's all right. Ever hear of a horse that could get that young wildcat out of the saddle? He clings as if he had claws. But—where did he get that red devil?"

"Terence ran him down—in the mountains—somewhere," she answered, speaking as one who had only half heard the question. "Two months of constant trailing to do it, I think. But oh, you're right! The horse is a devil! And sometimes I think—"

She stopped, shuddering. Vance had returned to the ranch only the day before after a long absence. More and more, after he had been away, he found it difficult to get in touch with things on the ranch. Once he had been a necessary part of the inner life. Now he was on the outside. Terence and Elizabeth were a perfectly completed circle in themselves.

CHAPTER 3

"IF TERRY worries you like this," suggested her brother kindly, "why don't you forbid these pranks?"

She looked at him as if in surprise.

"Forbid Terry?" she echoed, and then smiled. Decidedly this was her first tone, a soft tone that came from deep in her throat. Instinctively Vance contrasted it with the way she had spoken to him. But it was always this way when Terry was mentioned. For the first time he saw it clearly. It was amazing how blind he had been. "Forbid Terence? Vance, that devil of a horse is part of his life. He was on a hunting trip when he saw Le Sangre—"

"Good Lord, did they call the horse that?"

"A French-Canadian was the first to discover him, and he gave the name. And he's the color of blood, really. Well, Terence saw Le Sangre on a hilltop against the sky. And he literally went mad. Actually, he struck out on foot with his rifle and lived in the country and never stopped walking until he wore down Le Sangre somehow and brought him back hobbled—just skin and bones, and Terence not much more. Now Le Sangre is himself again, and he and Terence have a fight—like that—every day. I dream about it; the most horrible nightmares!"

"And you don't stop it?"

"My dear Vance, how little you know Terence! You couldn't tear that horse out of his life without breaking his heart. I *know!*"

"So you suffer, day by day?"

"I've done very little else all my life," said Elizabeth gravely. "And I've learned to bear pain."

He swallowed. Also, he was beginning to grow irritated. He had never before had a talk with Elizabeth that contained so many reefs that threatened shipwreck. He returned to the gist of their conversation rather too bluntly.

"But to continue, Elizabeth, any banker would lend me money on my prospects."

"You mean the property which will come to you when I die?"

He used all his power, but he could not meet her glance. "You know that's a nasty way to put it, Elizabeth."

"Dear Vance," she sighed, "a great many people say that I'm a hard woman. I suppose I am. And I like to look facts squarely in the face. Your prospects begin with my death, of course."

He had no answer, but bit his lip nervously and wished the ordeal would come to an end.

"Vance," she went on, "I'm glad to have this talk with you. It's something you have to know. Of course I'll see that during my life or my death you'll be provided for. But as for your main prospects, do you know where they are?"

"Well?"

She was needlessly brutal about it, but she had told him, her education had been one of pain.

"Your prospects are down there by the river on the back of Le Sangre."

Vance Cornish gasped.

"I'll show you what I mean, Vance. Come along."

The moment she rose, some of her age fell from her. Her carriage was erect. Her step was still full of spring and decision, as she led the way into the house. It was a big, solid, two-story building which the mightiest wind could not shake. Henry Cornish had merely founded the house, just as he had founded the ranch; the main portion of the work had been done by his daughter. And as they passed through, her stern old eye rested peacefully on the deep, shadowy vistas, and her foot fell with just pride on the splendid rising sweep of the staircase. They passed into the roomy vault of the upper hall and went down to the end. She took out a big key from her pocket and fitted it into the lock; then Vance dropped his hand on her arm. His voice lowered.

"You've made a mistake, Elizabeth. This is Father's room."

Ever since his death it had been kept unchanged, and practically unentered save for an occasional rare day of work to keep it in order. Now she nodded and resolutely turned the key and swung the door open. Vance went in with an exclamation of wonder. It was quite changed from the solemn old room and the brown, varnished woodwork which he remembered. Cream-tinted paint now made the walls cool and fresh. The solemn engravings no longer hung above the bookcases. And the bookcases themselves had been replaced with built-in shelves pleasantly filled with rich bindings, black and red and deep yellow-browns. A tall cabinet stood open at one side filled with rifles and shotguns of every description, and another cabinet was loaded with fishing apparatus. The stiff-backed chairs had given place to comfortable monsters of easy lines. Vance Cornish, as one in a dream, peered here and there.

"God bless us!" he kept repeating. "God bless us! But where's there a trace of Father?"

"I left it out," said Elizabeth huskily, "because this room is meant for—but let's go back. Do you remember that day twenty-four years ago when we took Jack Hollis's baby?"

"When *you* took it," he corrected. "I disclaim all share in the idea."

"Thank you," she answered proudly. "At any rate, I took the boy and called him Terence Colby."

"Why that name," muttered Vance, "I never could understand."

"Haven't I told you? No, and I hardly know whether to trust even you with the secret, Vance. But you remember we argued about it, and you said that blood would out; that the boy would turn out wrong; that before he was twenty-five he would have shot a man?"

"I believe the talk ran like that."

"Well, Vance, I started out with a theory; but the moment I had that baby in my arms, it became a matter of theory, plus, and chiefly plus. I kept remembering what you had said, and I was afraid. That was why I worked up the Colby idea."

"That's easy to see."

"It wasn't so easy to do. But I heard of the last of an old Virginia family who had died of consumption in Arizona. I traced his family. He was the last of it. Then it was easy to arrange a little story: Terence Colby had married a girl in Arizona, died shortly after; the girl died also, and I took the baby. Nobody can disprove what I say. There's not a living soul who knows that Terence is the son of Jack Hollis—except you and me."

"How about the woman I got the baby from?"

"I bought her silence until fifteen years ago. Then she died, and now Terry is convinced that he is the last representative of the Colby family."

She laughed with excitement and bekoned him out of the room and into another—Terry's room, farther down the hall. She pointed to a large photograph of a solemn-faced man on the wall. "You see that?"

"Who is it?"

"I got it when I took Terry to Virginia last winter—to see the old family estate and go over the ground of the historic Colbys."

She laughed again happily.

"Terry was wild with enthusiasm. He read everything he could lay his hands on about the Colbys. Discovered the year they landed in Virginia; how they fought in the Revolution;

how they fought and died in the Civil War. Oh, he knows every landmark in the history of 'his' family. Of course, I encouraged him."

"I know," chuckled Vance. "Whenever he gets in a pinch, I've heard you say: 'Terry, what should a Colby do?' "

"And," cut in Elizabeth, "you must admit that it has worked. There isn't a prouder, gentler, cleaner-minded boy in the world than Terry. Not blood. It's the blood of Jack Hollis. But it's what he thinks himself to be that counts. And now, Vance, admit that your theory is exploded."

He shook his head.

"Terry will do well enough. But wait till the pinch comes. You don't know how he'll turn out when the rub comes. *Then* blood will tell!"

She shrugged her shoulders angrily.

"You're simply being perverse now, Vance. At any rate, that picture is one of Terry's old 'ancestors,' Colonel Vincent Colby, of prewar days. Terry has discovered family resemblances, of course—same black hair, same black eyes, and a great many other things."

"But suppose he should ever learn the truth?" murmured Vance.

She caught her breath.

"That would be ruinous, of course. But he'll never learn. Only you and I know."

"A very hard blow, eh," said Vance, "if he were robbed of the Colby illusion and had Black Jack put in its place as a cold fact? But of course we'll never tell him."

Her color was never high. Now it became gray. Only her eyes remained burning, vivid, young, blazing out through the mask of age.

"Remember you said his blood would tell before he was twenty-five; that the blood of Black Jack would come to the surface; that he would have shot a man?"

"Still harping on that, Elizabeth? What if he does?"

"I'd disown him, throw him out penniless on the world, never see him again."

"You're a Spartan," said her brother in awe, as he looked on that thin, stern face. "Terry is your theory. If he disappoints you, he'll be simply a theory gone wrong. You'll cut him out of your life as if he were an algebraic equation and never think of him again."

"But he's *not* going wrong, Vance. Because, in ten days, he'll be twenty-five! And that's what all these changes mean. The moment it grows dark on the night of his twenty-fifth birthday, I'm going to take him into my father's room and turn it over to him."

He had listened to her patiently, a little wearied by her unusual flow of words. Now he came out of his apathy with a jerk. He laid his hand on Elizabeth's shoulder and turned her so that the light shone full in her face. Then he studied her.

"What do you mean by that, Elizabeth?"

"Vance," she said steadily, but with a touch of pity in her voice, "I have waited for a score of years, hoping that you'd settle down and try to do a man's work either here or somewhere else. You haven't done it. Yesterday Mr. Cornwall came here to draw up my will. By that will I leave you an annuity, Vance, that will take care of you in comfort; but I leave everything else to Terry Colby. That's why I've changed the room. The moment it grows dark ten days from today, I'm going to take Terry by the hand and lead him into the room and into the position of my father!"

The mask of youth which was Vance Cornish crumbled and fell away. A new man looked down at her. The firm flesh of his face became loose. His whole body was flabby. She had the feeling that if she pushed against his chest with the weight of her arm, he would topple to the floor. That weakness gradually passed. A peculiar strength of purpose grew in its place.

"Of course, this is a very shrewd game, Elizabeth. You want to wake me up. You're using the spur to make me work. I don't blame you for using the bluff, even if it's a rather cruel one. But, of course, it's impossible for you to be serious in what you say."

"Why impossible, Vance?"

"Because you know that I'm the last male representative of our family. Because you know my father would turn in his grave if he knew that an interloper, a foundling, the child of a murderer, a vagabond, had been made the heir to his estate. But you aren't serious, Elizabeth; I understand."

He swallowed his pride, for panic grew in him in proportion to the length of time she maintained her silence.

"As a matter of fact, I don't blame you for giving me a scare, my dear sister. I have been a shameless loafer. I'm going to reform and lift the burden of business off your shoulders—let you rest the remainder of your life."

It was the worst thing he could have said. He realized it the moment he had spoken. This forced, cowardly surrender was worse than brazen defiance, and he saw her lip curl. An idler is apt to be like a sullen child, except that in a grown man the child's sulky spite becomes a dark malice, all-embracing. For the very reason that Vance knew he was receiving what he deserved, and that this was the just reward for his thriftless years of idleness he began to hate Elizabeth with a cold, quiet hatred. There is something stimulating about any great passion. Now Vance felt his nerves soothed and calmed. His self-possession returned with a rush. He was suddenly able to smile into her face.

"After all," he said, "you're absolutely right. I've been a failure, Elizabeth—a rank, disheartening failure. You'd be foolish to trust the result of your life labors in my hands—entirely foolish. I admit that it's a shrewd blow to see the estate go to—Terry."

He found it oddly difficult to name the boy.

"But why not? Why not Terry? He's a clean youngster, and he may turn out very well—in spite of his blood. I hope so. The Lord knows you've given him every chance and the best start in the world. I wish him luck!"

He reached out his hand, and her bloodless fingers closed strongly over it.

"There's the old Vance talking," she said warmly, a mist across her eyes. "I almost thought that part of you had died."

He writhed inwardly. "By Jove, Elizabeth, think of that boy, coming out of nothing, everything poured into his hands—and now within ten days of his goal! Rather exciting, isn't it? Suppose he should stumble at the very threshold of his success? Eh?"

He pressed the point with singular insistence.

"Doesn't it make your heart beat, Elizabeth, when you think that he might fall—that he might do what I prophesied so long ago—shoot a man before he's twenty-five?"

She shrugged the supposition calmly away.

"My faith in him is based as strongly as the rocks, Vance.

But if he fell, after the schooling I've given him, I'd throw him out of my life—forever."

He paused a moment, studying her face with a peculiar eagerness. Then he shrugged in turn. "Tush! Of course, that's impossible. Let's go down."

CHAPTER 4

WHEN THEY reached the front porch, they saw Terence Colby coming up the terrace from the river road on Le Sangre. And a changed horse he was. One ear was forward as if he did not know what lay in store for him, but would try to be on the alert. One ear flagged warily back. He went slowly, lifting his feet with the care of a very weary horse. Yet, when the wind fluttered a gust of whirling leaves beside him, he leaped aside and stood with high head, staring, transformed in the instant into a creature of fire and wire-strung nerves. The rider gave to the side-spring with supple grace and then sent the stallion on up the hill.

Joyous triumph was in the face of Terry. His black hair was blowing about his forehead, for his hat was pushed back after the manner of one who has done a hard day's work and is ready to rest. He came close to the veranda, and Le Sangre lifted his fine head and stared fearlessly, curiously, with a sort of contemptuous pride, at Elizabeth and Vance.

"The killer is no longer a killer," laughed Terry. "Look him over, Uncle Vance. A beauty, eh?"

Elizabeth said nothing at all. But she rocked herself back and forth a trifle in her chair as she nodded. She glanced over the terrace, hoping that others might be there to see the triumph of her boy. Then she looked back at Terence. But Vance was regarding the horse.

"He might have a bit more in the legs, Terry."

"Not much more. A leggy horse can't stand mountain

work—or any other work, for that matter, except a ride in the park."

"I suppose you're right. He's a picture horse, Terry. And a devilish eye, but I see that you've beaten him."

"Beaten him?" He shook his head. "We reached a gentleman's agreement. As long as I wear spurs, he'll fight me till he gets his teeth in me or splashes my skull to bits with his heels. Otherwise he'll keep on fighting till he drops. But as soon as I take off the spurs and stop tormenting him, he'll do what I like. No whips or spurs for Le Sangre. Eh, boy?"

He held out the spurs so that the sun flashed on them. The horse stiffened with a shudder, and that forward look of a horse about to bolt came in his eyes.

"No, no!" cried Elizabeth.

But Terry laughed and dropped the spurs back in his pocket.

The stallion moved off, and Terry waved to them. Just as he turned, the mind of Vance Cornish raced back to another picture—a man with long black hair blowing about his face a gun in either hand, sweeping through a dusty street with shots barking behind him. It came suddenly as a revelation, and left him downheaded with the thought.

"What is it, Vance?" asked his sister, reaching out to touch his arm.

"Nothing." Then he added abruptly: "I'm going for a jaunt for a few days, Elizabeth."

She grew gloomy.

"Are you going to insist on taking it to heart this way?"

"Not at all. I'm going to be back here in ten days and drink Terry's long life and happiness across the birthday dinner table."

He marvelled at the ease with which he could make himself smile in her face.

"You noticed that—his gentleman's agreement with Le Sangre? I've made him detest fighting with the idea that only brute beasts fight—men argue and agree."

"I've noticed that he never has trouble with the cowpunchers."

"They've seen him box," chuckled Elizabeth. "Besides, Terry isn't the sort that troublemakers like to pick on. He has an ugly look when he's angry."

"H'm," murmured Vance. "I've noticed that. But as long

as he keeps to his fists, he'll do no harm. But what is the reason for surrounding him with guns, Elizabeth?"

"A very good reason. He loves them, you know. Anything from a shotgun to a derringer is a source of joy to Terence. And not a day goes by that he doesn't handle them."

"Certainly the effect of blood, eh?" suggested Vance.

She glanced sharply at him.

"You're determined to be disagreeable today, Vance. As a matter of fact, I've convinced him that for the very reason he is so accurate with a gun he must never enter a gun fight. The advantage would be too much on his side against any ordinary man. That appeals to Terry's sense of fair play. No, he's absolutely safe, no matter how you look at it."

"No doubt."

He looked away from her and over the valley. The day had worn into the late afternoon. Bear Creek ran dull and dark in the shadow, and Mount Discovery was robed in blue to the very edge of its shining crown of snow. In this dimmer, richer light the Cornish ranch had never seemed so desirable to Vance. It was not a ranch; it was a little kingdom. And Vance was the dispossessed heir.

He knew that he was being watched, however, and all that evening he was at his best. At the dinner table he guided the talk so that Terence Colby was the lion of the conversation. Afterward, when he was packing his things in his room for his journey of the next day, he was careful to sing at the top of his voice. He reaped a reward for this cautious acting, for the next morning, when he climbed into the buckboard that was to take him down the Blue Mountain road and over to the railroad, his sister came down the steps and stood beside the wagon.

"You *will* come back for the birthday party, Vance?" she pleaded.

"You want me to?"

"You were with me when I got Terry. In fact, you got him for me. And I want you to be here when he steps into his own."

In this he found enough to keep him thoughtful all the way to the railroad while the buckskins grunted up the grade and then spun away down the long slope beyond. It was one of those little ironies of fate that he should have picked up the very man who was to disinherit him some twenty-four years later.

He carried no grudge against Elizabeth, but he certainly retained no tenderness. Hereafter he would act his part as well as he could to extract the last possible penny out of her. And in the meantime he must concentrate on tripping up Terence Colby, alias Hollis.

Vance saw nothing particularly vicious in this. He had been idle so long that he rejoiced in a work which was within his mental range. It included scheming, working always behind the scenes, pulling strings to make others jump. And if he could trip Terry and actually make him shoot a man on or before that birthday, he had no doubt that his sister would actually throw the boy out of her house and out of her life. A woman who could give twenty-four years to a theory would be capable of grim things when the theory went wrong.

It was early evening when he climbed off the train at Garrison City. He had not visited the place since that cattle-buying trip of twenty-four years ago that brought the son of Black Jack into the affairs of the Cornish family. Garrison City had become a city. There were two solid blocks of brick buildings next to the station, a network of paved streets, and no less than three hotels. It was so new to the eye and so obviously full of the "booster" spirit that he was appalled at the idea of prying through this modern shell and getting back to the heart and the memory of the old days of the town.

At the restaurant he forced himself upon a grave-looking gentleman across the table. He found that the solemn-faced man was a travelling drummer. The venerable loafer in front of the blacksmith's shop was feeble-minded, and merely gaped at the name of Black Jack. The proprietor of the hotel shook his head with positive antagonism.

"Of course, Garrison City has its past," he admitted, "but we are living it down, and have succeeded pretty well. I think I've heard of a ruffian of the last generation named Jack Hollis; but I don't know anything, and I don't care to know anything, about him. But if you're interested in Garrison City, I'd like to show you a little plot of ground in a place that is going to be the center of the—"

Vance Cornish made his mind a blank, let the smooth current of words slip off his memory as from an oiled surface, and gave up Garrison City as a hopeless job. Nevertheless, it was the hotel proprietor who dropped a valuable hint.

"If you're interested in the early legends, why don't you go to the State Capitol? They have every magazine and every book that so much as mentions any place in the state."

So Vance Cornish went to the Capitol and entered the library. It was a sweaty task and a most discouraging one. The name "Black Jack" revealed nothing; and the name of Hollis was an equal blank, so far as the indices were concerned. He was preserved in legend only, and Vance Cornish could make no vital use of legend. He wanted something in cold print.

So he began an exhaustive search. He went through volume after volume, but though he came upon mention of Black Jack, he never reached the account of an eyewitness of any of those stirring holdups or train robberies.

And then he began on the old files of magazines. And still nothing. He was about to give up with four days of patient labor wasted when he struck gold in the desert—the very mine of information which he wanted.

"How I Painted Black Jack," by Lawrence Montgomery.

There was the photograph of the painter, to begin with— a man who had discovered the beauty of the deserts of the Southwest. But there was more—much more. It told how, in his wandering across the desert, he had hunted for something more than raw-colored sands and purple mesas blooming in the distance.

He had searched for a human being to fit into the picture and give the softening touch of life. But he never found the face for which he had been looking. And then luck came and tapped him on the shoulder. A lone rider came out of the dusk and the desert and loomed beside his campfire. The moment the firelight flushed on the face of the man, he knew this was the face for which he had been searching. He told how they fried bacon and ate it together; he told of the soft voice and the winning smile of the rider; he told of his eyes, unspeakably soft and unspeakably bold, and the agile, nervous hands, forever shifting and moving in the firelight.

The next morning he had asked his visitor to sit for a picture, and his request had been granted. All day he labored at the canvas, and by night the work was far enough along for him to dismiss his visitor. So the stranger asked for a small brush with black paint on it, and in the corner of the canvas drew in the words "Yours, Black Jack." Then he rode into the night.

Black Jack! Lawrence Montgomery had made up his pack and struck straight back for the nearest town. There he asked for tidings of a certain Black Jack, and there he got what he wanted in heaps. Everyone knew Black Jack—too well! There followed a brief summary of the history of the desperado and his countless crimes, unspeakable tales of cunning and courage and merciless vengeance taken.

Vance Cornish turned the last page of the article, and there was the reproduction of the painting. He held his breath when he saw it. The outlaw sat on his horse with his head raised and turned, and it was the very replica of Terence Colby as the boy had waved to them from the back of Le Sangre. More than a family, sketchy resemblance—far more.

There was the same large, dark eye; the same smile, half proud and half joyous; the same imperious lift of the head; the same bold carving of the features. There were differences, to be sure. The nose of Black Jack had been more cruelly arched, for instance, and his cheekbones were higher and more pronounced. But in spite of the dissimilarities the resemblance was more than striking. It might have stood for an actual portrait of Terence Colby masquerading in long hair.

When the full meaning of this photograph had sunk into his mind, Vance Cornish closed his eyes. "Eureka!" he whispered to himself.

There was something more to be done. But it was very simple. It merely consisted in covertly cutting out the pages of the article in question. Then, carefully, for fear of loss, he jotted down the name and date of the magazine, folded his stolen pages, and fitted them snugly into his breast pocket. That night he ate his first hearty dinner in four days.

CHAPTER 5

VANCE'S WORK was not by any means accomplished. Rather, it might be said that he was in the position of a man with a dangerous charge for a gun and no weapon to shoot it. He started out to find the gun.

In fact, he already had it in mind. Twenty-four hours later he was in Craterville. Five days out of the ten before the twenty-fifth birthday of Terence had elapsed, and Vance was still far from his goal, but he felt that the lion's share of the work had been accomplished.

Craterville was a day's ride across the mountains from the Cornish ranch, and it was the county seat. It was one of those towns which spring into existence for no reason that can be discovered, and cling to life generations after they should have died. But Craterville held one thing of which Vance Cornish was in great need, and that was Sheriff Joe Minter, familiarly called Uncle Joe. His reason for wanting the sheriff was perfectly simple. Uncle Joe Minter was the man who killed Black Jack Hollis.

He had been a boy of eighteen then, shooting with a rifle across a window sill. That shot had formed his life. He was now forty-two and he had spent the interval as the professional enemy of criminals in the mountains. For the glory which came from the killing of Black Jack had been sweet to the youthful palate of Minter, and he had cultivated his taste. He became the most dreaded manhunter in those districts where manhunting was most common. He had been sheriff at Craterville for a dozen years now, and still his supremacy was not even questioned.

Vance Cornish was lucky to find the sheriff in town presiding at the head of the long table of the hotel at dinner. He was a man of great dignity. He wore his stiff black hair, still untarnished by gray, very long, brushing it with difficulty to keep it behind his ears. This mass of black hair framed a long,

24

stern face, the angles of which had been made by years. But there was no sign of weakness. He had grown dry, not flabby. His mouth was a thin, straight line, and his fighting chin jutted out in profile.

He rose from his place to greet Vance Cornish. Indeed, the sheriff acted the part of master of ceremonies at the hotel, having a sort of silent understanding with the widow who owned the place. It was said that the sheriff would marry the woman sooner or later, he so loved to talk at her table. His talk doubled her business. Her table afforded him an audience; so they needed one another.

"You don't remember me," said Vance.

"I got a tolerable poor memory for faces," admitted the sheriff.

"I'm Cornish, of the Cornish ranch."

The sheriff was duly impressed. The Cornish ranch was a show place. He arranged a chair for Vance at his right, and presently the talk rose above the murmur to which it had been depressed by the arrival of this important stranger. The increasing noise made a background. It left Vance alone with the sheriff.

"And how do you find your work, sheriff?" asked Vance; for he knew that Uncle Joe Minter's great weakness was his love of talk. Everyone in the mountains knew it, for that matter.

"Dull," complained Minter. "Men ain't what they used to be, or else the law is a heap stronger."

"The men who enforce the law are," said Vance.

The sheriff absorbed this patent compliment with the blank eye of satisfaction and rubbed his chin.

"But they's been some talk of rustling, pretty recent. I'm waiting for it to grow and get ripe. Then I'll bust it."

He made an eloquent gesture which Vance followed. He was distinctly pleased with the sheriff. For Minter was wonderfully preserved. His face seemed five years younger than his age. His body seemed even younger—round, smooth, powerful muscles padding his shoulders and stirring down the length of his big arms. And his hands had that peculiar light restlessness of touch which Vance remembered to have seen —in the hands of Terence Colby, alias Hollis!

"And how's things up your way?" continued the sheriff.

"Booming. By the way, how long is it since you've seen the ranch?"

"Never been there. Bear Creek Valley has always been a quiet place since the Cornishes moved in; and they ain't been any call for a gent in my line of business up that way."

He grinned with satisfaction, and Vance nodded.

"If times are dull, why not drop over? We're having a celebration there in five days. Come and look us over."

"Maybe I might, and maybe I mightn't," said the sheriff. "All depends."

"And bring some friends with you," insisted Vance.

Then he wisely let the subject drop and went on to a detailed description of the game in the hills around the ranch. That, he knew, would bring the sheriff if anything would. But he mentioned the invitation no more. There were particular reasons why he must not press it on the sheriff any more than on others in Craterville.

The next morning, before traintime, Vance went to the post office and left the article on Black Jack addressed to Terence Colby at the Cornish ranch. The addressing was done on a typewriter, which completely removed any means of identifying the sender. Vance played with Providence in only one way. He was so eager to strike his blow at the last possible moment that he asked the postmaster to hold the letter for three days, which would land it at the ranch on the morning of the birthday. Then he went to the train.

His self-respect was increasing by leaps and bounds. The game was still not won, but, starting with absolutely nothing, in six days he had planted a charge which might send Elizabeth's twenty-four years of labor up in smoke.

He got off the train at Preston, the station nearest the ranch, and took a hired team up the road along Bear Creek Gorge. They debouched out of the Blue Mountains into the valley of the ranch in the early evening, and Vance found himself looking with new eyes on the little kingdom. He felt the happiness, indeed, of one who has lost a great prize and then put himself in a fair way of winning it back.

They dipped into the valley road. Over the tops of the big silver spruces he traced the outline of Sleep Mountain against the southern sky. Who but Vance, or the dwellers in the valley, would be able to duly appreciate such beauty? If there were any wrong in what he had done, this thought consoled him: the ends justified the means.

Now, as they drew closer, through the branches he made out glimpses of the dim, white front of the big house on the hill. That big, cool house with the kingdom spilled out at its feet, the farming lands, the pastures of the hills, and the rich forest of the upper mountains. Certainty came to Vance Cornish. He wanted the ranch so profoundly that the thought of losing it became impossible.

CHAPTER 6

BUT WHILE HE had been working at a distance, things had been going on apace at the ranch, a progress which had now gathered such impetus that he found himself incapable of checking it. The blow fell immediately after dinner that same evening. Terence excused himself early to retire to the mysteries of a new pump-gun. Elizabeth and Vance took their coffee into the library.

The night had turned cool, with a sharp wind driving the chill through every crack; so a few sticks were sending their flames crumbling against the big back log. The lamp glowing in the corner was the only other light, and when they drew their chairs close to the hearth, great tongues of shadows leaped and fell on the wall behind them. Vance looked at his sister with concern. There was a certain complacency about her this evening that told him in advance that she had formed a new plan with which she was well pleased. And he had come to dread her plans.

She always filled him with awe—and never more so than tonight, with her thin, homely face illuminated irregularly and by flashes. He kept watching her from the side, with glances.

"I think I know why you've gone away for these few days," she said.

"To get used to the new idea," he admitted with such frankness that she turned to him with unusual sympathy. "It was rather a shock at first."

"I know it was. And I wasn't diplomatic. There's too much man in me, Vance. Altogether too much, while you—"

She closed her lips suddenly. But he knew perfectly the unspoken words. She was about to suggest that there was too *little* man in him. He dropped his chin in his hand, partly for comfort and partly to veil the sneer. If she could have followed what he had done in the past six days!

"And you are used to the new idea?"

"You see that I'm back before the time was up and ahead of my promise," he said.

She nodded. "Which paves the way for another new idea of mine."

He felt that a blow was coming and nerved himself against the shock of it. But the preparation was merely like tensing one's muscles against a fall. When the shock came, it stunned him.

"Vance, I've decided to adopt Terence!"

His fingertips sank into his cheek, bruising the flesh. What would become of his six days of work? What would become of his cunning and his forethought? All destroyed at a blow. For if she adopted the boy, the very law would keep her from denying him afterward. For a moment it seemed to him that some devil must have forewarned her of his plans.

"You don't approve?" she said at last, anxiously.

He threw himself back in the chair and laughed. All his despair went into that hollow, ringing sound.

"Approve? It's a queer question to ask me. But let it go. I know I couldn't change you."

"I know that you have a right to advise," she said gently. "You are my father's son and you have a right to advise on the placing of his name."

He had to keep fighting against surging desires to throw his rage in her face. But he mastered himself, except for a tremor of his voice.

"When are you going to do it?"

"Tomorrow."

"Elizabeth, why not wait until after the birthday ceremony?"

"Because I've been haunted by peculiar fears, since our

last talk, that something might happen before that time. I've actually lain awake at night and thought about it! And I want to forestall all chances. I want to rivet him to me!"

He could see by her eagerness that her mind had been irrevocably made up, and that nothing could change her. She wanted agreement, not advice. And with consummate bitterness of soul he submitted to his fate.

"I suppose you're right. Call him down now and I'll be present when you ask him to join the circle—the family circle of the Cornishes, you know."

He could not school all the bitterness out of his voice, but she seemed too glad of his bare acquiescence to object to such trifles. She sent Wu Chi to call Terence down to them. He had apparently been in his shirt sleeves working at the gun. He came with his hands still faintly glistening from their hasty washing, and with the coat which he had just bundled into still rather bunched around his big shoulders. He came and stood against the massive, rough-finished stones of the fireplace looking down at Elizabeth. There had always been a sort of silent understanding between him and Vance. They never exchanged more words and looks than were absolutely necessary. Vance realized it more than ever as he looked up to the tall athletic figure. And he realized also that since he had last looked closely at Terence the latter had slipped out of boyhood and into manhood. There was that indescribable something about the set of the chin and the straight-looking eyes that spelled the difference.

"Terence," she said, "for twenty-four years you have been my boy."

"Yes, Aunt Elizabeth."

He acknowledged the gravity of this opening statement by straightening a little, his hand falling away from the stone against which he had been leaning. But Vance looked more closely at his sister. He could see the gleam of worship in her eyes.

"And now I want you to be something more. I want you to be my boy in the eyes of the law, so that when anything happens to me, your place won't be threatened."

He was straighter than ever.

"I want to adopt you, Terence!"

Somehow, in those few moments they had been gradually building to a climax. It was prodigiously heightened now by the silence of the boy. The throat of Vance tightened with excitement.

"I will be your mother, in the eyes of the law," she was explaining gently, as though it were a mystery which Terry could not understand. "And Vance, here, will be your uncle. You understand, my dear?"

What a world of brooding tenderness went into her voice! Vance wondered at it. But he wondered more at the stiff-standing form of Terence, and his silence; until he saw the tender smile vanish from the face of Elizabeth and alarm come into it. All at once Terence had dropped to one knee before her and taken her hands. And now it was he who was talking slowly, gently.

"All my life you've given me things, Aunt Elizabeth. You've given me everything. Home, happiness, love—everything that could be given. So much that you could never be repaid, and all I can do is to love you, you see, and honor you as if you were my mother, in fact. But there's just one thing that can't be given. And that's a name!"

He paused. Elizabeth was listening with a stricken face, and the heart of Vance thundered with his excitement. Vaguely he felt that there was something fine and clean and honorable in the heart of this youth which was being laid bare; but about that he cared very little. He was getting at facts and emotions which were valuable to him in the terms of dollars and cents.

"It makes me choke up," said Terence, "to have you offer me this great thing. It's a fine name, Cornish. But you know that I can't do it. It would be cowardly—a sort of rotten treason for me to change. It would be wrong. I know it would be wrong. I'm a Colby, Aunt Elizabeth. Every time that name is spoken, I feel it tingling down to my fingertips. I want to stand straighter, live cleaner. When I looked at the old Colby place in Virginia last year, it brought the tears to my eyes. I felt as if I were a product of that soil. Every fine thing that has ever been done by a Colby is a strength to me. I've studied them. And every now and then when I come to some brave thing they've done, I wonder if I could do it. And then I say to myself that I *must* be able to do just such things or else be a shame to my blood.

"Change my name? Why, I've gone all my life thanking God that I come of a race of gentlemen, clean-handed, and praying God to make me worthy of it. That name is like a whip over me. It drives me on and makes me want to do some fine big thing one of these days. Think of it! I'm the last of a race. I'm the end of it. The last of the Colbys! Why, when you think of it, you see how I can't possibly change, don't you? If I lost that, I'd lose the best half of myself and my self-respect! You understand, don't you? Not that I slight the name of Cornish for an instant. But even if names can be changed, blood can't be changed!"

She turned her head. She met the gleaming eyes of Vance, and then let her glance probe the fire and shadow of the hearth.

"It's all right, my dear," she said faintly. "Stand up."

"I've hurt you," he said contritely, leaning over her. "I feel—like a dog. Have I hurt you?"

"Not the least in the world. I only offered it for your happiness, Terry. And if you don't need it, there's no more to be said!"

He bent and kissed her forehead.

The moment he had disappeared through the tall doorway, Vance, past control, exploded.

"Of all the damnable exhibitions of pride in a young upstart, this—"

"Hush, hush!" said Elizabeth faintly. "It's the finest thing I've ever heard Terry say. But it frightens me, Vance. It frightens me to know that I've formed the character and the pride and the self-respect of that boy on—a lie! Pray God that he never learns the truth!"

CHAPTER 7

THERE WERE not many guests. Elizabeth had chosen them carefully from families which had known her father, Henry Cornish, when, in his reckless, adventurous way, he had been laying the basis of the Cornish fortune in the Rockies. Indeed, she was a little angry when she heard of the indiscriminate way in which Vance had scattered the invitations, particularly in Craterville.

But, as he said, he had acted so as to show her that he had entered fully into the spirit of the thing, and that his heart was in the right place as far as this birthday party was concerned, and she could not do otherwise than accept his explanation.

Some of the bidden guests, however, came from a great distance, and as a matter of course a few of them arrived the day before the celebration and filled the quiet rooms of the old house with noise. Elizabeth accepted them with resignation, and even pleasure, because they all had pleasant things to say about her father and good wishes to express for the destined heir, Terence Colby. It was carefully explained that this selection of an heir had been made by both Elizabeth and Vance, which removed all cause for remark. Vance himself regarded the guests with distinct amusement. But Terence was disgusted.

"What these true Westerners need," he said to Elizabeth later in the day, "is a touch of blood. No feeling of family or the dignity of family precedents out here."

It touched her shrewdly. More than once she had felt that Terry was on the verge of becoming a complacent prig. So she countered with a sharp thrust.

"You have to remember that you're a Westerner born and bred, my dear. A very Westerner yourself!"

"Birth is an accident—birthplaces, I mean," smiled Terence. "It's the blood that tells."

"Terry, you're a snob!" exclaimed Aunt Elizabeth.

"I hope not," he answered. "But look yonder, now!"

Old George Armstrong's daughter, Nelly, had gone up a tree like a squirrel and was laughing down through the branches at a raw-boned cousin on the ground beneath her.

"And what of it?" said Elizabeth. "That girl is pretty enough to please any man; and she's the type that makes a wife."

Terry rubbed his chin with his knuckles thoughtfully. It was the one family habit that he had contracted from Vance, much to the irritation of the latter.

"After all," said Terry, with complacency, "what are good looks with bad grammar?"

Elizabeth snorted literally and most unfemininely.

"Terence," she said, lessoning him with her bony, long forefinger, "you're just young enough to be wise about women. When you're a little older, you'll get sense. If you want white hands and good grammar, how do you expect to find a wife in the mountains?"

Terry answered with unshaken, lordly calm. "I haven't thought about the details. They don't matter. But a man must have standards of criticism."

"Standards your foot!" cried Aunt Elizabeth. "You insufferable young prig. That very girl laughing down through the branches—I'll wager she could set your head spinning in ten seconds if she thought it worth her while to try."

"Perhaps," smiled Terence. "In the meantime she has freckles and a vocabulary without growing pains."

"All men are fools," declared Aunt Elizabeth; "but boys are idiots, bless 'em! Terence, before you grow up you'll have sore toes from stumbling, take my word for it! Do you know what a wise man would do?"

"Well?"

"Go out and start a terrific flirtation with Nelly."

"For the sake of experience?" sighed Terence.

"Good heavens!" groaned Aunt Elizabeth. "Terry, you're impossible! Where are you going now?"

"Out to see El Sangre."

He went whistling out of the door, and she followed him with confused feelings of anger, pride, joy, and fear. She went to a side window and saw him go fearlessly into the corral where the man-destroying El Sangre was kept. And the big stallion, red fire in the sunshine, went straight to him and nosed at a hip pocket. They had already struck up a perfect understanding. Deeply she wondered at it.

She had never loved the mountains and their people and their ways. It had been a battle to fight. She had fought the battle, won, and gained a hollow victory. And watching Terry caress the great, beautiful horse, she knew vaguely that his heart, at least, was in tune with the wilderness.

"I wish to heaven, Terry," she murmured, "that you could find a master as El Sangre has done. You need teaching."

When she turned from the window, she found Vance watching her. He had a habit of obscurely melting into a background and looking out at her unexpectedly. All at once she knew that he had been there listening during all of her talk with Terence. Not that the talk had been of a peculiarly private nature, but it angered her. There was just a semblance of eavesdropping about the presence of Vance. For she knew that Terence unbosomed himself to her as he would do in the hearing of no other human being. However, she mastered her anger and smiled at her brother. He had taken all these recent changes which were so much to his disadvantage with a good spirit that astonished and touched her.

"Do you know what I'm going to give Terry for his birthday?" he said, sauntering toward her.

"Well?" A mention of Terence and his welfare always disarmed her completely. She opened her eyes and her heart and smiled at her brother.

"There's no set of Scott in the house. I'm going to give Terry one."

"Do you think he'll ever read the novels? I never could. That antiquated style, Vance, keeps me at arm's length."

"A stiff style because he wrote so rapidly. But there's the greatest body and bone of character. Except for his heroes. Terry reminds me of them, in a way. No thought, not very much feeling, but a great capacity for physical action."

"I think you'd like to be Terry's adviser," she said.

"I wouldn't aspire to the job," yawned Vance, "unless I could ride well and shoot well. If a man can't do that, he ceases to be a man in Terry's eyes. And if a woman can't talk pure English, she isn't a woman."

"That's because he's young," said Elizabeth.

"It's because he's a prig," sneered Vance. He had been drawn farther into the conversation than he planned; now he retreated carefully. "But another year or so may help him."

He retreated before she could answer, but he left her thoughtful, as he hoped to do. He had a standing theory that the only way to make a woman meditate is to keep her from talking. And he wanted very much to make Elizabeth meditate the evil in the son of Black Jack. Otherwise all his plans might be useless and his seeds of destruction fall on barren soil. He was intensely afraid of that, anyway. His hope was to draw the boy and the sheriff together on the birthday and guide the two explosives until they met on the subject of the death of Black Jack. Either Terry would kill the sheriff, or the sheriff would kill Terry. Vance hoped for the latter, but rather expected the former to be the outcome, and if it were, he was inclined to think that Elizabeth would sooner or later make excuses for Terry and take him back into the fold of her affections. Accordingly, his work was, in the few days that intervened, to plant all the seeds of suspicion that he could. Then, when the dénouement came, those seeds might blossom overnight into poison flowers.

In the late afternoon he took up his position in an easy chair on the big veranda. The mail was delivered, as a rule, just before dusk, one of the cow-punchers riding down for it. Grave fears about the loss of that all-important missive to Terry haunted him, for the postmaster was a doddering old fellow who was quite apt to forget his head. Consequently he was vastly relieved when the mail arrived and Elizabeth brought the familiar big envelope out to him, with its typewritten address.

"Looks like a business letter, doesn't it?" she asked Vance.

"More or less," said Vance, covering a yawn of excitement.

"But how on earth could any business—it's postmarked from Craterville."

"Somebody may have heard about his prospects; they're starting early to separate him from his money."

"Vance, how much talking did you do in Craterville?"

It was hard to meet her keen old eyes.

"Too much, I'm afraid," he said frankly. "You see, I've felt rather touchy about the thing. I want people to know that you and I have agreed on making Terry the heir to the ranch. I don't want anyone to suspect that we differed. I suppose I talked too much about the birthday plans."

She sighed with vexation and weighed the letter in her hand.

"I've half a mind to open it."

His heartbeat fluttered and paused.

"Go ahead," he urged, with well-assured carelessness.

She shook down the contents of the envelope preparatory to opening it.

"It's nothing but printed stuff, Vance. I can see that, through the envelope."

"But wait a minute, Elizabeth. It might anger Terry to have even his business mail opened. He's touchy, you know."

She hesitated, then shrugged her shoulders.

"I suppose you're right. Let it go." She laughed at her own concern over the matter. "Do you know, Vance, that sometimes I feel as if the whole world were conspiring to get a hand on Terry?"

CHAPTER 8

TERRY DID not come down for dinner. It was more or less of a calamity, for the board was quite full of early guests for the next day's festivities. Aunt Elizabeth shifted the burden of the entertainment onto the capable shoulders of Vance, who could please these Westerners when he chose. Tonight he decidedly chose. Elizabeth had never seen him in such high spirits. He could flirt good-humoredly and openly across the table at Nelly, or else turn and draw an anecdote from Nelly's father. He kept the reins in his hands and drove the talk along so smoothly that Elizabeth could sit in gloomy silence, unnoticed, at the farther end of the table. Her mind was up yonder in the room of Terry.

Something had happened, and it had come through that long business envelope with the typewritten address that seemed so harmless. One reading of the contents had brought Terry out of his chair with an exclamation. Then, without explanation of any sort, he had gone to his room and stayed there. She would have followed to find out what was the matter, but the requirements of dinner and her guests kept her downstairs.

Immediately after dinner Vance, at a signal from her, dexterously herded everyone into the living room and distributed them in comfort around the big fireplace; Elizabeth Cornish bolted straight for the room of Terence. She knocked and tried the door. To her astonishment, the knob turned, but the door did not open. She heard the click and felt the jar of the bolt. Terry had locked his door!

A little thing to make her heart fall, one would say, but

little things about Terry were great things to Elizabeth. In twenty-four years he had never locked his door. What could it mean?

It was a moment before she could call, and she waited breathlessly. She was reassured by a quiet voice that answered her: "Just a moment. I'll open."

The tone was so matter-of-fact that her heart, with one leap, came back to normal and tears of relief misted her eyes for an instant. Perhaps he was up here working out a surprise for the next day—he was full of tricks and surprises. That was unquestionably it. And he took so long in coming to the door because he was hiding the thing he had been working on. As for food, Wu Chi was his slave and would have smuggled a tray up to him. Presently the lock turned and the door opened.

She could not see his face distinctly at first, the light was so strong behind him. Besides, she was more occupied in looking for the tray of food which would assure her that Terry was not suffering from some mental crisis that had made him forget even dinner. She found the tray, sure enough, but the food had not been touched.

She turned on him with a new rush of alarm. And all her fears were realized. Terry had been fighting a hard battle and he was still fighting. About his eyes there was the look, half-dull and half-hard, that comes in the eyes of young people unused to pain. A worried, tense, hungry face. He took her arm and led her to the table. On it lay an article clipped out of a magazine. She looked down at it with unseeing eyes. The sheets were already much crumbled. Terry turned them to a full-page picture, and Elizabeth found herself looking down into the face of Black Jack, proud, handsome, defiant.

Had Vance been there, he might have recognized her actions. As she had done one day twenty-four years ago, now she turned and dropped heavily into a chair, her bony hands pressed to her shallow bosom. A moment later she was on her feet again, ready to fight, ready to tell a thousand lies. But it was too late. The revelation had been complete and she could tell by his face that Terence knew everything.

"Terry," she said faintly, "what on earth have you to do with that—"

"Listen, Aunt Elizabeth," he said, "you aren't going to fib about it, are you?"

"What in the world are you talking about?"

"Why were you so shocked?"

She knew it was a futile battle. He was prying at her inner mind with short questions and a hard, dry voice.

"It was the face of that terrible man. I saw him once before, you know. On the day—"

"On the day he was murdered!"

That word told her everything. "Murdered!" It lighted all the mental processes through which he had been going. Who in all the reaches of the mountain desert had ever before dreamed of terming the killing of the notorious Black Jack a "murder"?

"What are you saying, Terence? That fellow—"

"Hush! Look at us!"

He picked up the photograph and stood back so that the light fell sharply on his face and on the photograph which he held beside his head. He caught up a sombrero and jammed it jauntily on his head. He tilted his face high, with resolute chin. And all at once there were two Black Jacks, not one. He evidently saw all the admission that he cared for in her face. He took off the hat with a dragging motion and replaced the photograph on the table.

"I tried it in the mirror," he said quietly. "I wasn't quite sure until I tried it in the mirror. Then I knew, of course."

She felt him slipping out of her life.

"What shall I say to you, Terence?"

"Is that my real name?"

She winced. "Yes. Your real name."

"Good. Do you remember our talk of today?"

"What talk?"

He drew his breath with something of a groan.

"I said that what these people lacked was the influence of family—of old blood!"

He made himself smile at her, and Eliabeth trembled. "If I could explain—" she began.

"Ah, what is there to explain, Aunt Elizabeth? Except that you have been a thousand times kinder to me than I dreamed before. Why, I—I actually thought that you were rather honored by having a Colby under your roof. I really felt that I was bestowing something of a favor on you!"

"Terry, sit down!"

He sank into a chair slowly. And she sat on the arm of it with her mournful eyes on his face.

"Whatever your name may be, that doesn't change the man who wears the name."

He laughed softly. "And you've been teaching me steadily for twenty-four years that blood will tell? You can't change like this. Oh, I understand it perfectly. You determined to make me over. You determined to destroy my heritage and put the name of the fine old Colbys in its place. It was a brave thing to try, and all these years how you must have waited, and waited to see how I would turn out, dreading every day some outbreak of the bad blood! Ah, you have a nerve of steel, Aunt Elizabeth! How have you endured the suspense?"

She felt that he was mocking her subtly under this flow of compliment. But it was the bitterness of pain, not of reproach, she knew.

She said: "Why didn't you let me come up with you? Why didn't you send for me?"

"I've been busy doing a thing that no one could help me with. I've been burning my dreams." He pointed to a smoldering heap of ashes on the hearth.

"Terry!"

"Yes, all the Colby pictures that I've been collecting for the past fifteen years. I burned 'em. They don't mean anything to anyone else, and certainly they have ceased to mean anything to me. But when I came to Anthony Colby—the eighteen-twelve man, you know, the one who has always been my hero—it went pretty hard. I felt as if—I were burning my own personality. As a matter of fact, in the last couple of hours I've been born over again."

Terry paused. "And births are painful, Aunt Elizabeth!"

At that she cried out and caught his hand. "Terry dear! Terry dear! You break my heart!"

"I don't mean to. You mustn't think that I'm pitying myself. But I want to know the real name of my father. He must have had some name other than Black Jack. What was it?"

"Are you going to gather his memory to your heart, Terry?"

"I am going to find something about him that I can be

proud of. Blood will tell. I know that I'm not all bad, and there must have been good in Black Jack. I want to know all about him. I want to know about—his crimes."

He labored through a fierce moment of silent struggle while her heart went helplessly out to him.

"Because—I had a hand in every one of those crimes! Everything that he did is something that I might have done under the same temptation."

"But you're not all your father's son. You had a mother. A dear, sweet-faced girl—"

"Don't!" whispered Terry. "I suppose he broke—her heart?"

"She was a very delicate girl," she said after a moment.

"And now my father's name, please?"

"Not that just now. Give me until tomorrow night, Terry. Will you do that? Will you wait till tomorrow night, Terry? I'm going to have a long talk with you then, about many things. And I want you to keep this in mind always. No matter how long you live, the influence of the Colbys will never go out of your life. And neither will my influence, I hope. If there is anything good in me, it has gone into you. I have seen to that. Terry, you are not your father's son alone. All these other things have entered into your make-up. They're just as much a part of you as his blood."

"Ah, yes," said Terry. "But blood will tell!"

It was a mournful echo of a thing she had told him a thousand times.

CHAPTER 9

SHE WENT STRAIGHT down to the big living room and drew Vance away, mindless of her guests. He came humming until he was past the door and in the shadowy hall. Then he touched her arm, suddenly grown serious.

"What's wrong, Elizabeth?"

Her voice was low, vibrating with fierceness. And Vance blessed the dimness of the hall, for he could feel the blood recede from his face and the sweat stand on his forehead.

"Vance, if you've done what I think you've done, you're lower than a snake, and more poisonous and more treacherous. And I'll cut you out of my heart and my life. You know what I mean?"

It was really the first important crisis that he had ever faced. And now his heart grew small, cold. He knew, miserably, his own cowardice. And like all cowards, he fell back on bold lying to carry him through. It was a triumph that he could make his voice steady—more than steady. He could even throw the right shade of disgust into it.

"Is this another one of your tantrums, Elizabeth? By heavens, I'm growing tired of 'em. You continually throw in my face that you hold the strings of the purse. Well, tie them up as far as I'm concerned. I won't whine. I'd rather have that happen than be tyrannized over any longer."

She was much shaken. And there was a sting in this reproach that carried home to her; there was just a sufficient edge of truth to wound her. Had there been much light, she could have read his face; the dimness of the hall was saving Vance, and he knew it.

"God knows I'd like to believe that you haven't had anything to do with it. But you and I are the only two people in the world who know the secret of it—"

He pretended to guess. "It's something about Terence? Something about his father?"

Again she was disarmed. If he were guilty, it was strange that he should approach the subject so openly. And she began to doubt.

"Vance, he knows everything! Everything except the real name of Black Jack!"

"Good heavens!"

She strained her eyes through the shadows to make out his real expression; but there seemed to be a real horror in his restrained whisper.

"It isn't possible, Elizabeth!"

"It came in that letter. That letter I wanted to open, and which you persuaded me not to!" She mustered all her damning facts one after another. "And it was postmarked from Craterville. Vance, you have been in Craterville lately!"

He seemed to consider.

"Could I have told anyone? Could I, possibly? No, Elizabeth, I'll give you my word of honor that I've never spoken a syllable about that subject to anyone!"

"Ah, but what have you written?"

"I've never put pen to paper. But—how did it happen?"

He had control of himself now. His voice was steadier. He could feel her recede from her aggressiveness.

"It was dated after you left Craterville, of course. And— I can't stand imagining that you could be so low. Only, who else would have a motive?"

"But how was it done?"

"They sent him an article about his father and a picture of Black Jack that happens to look as much like Terry as two peas."

"Then I have it! If the picture looks like Terry, someone took it for granted that he'd be interested in the similarity. That's why it was sent. Unless they told him that he was really Black Jack's son. Did the person who sent the letter do that?"

"There was no letter. Only a magazine clipping and the photograph of the painting."

They were both silent. Plainly she had dismissed all idea of her brother's guilt.

"But what are we going to do, Elizabeth? And how has he taken it?"

"Like poison, Vance. He—he burned all the Colby pictures. Oh, Vance, twenty-four years of work are thrown away!"

"Nonsense! This will all straighten out. I'm glad he's found out. Sooner or later he was pretty sure to. Such things will come to light."

"Vance, you'll help me? You'll forgive me for accusing you, and you'll help me to keep Terry in hand for the next few days? You see, he declared that he will not be ashamed of his father."

"You can't blame him for that."

"God knows I blame no one but myself."

"I'll help you with every ounce of strength in my mind and body, my dear."

She pressed his hand in silence.

"I'm going up to talk with him now," he said. "I'm going

to do what I can with him. You go in and talk. And don't let them see that anything is wrong."

The door had not been locked again. He entered at the call of Terry and found him leaning over the hearth stirring up the pile of charred paper to make it burn more freely. A shadow crossed the face of Terry as he saw his visitor, but he banished it at once and rose to greet him. In his heart Vance was a little moved. He went straight to the younger man and took his hand.

"Elizabeth has told me," he said gently, and he looked with a moist eye into the face of the man who, if his plans worked out, would be either murderer or murdered before the close of the next day. "I am very sorry, Terence."

"I thought you came to congratulate me," said Terry, withdrawing his hand.

"Congratulate you?" echoed Vance, with unaffected astonishment.

"For having learned the truth," said Terry. "Also, for having a father who was a strong man."

Vance could not resist the opening.

"In a way, I suppose he was," he said dryly. "And if you look at it in that way, I *do* congratulate you, Terence!"

"You've always hated me, Uncle Vance," Terry declared. "I've known it all these years. And I'll do without your congratulations."

"You're wrong, Terry," said Vance. He kept his voice mild. "You're very wrong. But I'm old enough not to take offense at what a young spitfire says."

"I suppose you are," retorted Terry, in a tone which implied that he himself would never reach that age.

"And when a few years run by," went on Vance, "you'll change your viewpoint. In the meantime, my boy, let me give you this warning. No matter what you think about me, it is Elizabeth who counts."

"Thanks. You need have no fear about my attitude to Aunt Elizabeth. You ought to know that I love her, and respect her."

"Exactly. But you're headstrong, Terry. Very headstrong. And so is Elizabeth. Take your own case. She took you into the family for the sake of a theory. Did you know that?"

The boy stiffened. "A theory?"

"Quite so. She wished to prove that blood, after all, was

more talk than a vital influence. So she took you in and gave you an imaginary line of ancestors with which you were entirely contented. But, after all, it has been twenty-four years of theory rather than twenty-four years of Terry. You understand?"

"It's a rather nasty thing to hear," said Terence huskily. "Perhaps you're right. I don't know. Perhaps you're right."

"And if her theory is proved wrong—look out, Terry! She'll throw you out of her life without a second thought."

"Is that a threat?"

"My dear boy, not by any means. You think I have hated you? Not at all. I have simply been indifferent. Now that you are in more or less trouble, you see that I come to you. And hereafter if there should be a crisis, you will see who is your true friend. Now, good night!"

He had saved his most gracious speech until the very end, and after it he retired at once to leave Terence with the pleasant memory in his mind. For he had in his mind the idea of a perfect crime for which he would not be punished. He would turn Terry into a corpse or a killer, and in either case the youngster would never dream who had dealt the blow.

No wonder, then, as he went downstairs, that he stepped onto the veranda for a few moments. The moon was just up beyond Mount Discovery; the valley unfolded like a dream. Never had the estate seemed so charming to Vance Cornish, for he felt that his hand was closing slowly around his inheritance.

CHAPTER 10

THE SLEEP OF the night seemed to blot out the excitement of the preceding evening. A bright sun, a cool stir of air, brought in the next morning, and certainly calamity had never seemed farther from the Cornish ranch than it did on this day. All through the morning people kept arriving in ones and twos. Every buckboard on the place was commissioned to haul the guests around the smooth roads and show them the estate; and those who preferred were furnished with saddle horses from the stable to keep their own mounts fresh for their return trip. Vance took charge of the wagon parties; Terence himself guided the horsemen, and he rode El Sangre, a flashing streak of blood red.

The exercise brought the color to his face; the wind raised his spirits; and when the gathering at the house to wait for the big dinner began, he was as gay as any.

"That's the way with young people," Elizabeth confided to her brother. "Trouble slips off their minds."

And then the second blow fell, the blow on which Vance had counted for his great results. No less a person than Sheriff Joe Minter galloped up and threw his reins before the veranda. He approached Elizabeth with a high flourish of his hat and a profound bow, for Uncle Joe Minter affected the mannered courtesy of the "Southern" school. Vance had them in profile from the side, and his nervous glance flickered from one to the other. The sheriff was plainly pleased with what he had seen on his way up Bear Creek. He was also happy to be present at so large a gathering. But to Elizabeth his coming was like a death. Her brother could tell the difference between her forced cordiality and the real thing. She had his horse put up; presented him to the few people whom he had not met, and then left him posing for the crowd of admirers. Life to the sheriff was truly a stage. Then Elizabeth went to Vance.

"You saw?" she gasped.

"Sheriff Minter? What of it? Rather nervy of the old ass to come up here for the party; he hardly knows us."

"No, no! Not that! But don't you remember? Don't you remember what Joe Minter did?"

"Good Lord!" gasped Vance, apparently just recalling. "He killed Black Jack! And what will Terry do when he finds out?"

She grew still whiter, hearing him name her own fear.

"They mustn't meet," she said desperately. "Vance, if you're half a man you'll find some way of getting that pompous, windy idiot off the place."

"My dear! Do you want me to invite him to leave?"

"Something—I don't care what!"

"Neither do I. But I can't insult the fool. That type resents an insult with gunplay. We must simply keep them apart. Keep the sheriff from talking."

"Keep rain from falling!" groaned Elizabeth. "Vance, if you won't do anything, I'll go and tell the sheriff that he must leave!"

"You don't mean it!"

"Do you think that I'm going to risk a murder?"

"I suppose you're right," nodded Vance, changing his tactics with Machiavellian smoothness. "If Terry saw the man who killed his father, all his twenty-four years of training would go up in smoke and the blood of his father would talk in him. There'd be a shooting!"

She caught a hand to her throat. "I'm not so sure of that, Vance. I think he would come through this acid test. But I don't want to take chances."

"I don't blame you, Elizabeth," said her brother heartily. "Neither would I. But if the sheriff stays here, I feel that I'm going to win the bet that I made twenty-four years ago. You remember? That Terry would shoot a man before he was twenty-five?"

"Have I ever forgotten?" she said huskily. "Have I ever let it go out of my mind? But it isn't the danger of Terry shooting. It's the danger of Terry being shot. If he should reach for a gun against the sheriff—that professional man-killer— Vance, something has to be done!"

"Right," he nodded. "I wouldn't trust Terry in the face of such a temptation to violence. Not for a moment!"

The natural stubbornness on which he had counted hardened in her face.

"I don't know."

"It would be an acid test, Elizabeth. But perhaps now is the time. You've spent twenty-four years training him. If he isn't what he ought to be now, he never will be, no doubt."

"It may be that you're right," she said gloomily. "Twenty-four years! Yes, and I've filled about half of my time with Terry and his training. Vance, you *are* right. If he has the elements of a mankiller in him after what I've done for him, then he's a hopeless case. The sheriff shall stay! The sheriff shall stay!"

She kept repeating it, as though the repetition of the phrase might bring her courage. And then she went back among her guests.

As for Vance, he remained skillfully in the background that day. It was peculiarly vital, this day of all days, that he should not be much in evidence. No one must see in him a controlling influence.

In the meantime he watched his sister with a growing admiration and with a growing concern. Instantly she had a problem on her hands. For the moment Terence heard that the great sheriff himself had joined the party, he was filled with happiness. Vance watched them meet with a heart swelling with happiness and surety of success. Straight through a group came Terry, weaving his way eagerly, and went up to the sheriff. Vance saw Elizabeth attempt to detain him, attempt to send him on an errand. But he waved her suggestion away for a moment and made for the sheriff. Elizabeth, seeing that the meeting could not be avoided, at least determined to be present at it. She came up with Terence and presented him.

"Sheriff Minter, this is Terence Colby."

"I've heard of you, Colby," said the sheriff kindly. And he waited for a response with the gleaming eye of a vain man. There was not long to wait.

"You've really heard of me?" said Terry, immensely pleased. "By the Lord, I've heard of *you*, sheriff! But, of course, everybody has."

"I dunno, son," said the sheriff benevolently. "But I been drifting around a tolerable long time, I guess."

"Why," said Terry, with a sort of outburst, "I've simply eaten up everything I could gather. I've even read about you in magazines!"

"Well, now you don't say," protested the sheriff. "In magazines?"

And his eye quested through the group, hoping for other listeners who might learn how broadly the fame of their sheriff was spread.

"That Canning fellow who travelled out West and ran into you and was along while you were hunting down the Garrison boys. I read his article."

The sheriff scratched his chin. "I disremember him. Canning? Canning? Come to think of it, I *do* remember him. Kind of a small man with washed-out eyes. Always with a notebook on his knee. I got sick of answering all that gent's questions, I recollect. Yep, he was along when I took the Garrison boys, but that little party didn't amount to much."

"*He* thought it did," said Terry fervently. "Said it was the bravest, coolest-headed, cunningest piece of work he'd ever seen done. Perhaps you'll tell me some of the other things—the things you count big?"

"Oh, I ain't done nothing much, come to think of it. All pretty simple, they looked to me, when I was doing them. Besides, I ain't much of a hand at talk!"

"Ah," said Terry, "you'd talk well enough to suit me, sheriff!"

The sheriff had found a listener after his own heart.

"They ain't nothing but a campfire that gives a good light to see a story by—the kind of stories I got to tell," he declared. "Some of these days I'll take you along with me on a trail, son, if you'd like—and most like I'll talk your arm off at night beside the fire. Like to come?"

"Like to?" cried Terry. "I'd be the happiest man in the mountains!"

"Would you, now? Well, Colby, you and me might hit it off pretty well. I've heard tell you ain't half bad with a rifle and pretty slick with a revolver, too."

"I practice hard," said Terry frankly. "I love guns."

"Good things to love, and good things to hate, too," philosophized the sheriff. "But all right in their own place, which ain't none too big, these days. The old times is gone when a man went out into the world with a hoss under him, and a pair of Colts strapped to his waist, and made his own way. Them days is gone, and our younger boys is going to pot!"

"I suppose so," admitted Terry.

"But you got a spark in you, son. Well, one of these days we'll get together. And I hear tell you got El Sangre?"

"I was lucky," said Terry.

"That's a sizable piece of work, Colby. I've seen twenty that run El Sangre, and never even got close enough to eat his dust. Nacheral pacer, right enough. I've seen him kite across country like a train! And his mane and tail blowing like smoke!"

"I got him with patience. That was all."

"S'pose we take a look at him?"

"By all means. Just come along with me."

Elizabeth struck in.

"Just a moment, Terence. There's Mr. Gainor, and he's been asking to see you. You can take the sheriff out to see El Sangre later. Besides, half a dozen people want to talk to the sheriff, and you mustn't monopolize him. Miss Wickson begged me to get her a chance to talk to you—the real Sheriff Minter. Do you mind?"

"Pshaw," said the sheriff. "I ain't no kind of a hand at talking to the womenfolk. Where is she?"

"Down yonder, sheriff. Shall we go?"

"The old lady with the cane?"

"No, the girl with the bright hair."

"Doggone me," muttered the sheriff. "Well, let's saunter down that way."

He waved to Terence, who, casting a black glance in the direction of Mr. Gainor, went off to execute Elizabeth's errand. Plainly Elizabeth had won the first engagement, but Vance was still confident. The dinner table would tell the tale.

CHAPTER 11

ELIZABETH LEFT the ordering of the guests at the table to Vance, and she consulted him about it as they went into the dining room. It was a long, low-ceilinged room, with more windows than wall space. It opened onto a small porch, and below the porch was the garden which had been the pride of Henry Cornish. Beside the tall glass doors which led out onto the porch she reviewed the seating plans of Vance.

"You at this end and I at the other," he said. "I've put the sheriff beside you, and right across from the sheriff is Nelly. She ought to keep him busy. The old idiot has a weakness for pretty girls, and the younger the better, it seems. Next to the sheriff is Mr. Gainor. He's a political power, and what time the sheriff doesn't spend on you and on Nelly he certainly will give to Gainor. The arrangement of the rest doesn't matter. I simply worked to get the sheriff well-pocketed and keep him under your eye."

"But why not under yours, Vance? You're a thousand times more diplomatic than I am."

"I wouldn't take the responsibility, for, after all, this may turn out to be a rather solemn occasion, Elizabeth."

"You don't think so, Vance?"

"I pray not."

"And where have you put Terence?"

"Next to Nelly, at your left."

"Good heavens, Vance, that's almost directly opposite the sheriff. You'll have them practically facing each other."

It was the main thing he was striving to attain. He placated her carefully.

"I had to. There's a danger. But the advantage is huge. You'll be there between them, you might say. You can keep the table talk in hand at that end. Flash me a signal if you're in trouble, and I'll fire a question down the table at the sheriff or Terry, and get their attention. In the meantime you can draw Terry into talk with you if he begins to ask the sheriff what you consider leading questions. In that way, you'll keep the talk a thousand leagues away from the death of Black Jack."

He gained his point without much more trouble. Half an hour later the table was surrounded by the guests. It was a table of baronial proportions, but twenty couples occupied every inch of the space easily. Vance found himself a greater distance than he could have wished from the scene of danger, and of electrical contact.

At least four zones of cross-fire talk intervened, and the talk at the farther end of the table was completely lost to him, except when some new and amazing dish, a triumph of Wu Chi's fabrication, was brought on, and an appreciative wave of silence attended it.

Or again, the mighty voice of the sheriff was heard to bellow forth in laughter of heroic proportions.

Aside from that, there was no information he could gather except by his eyes. And chiefly, the face of Elizabeth. He knew her like a book in which he had often read. Twice he read the danger signals. When the great roast was being removed, he saw her eyes widen and her lips contract a trifle, and he knew that someone had come very close to the danger line indeed. Again when dessert was coming in bright shoals on the trays of the Chinese servants, the glance of his sister fixed on him down the length of the table with a grim appeal. He made a gesture of helplessness. Between them four distinct groups into which the table talk had divided were now going at full blast. He could hardly have made himself heard at the other end of the table without shouting.

Yet that crisis also passed away. Elizabeth was working hard, but as the meal progressed toward a close, he began to worry. It had seemed impossible that the sheriff could actually sit this length of time in such an assemblage without launching into the stories for which he was famous. Above all, he would be sure to tell how he had started on his career as a manhunter by relating how he slew Black Jack.

Once the appalling thought came to Vance that the story must have been told during one of those moments when his sister had shown alarm. The crisis might be over, and Terry had indeed showed a restraint which was a credit to Elizabeth's training. But by the hunted look in her eyes, he knew that the climax had not yet been reached, and that she was continually fighting it away.

He writhed with impatience. If he had not been a fool, he would have taken that place himself, and then he could have seen to it that the sheriff, with dexterous guiding, should approach the fatal story. As it was, how could he tell that Elizabeth might not undo all his plans and cleverly keep the sheriff away from his favorite topic for an untold length of time? But as he told his sister, he wished to place all the seeming responsibility on her own shoulders. Perhaps he had played too safe.

The first ray of hope came to him as coffee was brought in. The prodigious eating of the cattlemen and miners at the table had brought them to a stupor. They no longer talked, but puffed with unfamiliar awkwardness at the fine Havanas which Vance had provided. Even the women talked less, having worn off the edge of the novelty of actually dining at the table of Elizabeth Cornish. And since the hostess was occupied solely with the little group nearest her, and there was no guiding mind to pick up the threads of talk in each group and maintain it, this duty fell more and more into the hands of Vance. He took up his task with pleasure.

Farther and farther down the table extended the sphere of

his mild influence. He asked Mr. Wainwright to tell the story of how he treed the bear so that the tenderfoot author could come and shoot it. Mr. Wainwright responded with gusto. The story was a success. He varied it by requesting young Dobel to describe the snowslide which had wiped out the Vorheimer shack the winter before.

Young Dobel did well enough to make the men grunt at the end, and he brought several little squeals of horror from the ladies.

All of this was for a purpose. Vance was setting the precedent, and they were becoming used to hearing stories. At the end of each tale the silence of expectation was longer and wider. Finally, it reached the other end of the table, and suddenly the sheriff discovered that tales were going the rounds, and that he had not yet been heard. He rolled his eye with an inward look, and Vance knew that he was searching for some smooth means of introducing one of his yarns.

Victory!

But here Elizabeth cut trenchantly into the heart of the conversation. She had seen and understood. She shot home half a dozen questions with the accuracy of a marksman, and beat up a drumfire of responses from the ladies which, for a time, rattled up and down the length of the table. The sheriff was biting his mustache thoughtfully.

It was only a momentary check, however. Just at the point where Vance began to despair of ever effecting his goal, the silence began again as lady after lady ran out of material for the nonce. And as the silence spread, the sheriff was visibly gathering steam.

Again Elizabeth cut in. But this time there was only a sporadic chattering in response. Coffee was steaming before them, Wu Chi's powerful, thick, aromatic coffee, which only he knew how to make. They were in a mood, now, to hear stories, that tableful of people. An expected ally came to the aid of Vance. It was Terence, who had been eating his heart out during the silly table talk of the past few minutes. Now he seized upon the first clear opening.

"Sheriff Minter, I've heard a lot about the time you ran down Johnny Garden. But I've never had the straight of it. Won't you tell us how it happened?"

"Oh," protested the sheriff, "it don't amount to much."

Elizabeth cast one frantic glance at her brother, and strove to edge into the interval of silence with a question directed at Mr. Gainor. But he shelved that question; the whole table was obviously waiting for the great man to speak. A dozen appeals for the yarn poured in.

"Well," said the sheriff, "if you folks are plumb set on it, I'll tell you just how it come about."

There followed a long story of how Johnny Garden had announced that he would ride down and shoot up the sheriff's own town, and then get away on the sheriff's own horse— and how he did it. And how the sheriff was laughed at heartily by the townsfolk, and how the whole mountain district joined in the laughter. And how he started out single-handed in the middle of winter to run down Johnny Garden, and struck through the mountains, was caught above the timberline in a terrific blizzard, kept on in peril of his life until he barely managed to reach the timber again on the other side of the ridge. How he descended upon the hiding-place of Johnny Garden, found Johnny gone, but his companions there, and made a bargain with them to let them go if they would consent to stand by and offer no resistance when he fought with Johnny on the latter's return. How they were as good as their word and how, when Johnny returned, they stood aside and let Johnny and the sheriff fight it out. How the sheriff beat Johnny to the draw, but was wounded in the left arm while Johnny fired a second shot as he lay dying on the floor of the lean-to. How the sheriff's wound was dressed by the companions of the dead Johnny, and how he was safely dismissed with honor, as between brave men, and how afterwards he hunted those same men down one by one.

It was quite a long story, but the audience followed it with a breathless interest.

"Yes, sir," concluded the sheriff, as the applause of murmurs fell off. "And from yarns like that one you wouldn't never figure it that I was the son of a minister brung up plumb peaceful. Now, would you?"

And again, to the intense joy of Vance, it was Terry who brought the subject back, and this time the subject of all subjects which Elizabeth dreaded, and which Vance longed for.

"Tell us how you came to branch out, Sheriff Minter?"

"It was this way," began the sheriff, while Elizabeth cast

at Vance a glance of frantic and weary appeal, to which he responded with a gesture which indicated that the cause was lost.

"I was brung up mighty proper. I had a most amazing lot of prayers at the tip of my tongue when I wasn't no more'n knee-high to a grasshopper. But when a man has got a fire in him, they ain't no use trying to smother it. You either got to put water on it or else let it burn itself out.

"My old man didn't see it that way. When I got to cutting up he'd try to smother it, and stop me by saying: 'Don't!' Which don't accomplish nothing with young gents that got any spirit. Not a damn thing—asking your pardon, ladies! Well, sirs, he kept me in harness, you might say, and pulling dead straight down the road and working hard and faithful. But all the time I'd been saving up steam, and swelling and swelling and getting pretty near ready to burst.

"Well, sirs, pretty soon—we was living in Garrison City them days, when Garrison wasn't near the town that it is now—along comes word that Jack Hollis is around. A lot of you younger folks ain't never heard nothing about him. But in his day Jack Hollis was as bad as they was made. They was nothing that Jack wouldn't turn to real handy, from shootin' up a town to sticking up a train or a stage. And he done it all just about as well. He was one of them universal experts. He could blow a safe as neat as you'd ask. And if it come to a gun fight, he was greased lightning with a flying start. That was Jack Hollis."

The sheriff paused to draw breath.

"Perhaps," said Elizabeth Cornish, white about the lips, "we had better go into the living room to hear the rest of the sheriff's story?"

It was not a very skillful diversion, but Elizabeth had reached the point of utter desperation. And on the way into the living room unquestionably she would be able to divert Terry to something else. Vance held his breath.

And it was Terry who signed his own doom.

"We're very comfortable here, Aunt Elizabeth. Let's not go in till the sheriff has finished his story."

The sheriff rewarded him with a flash of gratitude, and Vance settled back in his chair. The end could not, now, be far away.

CHAPTER 12

"I WAS SAYING," proceeded the sheriff, "that they scared their babies in these here parts with the name of Jack Hollis. Which they sure done. Well, sir, he was bad."

"Not all bad, surely," put in Vance. "I've heard a good many stories about the generosity of—"

He was anxious to put in the name of Black Jack, since the sheriff was sticking so close to "Jack Hollis," which was a name that Terry had not yet heard for his dead father. But before he could get out the name, the sheriff, angry at the interruption, resumed the smooth current of his tale with a side flash at Vance.

"Not all bad, you say? Generous? Sure he was generous. Them that live outside the law has got to be generous to keep a gang around 'em. Not that Hollis ever played with a gang much, but he had hangers-on all over the mountains and gents that he had done good turns for and hadn't gone off and talked about it. But that was just common sense. He knew he'd need friends that he could trust if he ever got in trouble. If he was wounded, they had to be someplace where he could rest up. Ain't that so? Well, sir, that's what the goodness of Jack Hollis amounted to. No, sir, he was bad. Plumb bad and all bad!

"But he had them qualities that a young gent with an imagination is apt to cotton to. He was free with his money. He dressed like a dandy. He'd gamble with hundreds, and then give back half of his winnings if he'd broke the gent that run the bank. Them was the sort of things that Jack Hollis would do. And I had my head full of him. Well, about the time that he come to the neighborhood, I sneaked out of the house one night and went off to a dance with a girl that I was sweet on. And when I come back, I found Dad waiting up for me ready to skin me alive. He tried to give me a clubbing. I kicked the stick out of his hands and swore that I'd leave and never come back. Which I never done, living up to my word proper.

"But when I found myself outside in the night, I says to myself: 'Where shall I go now?'

"And then, being sort of sick at the world, and hating Dad particular, I decided to go out and join Jack Hollis. I was going to go bad. Mostly to cut up Dad, I reckon, and not because I wanted to particular.

"It wasn't hard to find Jack Hollis. Not for a kid my age that was sure not to be no officer of the law. Besides, they didn't go out single and hunt for Hollis. They went in gangs of a half a dozen at a time, or more if they could get 'em. And even then they mostly got cleaned up when they cornered Hollis. Yes, sir, he made life sad for the sheriffs in them parts that he favored most.

"I found Jack toasting bacon over a fire. He had two gents with him, and they brung me in, finding me sneaking around like a fool kid instead of walking right into camp. Jack sized me up a minute. He was a fine-looking boy, was Hollis. He gimme a look out of them fine black eyes of his which I won't never forget. Aye, a handsome scoundrel, that Hollis!"

Elizabeth Cornish sank back in her chair and covered her eyes with her hands for a moment. To the others it seemed that she was merely rubbing weary eyes. But her brother knew perfectly that she was near to fainting.

He looked at Terry and saw that the boy was following the tale with sparkling eyes.

"I like what you say about this Hollis, sheriff," he ventured softly.

"Do you? Well, so did I like what I seen of him that night, for all I knew that he was a no-good, man-killing, heartless sort. I told him right off that I wanted to join him. I even up and give him an exhibition of shooting.

"What do you think he says to me? 'You go home to your ma, young man!'

"That's what he said.

" 'I ain't a baby,' says I to Jack Hollis. 'I'm a grown man. I'm ready to fight your way.'

" 'Any fool can fight,' says Jack Hollis. 'But a gent with any sense don't have to fight. You can lay to that, son!'

" 'Don't call me son,' says I. 'I'm older than you was when you started out.'

" 'I'd had my heart busted before I started,' says Jack Hollis to me. 'Are you as old as that, son? You go back home and don't bother me no more. I'll come back in five years and see if you're still in the same mind!'

"And that was what I seen of Jack Hollis.

"I went back into town—Garrison City. I slept over the stables the rest of that night. The next day I loafed around town not hardly noways knowing what I was going to do.

"Then I was loafing around with my rifle, like I was going out on a hunting trip that afternoon. And pretty soon I heard a lot of noise coming down the street, guns and what not. I look out the window and there comes Jack Hollis, hell-bent! Jack Hollis! And then it pops into my head that they was a big price, for them days, on Jack's head. I picked up my gun and eased it over the sill of the window and got a good bead.

"Jack turned in his saddle—"

There was a faint groan from Elizabeth Cornish. All eyes focused on her in amazement. She mustered a smile. The story went on.

"When Jack turned to blaze away at them that was piling out around the corner of the street, I let the gun go, and I drilled him clean. Great sensation, gents, to have a life under your trigger. Just beckon one mite of an inch and a life goes scooting up to heaven or down to hell. I never got over seeing Hollis spill sidewise out of that saddle. There he was a minute before better'n any five men when it come to fighting. And now he wasn't nothing but a lot of trouble to bury. Just so many pounds of flesh. You see? Well, sir, the price on Black Jack set me up in life and gimme my start. After that I sort of specialized in manhunting, and I've kept on ever since."

Terry leaned across the table, his left arm outstretched to call the sheriff's attention.

"I didn't catch that last name, sheriff," he said.

The talk was already beginning to bubble up at the end of the sheriff's tale. But there was something in the tone of the boy that cut through the talk to its root. People were suddenly looking at him out of eyes which were very wide indeed. And it was not hard to find a reason. His handsome face was colorless, like a carving from the stone, and under his knitted brows his black eyes were ominous in the shadow. The sheriff frankly gaped at him. It was another man who sat across the table in the chair where the ingenuous youth had been a moment before.

"What name? Jack Hollis?"

"I think the name you used was Black Jack, sheriff?"

"Black Jack? Sure. That was the other name for Jack Hollis. He was mostly called Black Jack for short, but that was chiefly among his partners. Outside he was called Jack Hollis, which was his real name."

Terence rose from his chair, more colorless than ever, the knuckles of one hand resting upon the table. He seemed very tall, years older, grim.

"Terry!" called Elizabeth Cornish softly.

It was like speaking to a stone.

"Gentlemen," said Terry, though his eyes never left the face of the sheriff, and it was obvious that he was making his speech to one pair of ears alone. "I have been living among you under the name of Colby—Terence Colby. It seems an appropriate moment to say that this is not my name. After what the sheriff has just told you it may be of interest to know that my real name is Hollis. Terence Hollis is my name and my father was Jack Hollis, commonly known as Black Jack, it seems from the story of the sheriff. I also wish to say that I am announcing my parentage not because I wish to apologize for it—in spite of the rather remarkable narrative of the sheriff—but because I am proud of it."

He lifted his head while he spoke. And his eye went boldly, calmly down the table.

"This could not have been expected before, because none of you knew my father's name. I confess that I did not know it myself until a very short time ago. Otherwise I should not have listened to the sheriff's story until the end. Hereafter, however, when any of you are tempted to talk about Black or Jack Hollis, remember that his son is alive—and in good health!"

He hung in his place for an instant as though he were ready to hear a reply. But the table was stunned. Then Terry turned on his heel and left the room.

It was the signal for a general upstarting from the table, a pushing back of chairs, a gathering around Elizabeth Cornish. She was as white as Terry had been while he talked. But there was a gathering excitement in her eye, and happiness. The sheriff was full of apologies. He would rather have had his tongue torn out by the roots than to have offended her or the young man with his story.

She waved the sheriff's apology aside. It was unfortunate, but it could not have been helped. They all realized that. She guided her guests into the living room, and on the way she managed to drift close to her brother.

Her eyes were on fire with her triumph.

"You heard, Vance? You saw what he did?"

There was a haunted look about the face of Vance, who had seen his high-built schemes topple about his head.

"He did even better than I expected, Elizabeth. Thank heaven for it!"

CHAPTER 13

TERENCE HOLLIS had gone out of the room and up the stairs like a man stunned or walking in his sleep. Not until he stepped into the familiar room did the blood begin to return to his face, and with the warmth there was a growing sensation of uneasiness.

Something was wrong. Something had to be righted. Gradually his mind cleared. The thing that was wrong was that the man who had killed his father was now under the same roof with him, had shaken his hand, had sat in bland complacency and looked in his face and told of the butchery.

Butchery it was, according to Terry's standards. For the sake of the price on the head of the outlaw, young Minter had shoved his rifle across a window sill, taken his aim, and with no risk to himself had shot down the wild rider. His heart stood up in his throat with revulsion at the thought of it. Murder, horrible, and cold-blooded, the more horrible because it was legal.

Something had to be done. What was it?

And when he turned, what he saw was the gun cabinet with a shimmer of light on the barrels. Then he knew. He selected his favorite Colt and drew it out. It was loaded, and the action in perfect condition. Many and many an hour he had practiced and blazed away hundreds of rounds of ammunition with it. It responded to his touch like a muscular part of his own body.

He shoved it under his coat, and walking down the stairs again the chill of the steel worked through to his flesh. He went back to the kitchen and called out Wu Chi. The latter came shuffling in his slippers, nodding, grinning in anticipation of compliments.

"Wu," came the short demand, "can you keep your mouth shut and do what you're told to do?"

"Wu try," said the Chinaman, grave as a yellow image instantly.

"Then go to the living room and tell Mr. Gainor and Sheriff Minter that Mr. Harkness is waiting for them outside and wishes to see them on business of the most urgent nature. It will only be the matter of a moment. Now go. Gainor and the sheriff. Don't forget."

He received a scared glance, and then went out onto the veranda and sat down to wait.

That was the right way, he felt. His father would have called the sheriff to the door, in a similar situation, and after one brief challenge they would have gone for their guns. But there was another way, and that was the way of the Colbys. Their way was right. They lived like gentlemen, and, above all, they fought always like gentlemen.

Presently the screen door opened, squeaked twice, and then closed with a hum of the screen as it slammed. Steps approached him. He got up from the chair and faced them, Gainor and the sheriff. The sheriff had instinctively put on his hat, like a man who does not understand the open air with an uncovered head. But Gainor was uncovered, and his white hair glimmered.

He was a tall, courtly old fellow. His ceremonious address had won him much political influence. Men said that Gainor was courteous to a dog, not because he respected the dog, but because he wanted to practice for a man. He had always the correct rejoinder, always did the right thing. He had a thin, stern face and a hawk nose that gave him a cast of ferocity in certain aspects.

It was to him that Terry addressed himself.

"Mr. Gainor," he said, "I'm sorry to have sent in a false message. But my business is very urgent, and I have a very particular reason for not wishing to have it known that I have called you out."

The moment he rose out of the chair and faced them, Gainor had stopped short. He was quite capable of fast thinking, and now his glance flickered from Terry to the sheriff and back again. It was plain that he had shrewd suspicions as to the purpose behind that call. The sheriff was merely confused. He flushed as much as his tanned-leather skin permitted. As for Terry, the moment his glance fell on the sheriff he felt his muscles jump into hard ridges, and an almost uncontrollable desire to go at the throat of the other seized him. He quelled that desire and fought it back with a chill of fear.

"My father's blood working out!" he thought to himself.

And he fastened his attention on Mr. Gainor and tried to shut the picture of the sheriff out of his brain. But the desire to leap at the tall man was as consuming as the passion for water in the desert. And with a shudder of horror he found himself without a moral scruple. Just behind the thin partition of his will power there was a raging fury to get at Joe Minter. He wanted to kill. He wanted to snuff that life out as the life of Black Jack Hollis had been snuffed.

He excluded the sheriff deliberately from his attention and turned fully upon Gainor.

"Mr. Gainor, will you be kind enough to go over to that grove of spruce where the three of us can talk without any danger of interruption?"

Of course, that speech revealed everything. Gainor stiffened a little and the tuft of beard which ran down to a point on his chin quivered and jutted out. The sheriff seemed to feel nothing more than a mild surprise and curiosity. And the three went silently, side by side, under the spruce. They were glorious trees, strong of trunk and nobly proportioned. Their tops were silver-bright in the sunshine. Through the lower branches the light was filtered through layer after layer of shadow, until on the ground there were only a few patches of light here and there, and these were no brighter than silver moonshine, and seemed to be without heat. Indeed, in the mild shadow among the trees lay the chill of the mountain air which seems to lurk in covert places waiting for the night.

It might have been this chill that made Terry button his coat closer about him and tremble a little as he entered the shadow. The great trunks shut out the world in a scattered wall. There was a narrow opening here among the trees at the very center. The three were in a sort of gorge of which the solemn spruce trees furnished the sides, the cold blue of the mountain skies was just above the lofty tree-tips, and the wind kept the pure fragrance of the evergreens stirring about them. The odor is the soul of the mountains. A great surety had come to Terry that this was the last place he would ever see on earth. He was about to die, and he was glad, in a dim sort of way, that he should die in a place so beautiful. He looked at the sheriff, who stood calm but puzzled, and at Gainor, who was very grave, indeed, and returned his look with one of infinite pity, as though he knew and understood and acquiesced, but was deeply grieved that it must be so.

"Gentlemen," said Terry, making his voice light and cheerful as he felt that the voice of a Colby should be at such a time, being about to die. "I suppose you understand why I have asked you to come here?"

"Yes," nodded Gainor.

"But I'm damned if I do," said the sheriff frankly.

Terry looked upon him coldly. He felt that he had not the slightest chance of killing this professional manslayer, but at least he would do his best—for the sake of Black Jack's memory. But to think that his life—his mind—his soul—all that was dear to him and all that he was dear to, should ever lie at the command of the trigger of this hard, crafty, vain, and unimportant fellow! He writhed at the thought. It made him stand stiffer. His chin went up. He grew literally taller before their eyes, and such a look came on his face that the sheriff instinctively fell back a pace.

"Mr. Gainor," said Terry, as though his contempt for the sheriff was too great to permit his speaking directly to Minter, "will you explain to the sheriff that my determination to have satisfaction does not come from the fact that he killed my father, but because of the manner of the killing? To the sheriff it seems justifiable. To me it seems a murder. Having that thought, there is only one thing to do. One of us must not leave this place!"

Gainor bowed, but the sheriff gaped.

"By the eternal!" he scoffed. "This sounds like one of them duels of the old days. This was the way they used to talk!"

"Gentlemen," said Gainor, raising his long-fingered hand, "it is my solemn duty to admonish you to make up your differences amicably."

"Whatever that means," sneered the sheriff. "But tell this young fool that's trying to act like he couldn't see me or hear me—tell him that I don't carry no grudge ag'in' him, that I'm sorry he's Black Jack's son, but that it's something he can live down, maybe. And I'll go so far as to say I'm sorry that I done all that talking right to his face. But farther than that I won't go. And if all this is leading up to a gun-play, by God, gents, the minute a gun comes into my hand I shoot to kill, mark you that, and don't you never forget it!"

Mr. Gainor had remained with his hand raised during this outbreak. Now he turned to Terry.

"You have heard?" he said. "I think the sheriff is going quite a way toward you, Mr. Colby."

"Hollis!" gasped Terry. "Hollis is the name, sir!"

"I beg your pardon," said Gainor. "Mr. Hollis it is! Gentlemen, I assure you that I feel for you both. It seems, however, to be one of those unfortunate affairs when the mind must stop its debate and physical action must take up its proper place. I lament the necessity, but I admit it, even though the law does not admit it. But there are unwritten laws, sirs, unwritten laws which I for one consider among the holies of holies."

Palpably the old man was enjoying every minute of his own talk. It was not his first affair of this nature. He came out of an early and more courtly generation where men drank together in the evening by firelight and carved one another in the morning with glimmering bowie knives.

"You are both," he protested, "dear to me. I esteem you both as men and as good citizens. And I have done my best to open the way for peaceful negotiations toward an understanding. It seems that I have failed. Very well, sirs. Then it must be battle. You are both armed? With revolvers?"

"Nacher'ly," said the sheriff, and spat accurately at a blaze on the tree trunk beside him. He had grown very quiet.

"I am armed," said Terry calmly, "with a revolver."

"Very good."

The hand of Gainor glided into his bosom and came forth

bearing a white handkerchief. His right hand slid into his coat and came forth likewise—bearing a long revolver.

"Gentlemen," he said, "the first man to disobey my directions I shall shoot down unquestioningly, like a dog. I give you my solemn word for it!"

And his eye informed them that he would enjoy the job.

He continued smoothly: "This contest shall accord with the only terms by which a duel with guns can be properly fought. You will stand back to back with your guns not displayed, but in your clothes. At my word you will start walking in the opposite directions until my command 'Turn!' and at this command you will wheel, draw your guns, and fire until one man falls—or both!"

He sent his revolver through a peculiar, twirling motion and shook back his long white hair.

"Ready, gentlemen, and God defend the right!"

CHAPTER 14

THE TALK was fitful in the living room. Elizabeth Cornish did her best to revive the happiness of her guests, but she herself was a prey to the same subdued excitement which showed in the faces of the others. A restraint had been taken away by the disappearance of both the storm centers of the dinner—the sheriff and Terry. Therefore it was possible to talk freely. And people talked. But not loudly. They were prone to gather in little familiar groups and discuss in a whisper how Terry had risen and spoken before them. Now and then someone, for the sake of politeness, strove to open a general theme of conversation, but it died away like a ripple on a placid pond.

"But what I can't understand," said Elizabeth to Vance when she was able to maneuver him to her side later on, "is why they seem to expect something more."

Vance was very grave and looked tired. The realization

that all his cunning, all his work, had been for nothing, tormented him. He had set his trap and baited it, and it had worked perfectly—save that the teeth of the trap had closed over thin air. At the dénouement of the sheriff's story there should have been the barking of two guns and a film of gunpowder smoke should have gone tangling to the ceiling. Instead there had been the formal little speech from Terry— and then quiet. Yet he had to mask and control his bitterness; he had to watch his tongue in talking with his sister.

"You see," he said quietly, "they don't understand. They can't see how fine Terry is in having made no attempt to avenge the death of his father. I suppose a few of them think he's a coward. I even heard a little talk to that effect!"

"Impossible!" cried Elizabeth.

She had not thought of this phase of the matter. All at once she hated the sheriff.

"It really is possible," said Vance. "You see, it's known that Terry never fights if he can avoid it. There never has been any real reason for fighting until today. But you know how gossip will put the most unrelated facts together, and make a complete story in some way."

"I wish the sheriff were dead!" moaned Elizabeth. "Oh, Vance, if you only hadn't gone near Craterville! If you only hadn't distributed those wholesale invitations!"

It was almost too much for Vance—to be reproached after so much of the triumph was on her side—such a complete victory that she herself would never dream of the peril she and Terry had escaped. But he had to control his irritation. In fact, he saw his whole life ahead of him carefully schooled and controlled. He no longer had anything to sell. Elizabeth had made a mock of him and shown him that he was hollow, that he was living on her charity. He must all the days that she remained alive keep flattering her, trying to find a way to make himself a necessity to her. And after her death there would be a still harder task. Terry, who disliked him pointedly, would then be the master, and he would face the bitter necessity of cajoling the youngster whom he detested. A fine life, truly! An almost noble anguish of the spirit came upon Vance. He was urged to the very brink of the determination to thrust out into the world and make his own living. But he recoiled from that horrible idea in time.

"Yes," he said, "that was the worst step I ever took. But

I was trying to be wholehearted in the Western way, my dear, and show that I had entered into the spirit of things."

"As a matter of fact," sighed Elizabeth, "you nearly ruined Terry's life—and mine!"

"Very near," said the penitent Vance. "But then—you see how well it has turned out? Terry has taken the acid test, and now you can trust him under any—"

The words were literally blown off ragged at his lips. Two revolver shots exploded at them. No one gun could have fired them. And there was a terrible significance in the angry speed with which one had followed the other, blending, so that the echo from the lofty side of Sleep Mountain was but a single booming sound. In that clear air it was impossible to tell the direction of the noise.

Everyone in the room seemed to listen stupidly for a repetition of the noises. But there was no repetition.

"Vance," whispered Elizabeth in such a tone that the coward dared not look into her face. "It's happened!"

"What?" He knew, but he wanted the joy of hearing it from her own lips.

"It has happened," she whispered in the same ghostly voice. "But which one?"

That was it. Who had fallen—Terry, or the sheriff? A long, heavy step crossed the little porch. Either man might walk like that.

The door was flung open. Terence Hollis stood before them.

"I think that I've killed the sheriff," he said simply. "I'm going up to my room to put some things together; and I'll go into town with any man who wishes to arrest me. Decide that between yourselves."

With that he turned and walked away with a step as deliberately unhurried as his approach had been. The manner of the boy was more terrible than the thing he had done. Twice he had shocked them on the same afternoon. And they were just beginning to realize that the shell of boyhood was being ripped away from Terence Colby. Terence Hollis, son of Black Jack, was being revealed to them.

The men received the news with utter bewilderment. The sheriff was as formidable in the opinion of the mountains as some Achilles. It was incredible that he should have fallen. And naturally a stern murmur rose: "Foul play!"

Since the first vigilante days there has been no sound in all the West so dreaded as that deep-throated murmur of angry, honest men. That murmur from half a dozen law-abiding citizens will put the fear of death in the hearts of a hundred outlaws. The rumble grew, spread: "Foul play." And they began to look to one another, these men of action.

Only Elizabeth was silent. She rose to her feet, as tall as her brother, without an emotion on her face. And her brother would never forget her.

"It seems that you've won, Vance. It seems that blood will out, after all. The time is not quite up—and you win the bet!"

Vance shook his head as though in protest and struck his hand across his face. He dared not let her see the joy that contorted his features. Triumph here on the very verge of defeat! It misted his eyes. Joy gave wings to his thoughts. He was the master of the valley.

"But—you'll think before you do anything, Elizabeth?"

"I've done my thinking already—twenty-four years of it. I'm going to do what I promised I'd do."

"And that?"

"You'll see and hear in time. What's yonder?"

The men were rising, one after another, and bunching together. Before Vance could answer, there was a confusion in the hall, running feet here and there. They heard the hard, shrill voice of Wu Chi chattering directions and the guttural murmurs of his fellow servants as they answered. Someone ran out into the hall and came back to the huddling, stirring crowd in the living room.

"He's not dead—but close to it. Maybe die any minute—maybe live through it!"

That was the report.

"We'll get young Hollis and hold him to see how the sheriff comes out."

"Aye, we'll get him!"

All at once they boiled into action and the little crowd of men thrust for the big doors that led into the hall. They cast the doors back and came directly upon the tall, white-headed figure of Gainor.

CHAPTER 15

GAINOR'S DIGNITY split the force of their rush. They recoiled as water strikes on a rock and divides into two meager swirls. And when one or two went past him on either side, he recalled them.

"Boys, there seems to be a little game on hand. What is it?"

Something repelling, coldly inquiring in his attitude and in his voice. They would have gone on if they could, but they could not. He held them with a force of knowledge of things that they did not know. They were remembering that this man had gone out with the sheriff to meet, apparently, his death. And yet Gainor, a well-tried friend of the sheriff, seemed unexcited. They had to answer his question, and how could they lie when he saw them rushing through a door with revolvers coming to brown, skillful hands? It was someone from the rear who made the confession.

"We're going to get young Black Jack!"

That was it. The speech came out like the crack of a gun, clearing the atmosphere. It told every man exactly what was in his own mind, felt but not confessed. They had no grudge against Terry, really. But they were determined to hang the son of Black Jack. Had it been a lesser deed, they might have let him go. But his victim was too distinguished in their society. He had struck down Joe Minter; the ghost of the great Black Jack himself seemed to have stalked out among them.

"You're going to get young Terry Hollis?" interpreted Gainor, and his voice rose and rang over them. Those who had slipped past him on either side came back and faced him. In the distance Elizabeth had not stirred. Vance kept watching her face. It was cold as ice, unreadable. He could not believe that she was allowing this lynching party to organize under her own roof—a lynching party aimed at Terence. It began to grow in him that he had gained a greater victory than he imagined.

"If you aim at Terry," went on Gainor, his voice even louder, "you'll have to aim at me, too. There's going to be no lynching bee, my friends!"

The women had crowded back in the room. They made a little bank of stir and murmur around Elizabeth.

"Gentlemen," said Gainor, shaking his white hair back again in his imposing way, "there has been no murder. The sheriff is not going to die. There has been a disagreement between two men of honor. The sheriff is now badly wounded. I think that is all. Does anybody want to ask questions about what has happened?"

There was a bustle in the group of men. They were putting away the weapons, not quite sure what they could do next.

"I am going to tell you exactly what has happened," said Gainor. "You heard the unfortunate things that passed at the table today. What the sheriff said was not said as an insult; but under the circumstances it became necessary for Terence Hollis to resent what he had heard. As a man of honor he could not do otherwise. You all agree with me in that?"

They grunted a grudging assent. There were ways and ways of looking at such things. The way of Gainor was a generation old. But there was something so imposing about the old fellow, something which breathed the very spirit of honor and fair play, that they could not argue the point.

"Accordingly Mr. Hollis sent for the sheriff. Not to bring him outdoors and shoot him down in a sudden gunplay, nor to take advantage of him through a surprise—as a good many men would have been tempted to do, my friends, for the sheriff has a wide reputation as a handler of guns of all sorts. No, sir, he sent for me also, and he told us frankly that the bad blood between him and the sheriff must be spent. You understand? By the Lord, my friends, I admired the fine spirit of the lad. He expected to be shot rather than to drop the sheriff. I could tell that by his expression. But his eye did not falter. It carried me back to the old days—to old days, sirs!"

There was not a murmur in the entire room. The eye of Elizabeth Cornish was fire. Whether with anger or pride, Vance could not tell. But he began to worry.

"We went over to the group of silver spruce near the house. I gave them the directions. They came and stood together, back to back, with their revolvers not drawn. They began to walk away in opposite directions at my command.

"When I called 'Turn,' they wheeled. My gun was ready to shoot down the first man guilty of foul play—but there was no attempt to turn too soon, before the signal. They whirled, snatching out their guns—and the revolver of the sheriff hung in his clothes!"

A groan from the little crowd.

"Although, upon my word," said Gainor, "I do not think that the sheriff could have possibly brought out his gun as swiftly as Terence Hollis did. His whirl was like the spin of a top, or the snap of a whiplash, and as he snapped about, the revolver was in his hand, not raised to draw a bead, but at his hip. The sheriff set his teeth—but Terry did not fire!"

A bewildered murmur from the crowd.

"No, my friends," cried Gainor, his voice quivering, "he did not fire. He dropped the muzzle of his gun—and waited. By heaven, my heart went out to him. It was magnificent."

The thin, strong hand of Elizabeth closed on the arm of Vance. "That was a Colby who did that!" she whispered.

"The sheriff gritted his teeth," went on Gainor, "and tore out his gun. All this pause had been such a space as is needed for an eyelash to flicker twice. Out shot the sheriff's Colt. And then, and not until then, did the muzzle of Terry's revolver jerk up. Even after that delay he beat the sheriff to the trigger. The two shots came almost together, but the sheriff was already falling when he pulled his trigger, and his aim was wild.

"He dropped on one side, the revolver flying out of his hand. I started forward, and then I stopped. By heaven, the sheriff had stretched out his arm and picked up his gun again. He was not through fighting.

"A bulldog spirit, you say? Yes! And what could I do? It was the sheriff's right to keep on fighting as long as he wished. And it was the right of Terence to shoot the man full of holes the minute his hand touched the revolver again.

"I could only stand still. I saw the sheriff raise his revolver. It was an effort of agony. But he was still trying to kill. And I nerved myself and waited for the explosion of the gun of Terence. I say I nerved myself for that shock, but the gun did not explode. I looked at him in wonder. My friends, he was putting up his gun and quietly looking the sheriff in the eye!

"At that I shouted to him, I don't know what. I shouted to the sheriff not to fire. Too late. The muzzle of the gun was already tilting up, the barrel was straightening. And then the gun fell from Minter's hand and he dropped on his side. His strength had failed him at the last moment.

"But I say, sirs, that what Terence Hollis did was the finest thing I have ever seen in my life, and I have seen fine things done by gentlemen before. There may be unpleasant associations with the name of Terry's father. I, for one, shall never carry over those associations to the son. Never! He has my hand, my respect, my esteem in every detail. He is a gentleman, my friends! There is nothing for us to do. If the sheriff is unfortunate and the wound should prove fatal, Terence will give himself up to the law. If he lives, he will be the first to tell you to keep your hands off the boy!"

He ended in a little silence. But there was no appreciative burst of applause from those who heard him. The fine courage of Terence was, to them, merely the iron nerve of the man-killer, the keen eye and the judicious mind which knew that the sheriff would collapse before he fired his second shot. And this courtesy before the first shot was simply the surety of the man who knew that no matter what advantage he gave to his enemy, his own speed of hand would more than make up for it.

Gainor, reading their minds, paid no more heed to them. He went straight across the room and took the hand of Elizabeth.

"Dear Miss Cornish," he said so that all could hear, "I congratulate you for the man you have given us in Terence Hollis."

Vance, watching, saw the tears of pleasure brighten the eyes of his sister.

"You are very kind," she said. "But now I must see Sheriff Minter and be sure that everything is done for him."

It seemed that the party took this as a signal for dismissal. As she went across the room, there were a dozen hasty adieus, and soon the guests were streaming towards the doors.

Vance and Elizabeth and Gainor went to the sheriff. He had been installed in a guest room. His eyes were closed, his arms outstretched. A thick, telltale bandage was wrapped about his breast. And Wu Chi, skillful in such matters from a long experience, was sliding about the room in his whispering slippers. The sheriff did not open his eyes when Elizabeth tried his pulse. It was faint, but steady.

He had been shot through the body and the lungs grazed, for as he breathed there was a faint bubble of blood that grew and swelled and burst on his lips at every breath. But he lived, and he would live unless there were an unnecessary change for the worse. They went softly out of the room again. Elizabeth was grave. Mr. Gainor took her hand.

"I think I know what people are saying now, and what they will say hereafter. If Terry's father were any other than Hollis, this affair would soon be forgotten, except as a credit to him. But even as it is, he will live this matter down. I want to tell you again, Miss Cornish, that you have reason to be proud of him. He is the sort of man I should be proud to have in my own family. Madam, good-by. And if there is anything in which I can be of service to you or to Terence, call on me at any time and to any extent."

And he went down the hall with a little swagger. Mr. Gainor felt that he had risen admirably to a great situation. As a matter of fact, he had.

Elizabeth turned to Vance.

"I wish you'd find Terence," she said, "and tell him that I'm waiting for him in the library."

CHAPTER 16

VANCE WENT GLOOMILY to the room of Terry and called him out. The boy was pale, but perfectly calm, and he looked older, much older.

"There was a great deal of talk," said Vance—he must make doubly sure of Terence now. "And they even started a little lynching party. But we stopped all that. Gainor made a very nice little speech about you. And now Elizabeth is waiting for you in the library."

Terry bit his lip.

"And she?" he asked anxiously.

"There's nothing to worry about," Vance assured him. "She'll probably read you a curtain lecture. But at heart she's proud of you because of the way Gainor talked. You can't do anything wrong in my sister's eyes."

Terry breathed a great sigh of relief.

"But I'm not ashamed of what I've done. I'm really not, Uncle Vance. I'm afraid that I'd do it over again, under the same circumstances."

"Of course you would. Of course you would, my boy. But you don't have to blurt that out to Elizabeth, do you? Let her think it was the overwhelming passion of the moment; something like that. A woman likes to be appealed to, not defied. Particularly Elizabeth. Take my advice. She'll open her arms to you after she's been stern as the devil for a moment."

The boy caught his hand and wrung it.

"By the Lord, Uncle Vance," he said, "I certainly appreciate this!"

"Tush, Terry, tush!" said Vance. "You'll find that I'm with you and behind you in more ways than you'd ever guess."

He received a grateful glance as they went down the broad stairs together. At the door to the library Vance turned away, but Elizabeth called to him and asked him in. He entered behind Terence Hollis, and found Elizabeth sitting in her father's big chair under the window, looking extremely fragile and very erect and proud. Across her lap was a legal-looking document.

Vance knew instantly that it was the will she had made up in favor of Terence. He had been preparing himself for the worst, but at this his heart sank. He lowered himself into a chair. Terence had gone straight to Elizabeth.

"I know I've done a thing that will cut you deeply, Aunt Elizabeth," he said. "I'm not going to ask you to see any justice on my side. I only want to ask you to forgive me, because—"

Elizabeth was staring straight at and through her protégé.

"Are you done, Terence?"

This time Vance was shocked into wide-eyed attention. The voice of Elizabeth was hard as iron. It brought a corresponding stiffening of Terence.

"I'm done," he said, with a certain ring to his voice that Vance was glad to hear.

It brought a flush into the pale cheeks of Elizabeth.

"It is easy to see that you're proud of what you have done, Terence."

"Yes," he answered with sudden defiance, "I am proud. It's the best thing I've ever done. I regret only one part of it."

"And that?"

"That my bullet didn't kill him!"

Elizabeth looked down and tapped the folded paper against her fingertips. Whether it was mere thoughtfulness or a desire to veil a profound emotion from Terence, her brother could not tell. But he knew that something of importance was in the air. He scented it as clearly as the smoke of a forest fire.

"I thought," she said in her new and icy manner, "that that would be your one regret."

She looked suddenly up at Terence.

"Twenty-four years," she said, "have passed since I took you into my life. At that time I was told that I was doing a rash thing, a dangerous thing—that before your twenty-fifth birthday the bad blood would out; that you would, in short, have shot a man. And the prophecy has come true. By an irony of chance it has happened on the very last day. And by another irony you picked your victim from among the guests under my roof!"

"Victim?" cried Terry hoarsely. "Victim, Aunt Elizabeth?"

"If you please," she said quietly, "not that name again, Terence. I wish you to know exactly what I have done. Up to this time I have given you a place in my affections. I have tried to the best of my skill to bring you up with a fitting education. I have given you what little wisdom and advice I have to give. Today I had determined to do much more. I had a will made out—this is it in my hands—and by the terms of this will I made you my heir—the heir to the complete Cornish estate aside from a comfortable annuity to Vance."

She looked him in the eye, ripped the will from end to end, and tossed the fragments into the fire. There was a sharp cry from Vance, who sprang to his feet. It was the thrill of an unexpected triumph, but his sister took it for protest.

"Vance, I haven't used you well, but from now on I'm going to change. As for you, Terence, I don't want you near me any longer than may be necessary. Understand that I expect to provide for you. I haven't raised you merely to cast you down suddenly. I'm going to establish you in business, see that you are comfortable, supply you with an income that's respectable, and then let you drift where you will.

"My own mind is made up about your end before you take a step across the threshold of my house. But I'm still going to give you every chance. I don't want to throw you out suddenly, however. Take your time. Make up your mind what you want to do and where you are going. Take all the time you wish for such a conclusion. It's important, and it needs time for such a decision. When that decision is made, go your way. I never wish to hear from you again. I want no letters, and I shall certainly refuse to see you."

Every word she spoke seemed to be a heavier blow than the last, and Terence bowed under the accumulated weight. Vance could see the boy struggle, waver between fierce pride and desperate humiliation and sorrow. To Vance it was clear that the stiff pride of Elizabeth as she sat in the chair was a brittle strength, and one vital appeal would break her to tears. But the boy did not see. Presently he straightened, bowed to her in the best Colby fashion, and turned on his heel. He went out of the room and left Vance and his sister facing one another, but not meeting each other's glances.

"Elizabeth," he said at last, faintly—he dared not persuade too much lest she take him at his word. "Elizabeth, you don't mean it. It was twenty-four years ago that you passed your word to do this if things turned out as they have. Forget your promise. My dear, you're still wrapped up in Terry, no matter what you have said. Let me go and call him back. Why should you torture yourself for the sake of your pride?"

He even rose, not too swiftly, and still with his eyes upon her. When she lifted her hand, he willingly sank back into his chair.

"You're a very kind soul, Vance. I never knew it before. I'm appreciating it now almost too late. But what I have done shall stand!"

"But, my dear, the pain—is it worth—"

"It means that my life is a wreck and a ruin, Vance. But I'll stand by what I've done. I won't give way to the extent of a single scruple."

And the long, bitter silence which was to last so many days at the Cornish ranch began. And still they did not look into one another's eyes. As for Vance, he did not wish to. He was seeing a bright future. Not long to wait; after this blow she would go swiftly to her grave.

He had barely reached that conclusion when the door opened again. Terry stood before them in the old, loose, disreputable clothes of a cow-puncher. The big sombrero swung in his right hand. The heavy Colt dragged down in its holster over his right hip. His tanned face was drawn and stern.

"I won't keep you more than a moment," he said. "I'm leaving. And I'm leaving with nothing of yours. I've already taken too much. If I live to be a hundred, I'll never forgive myself for taking your charity these twenty-four years. For what you've spent maybe I can pay you back one of these days, in money. But for all the time and—patience—you've spent on me I can never repay you. I know that. At least, here's where I stop piling up a debt. These clothes and this gun come out of the money I made punching cows last year. Outside I've got El Sangre saddled with a saddle I bought out of the same money. They're my start in life, the clothes I've got on and the gun and the horse and the saddle. So I'm starting clean—Miss Cornish!"

Vance saw his sister wince under that name from the lips of Terry. But she did not speak.

"There'll be no return," said Terence sadly. "My trail is an out trail. Good-by again." And so he was gone.

CHAPTER 17

DOWN THE BEAR CREEK road Terence Hollis rode as he had never ridden before. To be sure, it was not the first time that El Sangre had stretched to the full his mighty strength, but on those other occasions he had fought the burst of speed, straining back in groaning stirrup leathers, with his full weight wresting at the bit. Now he let the rein play to such a point that he was barely keeping the power of the stallion in touch. He lightened his weight as only a fine horseman can do, shifting a few vital inches forward, and with the burden falling more over his withers, El Sangre fled like a racer down the valley. Not that he was fully extended. His head was not stretched out as a cow-pony's head is stretched when he runs; he held it rather high, as though he carried in his big heart a reserve strength ready to be called on for any emergency. For all that, it was running such as Terry had never known.

The wind became a blast, jerking the brim of his sombrero up and whistling in his hair. He was letting the shame, the grief, the thousand regrets of that parting with Aunt Elizabeth be blown out of his soul. His mind was a whirl; the thoughts became blurs. As a matter of fact, Terry was being reborn.

He had lived a life perfectly sheltered. The care of Elizabeth Cornish had surrounded him as the Blue Mountains and Sleep Mountain surrounded Bear Valley and fenced off the full power of the storm winds. The reality of life had never reached him. Now, all in a day, the burden was placed on his back, and he felt the spur driven home to the quick. No wonder that he winced, that his heart contracted.

But now that he was awakening, everything was new. Uncle Vance, whom he had always secretly despised, now seemed a fine character, gentle, cultured, thoughtful of others. Aunt Elizabeth Cornish he had accepted as a sort of natural fact, as though there were a blood tie between them. Now he was suddenly aware of twenty-four years of patient love. The sorrow of it, that only the loss of that love should have brought him realization of it. Vague thoughts and aspirations formed in his mind. He yearned toward some large and heroic deed which should re-establish himself in her respect. He wished to find her in need, in great trouble, free her from some crushing burden with one perilous effort, lay his homage at her feet.

All of which meant that Terry Hollis was a boy—a bewildered, heart-stricken boy. Not that he would have undone what he had done. It seemed to him inevitable that he should resent the story of the sheriff and shoot him down or be shot down himself. All that he regretted was that he had remained mute before Aunt Elizabeth, unable to explain to her a thing which he felt so keenly. And for the first time he realized the flinty basis of her nature. The same thing that enabled her to give half a lifetime to the cherishing of a theory, also enabled her to cast all the result of that labor out of her life. It stung him again to the quick every time he thought of it. There was something wrong. He felt that a hundred hands of affection gave him hold on her. And yet all those grips were brushed away.

The torment was setting him on fire. And the fire was burning away the smug complacency which had come to him during his long life in the valley.

When El Sangre pulled out of his racing gallop and struck out up a slope at his natural gait, the ground-devouring pace, Terry Hollis was panting and twisting in the saddle as though the labor of the gallop had been his. They climbed and climbed, and still his mind was involved in a haze of thought. It cleared when he found that there were no longer high mountains before him. He drew El Sangre to a halt with a word. The great stallion turned his head as he paused and looked back to his master with a confiding eye as though waiting willingly for directions. And all at once the heart of Terence went out to the blood-bay as it had never gone before to any creature, dumb or human. For El Sangre had known such pain as he himself was learning at this moment. El Sangre was giving him true trust, true love, and asking him for no return.

The stallion, following his own will, had branched off from the Bear Creek trail and climbed through the lower range of the Blue Peaks. They were standing now on a mountaintop.

The red of the sunset filled the west and brought the sky close to them with the lower drifts of stained clouds. Eastward the winding length of Bear Creek was turning pink and purple. The Cornish ranch had never seemed so beautiful to Terry as it was at this moment. It was a kingdom, and he was leaving, the disinherited heir.

He turned west to the blare of the sunset. Blue Mountains tumbled away in lessening ranges—beyond was Craterville, and he must go there today. That was the world to him just then. And something new passed through Terry. The world was below him; it lay at his feet with its hopes and its battles. And he was strong for the test. He had been living in a dream. Now he would live in fact. And it was glorious to live!

And when his arms fell, his right hand lodged instinctively on the butt of his revolver. It was a prophetic gesture, but there, again, was something that Terry Hollis did not understand.

He called to El Sangre softly. The stallion responded with the faintest of whinnies to the vibrant power in the voice of the master; and at that smooth, effortless pace, he glided down the hillside, weaving dexterously among the jagged outcroppings of rock. A period had been placed after Terry's old life. And this was how he rode into the new.

The long and ever-changing mountain twilight began as he wound through the lower ranges. And when the full dark came, he broke from the last sweep of foothills and El Sangre roused to a gallop over the level toward Craterville.

He had been in the town before, of course. But he felt this evening that he had really never seen it before. On other days what existed outside of Bear Valley did not very much matter. That was the hub around which the rest of the world revolved, so far as Terry was concerned. It was very different now. Craterville, in fact, was a huddle of broken-down houses among a great scattering of boulders with the big mountains plunging up on every side to the dull blue of the night sky.

But Craterville was also something more. It was a place where several hundred human beings lived, any one of whom might be the decisive influence in the life of Terry. Young men and old men were in that town, cunning and strength; old crones and lovely girls were there. Whom would he meet? What should he see? A sudden kindness toward others poured through Terry Hollis. After all, every man might be a treasure to him. A queer choking came in his throat when he thought of all that he had missed by his contemptuous aloofness.

One thing gave him check. This was primarily the sheriff's town, and by this time they knew all about the shooting. But what of that? He had fought fairly, almost too fairly.

He passed the first shapeless shack. The hoofs of El Sangre bit into the dust, choking and red in daylight, and acrid of scent by the night. All was very quiet except for a stir of voices in the distance here and there, always kept hushed as though the speaker felt and acknowledged the influence of the profound night in the mountains. Someone came down the street carrying a lantern. It turned his steps into vast spokes of shadows that rushed back and forth across the houses with the swing of the light. The lantern light gleamed on the stained flank of El Sangre.

"Halloo, Jake, that you?"

The man with the lantern raised it, but its light merely served to blind him. Terry passed on without a word and heard the other mutter behind him: "Some damn stranger!"

Perhaps strangers were not welcome in Craterville. At least, it seemed so when he reached the hotel after putting up his horse in the shed behind the old building. Half a dozen dark forms sat on the veranda talking in the subdued voices which he had noted before. Terry stepped through the lighted doorway. There was no one inside.

"Want something?" called a voice from the porch. The widow Rickson came in to him.

"A room, please," said Terry.

But she was gaping at him. "You! Terence—Hollis!"

A thousand things seemed to be in that last word, which she brought out with a shrill ring of her voice. Terry noted that the talking on the porch was cut off as though a hand had been clapped over the mouth of every man.

He recalled that the widow had been long a friend of the sheriff and he was suddenly embarrassed.

"If you have a spare room, Mrs. Rickson. Otherwise, I'll find—"

Her manner had changed. It became as strangely ingratiating as it had been horrified, suspicious, before.

"Sure I got a room. Best in the house, if you want it. And —you'll be hungry, Mr.—Hollis?"

He wondered why she insisted so savagely on that new-found name? He admitted that he was very hungry from his ride, and she led him back to the kitchen and gave him cold ham and coffee and vast slices of bread and butter.

She did not talk much while he ate, and he noted that she asked no questions. Afterwards she led him through the silence of the place up to the second story and gave him a room at the corner of the building. He thanked her. She paused at the door with her hand on the knob, and her eyes fixed him through and through with a glittering, hostile stare. A wisp of gray hair had fallen across her cheek, and there it was plastered to the skin with sweat, for the evening was warm.

"No trouble," she muttered at length. "None at all. Make yourself to home, Mr.—Hollis!"

CHAPTER 18

WHEN THE DOOR closed on her, Terry remained standing in the middle of the room watching the flame in the oil lamp she had lighted flare and rise at the corner, and then steady down to an even line of yellow; but he was not seeing it; he was listening to that peculiar silence in the house. It seemed to have spread over the entire village, and he heard no more of those casual noises which he had noticed on his coming.

He went to the window and raised it to let whatever wind was abroad enter the musty warmth of the room. He raised the sash with stealthy caution, wondering at his own stealthiness. And he was oddly glad when the window rose without a squeak. He leaned out and looked up and down the street. It was unchanged. Across the way a door flung open, a child darted out with shrill laughter and dodged about the corner of the house, escaping after some mischief.

After that the silence again, except that before long a murmur began on the veranda beneath him where the half-dozen obscure figures had been sitting when he entered. Why should they be mumbling to themselves? He thought he could distinguish the voice of the widow Rickson among the rest, but he shrugged that idle thought away and turned back into his room.

He sat down on the side of the bed and pulled off his boots, but the minute they were off he was ill at ease. There was something oppressive about the atmosphere of this rickety old hotel. What sort of a world was this he had entered, with its whispers, its cold glances?

He cast himself back on his bed, determined to be at ease. Nevertheless, his heart kept bumping absurdly. Now, Terry began to grow angry. With the feeling that there was danger in the air of Craterville—for him—there came a nervous setting of the muscles, a desire to close on someone and throttle the secret of this hostility. At this point he heard a light tapping at the door. Terry sat bolt upright on the bed.

There are all kinds of taps. There are bold, heavy blows on the door that mean danger without; there are careless, conversational rappings; but this was a furtive tap, repeated after a pause as though it contained a code message.

First there was a leap of fear—then cold quiet of the nerves. He was surprised at himself. He found himself stepping into whatever adventure lay toward him with the lifting of the spirits. It was a stimulus.

He called cheerfully: "Come in!"

And the moment he had spoken he was off the bed, noiselessly, and half the width of the room away. It had come to him as he spoke that it might be well to shift from the point from which his voice had been heard.

The door opened swiftly—so swiftly was it opened and closed that it made a faint whisper in the air, oddly like a sigh. And there was no click of the lock either in the opening or the closing. Which meant an incalculably swift and dexterous manipulation with the fingers. Terry found himself facing a short-throated man with heavy shoulders; he wore a shapeless black hat bunched on his head as though the whole hand had grasped the crown and shoved the hat into place. It sat awkwardly to one side. And the hat typified the whole man. There was a sort of shifty readiness about him. His eyes flashed in the lamplight as they glanced at the bed, and then flicked back toward Terry. And a smile began somewhere in his face and instantly went out. It was plain that he had understood the maneuver.

He continued to survey Terry insolently for a moment without announcing himself. Then he seated: "You're him, all right!"

"Am I?" said Terry, regarding this unusual visitor with increasing suspicion. "But I'm afraid you have me at a disadvantage."

The big-shouldered man raised a stubby hand. He had an air of one who deprecates, and at the same time lets another into a secret. He moved across the room with short steps that made no sound, and gave him a peculiar appearance of drifting rather than walking. He picked up a chair and placed it down on the rug beside the bed and seated himself in it.

Aside from the words he had spoken, since he entered the room he had made no more noise than a phantom.

"You're him, all right," he repeated, balancing back in the chair. But he gathered his toes under him, so that he remained continually poised in spite of the seeming awkwardness of his position.

"Who am I?" asked Terry.

"Why, Black Jack's kid. It's printed in big type all over you."

His keen eyes continued to bore at Terry as though he were striving to read features beneath a mask. Terry could see his visitor's face more clearly now. It was square, with a powerfully muscled jaw and features that had a battered look. Suddenly he teetered forward in his chair and dropped his elbows aggressively on his knees.

"D'you know what they're talking about downstairs?"

"Haven't the slightest idea."

"You ain't! The old lady is trying to fix up a bad time for you."

"She's raising a crowd?"

"Doing her best. I dunno what it'll come to. The boys are stirring a little. But I think it'll be all words and no action. Four-flushers, most of 'em. Besides, they say you bumped old Minter for a goal; and they don't like the idea of messing up with you. They'll just talk. If they try anything besides their talk—well, you and me can fix 'em!"

Terry slipped into the only other chair which the room pro-

vided, but he slid far down in it, so that his holster was free
and the gun butt conveniently under his hand.

"You seem a charitable sort," he said. "Why do you throw
in with me?"

"And you don't know who I am?" said the other.

He chuckled noiselessly, his mouth stretching to remarkable proportions.

"I'm sorry," said Terry.

"Why, kid, I'm Denver. I'm your old man's pal, Denver!
I'm him that done the Silver Junction job with old Black
Jack, and a lot more jobs, when you come to that!"

He laughed again. "They were getting sort of warm for
me out in the big noise. So I grabbed me a side-door Pull-
man and took a trip out to the old beat. And think of bumping into Black Jack's boy right off the bat!"

He became more sober. "Say, kid, ain't you got a glad
hand for me? Ain't you ever heard Black Jack talk?"

"He died," said Terry soberly, "before I was a year old."

"The hell!" murmured the other. "The hell! Poor kid. That
was a rotten lay, all right. If I'd known about that, I'd of—
but I didn't. Well, let it go. Here we are together. And you're
the sort of a sidekick I need. Black Jack, we're going to trim
this town to a fare-thee-well!"

"My name is Hollis," said Terry. "Terence Hollis."

"Terence hell," snorted the other. "You're Black Jack's
kid, ain't you? And ain't his moniker good enough for you
to work under? Why, kid, that's a trademark most of us
would give ten thousand cash for!"

He broke off and regarded Terry with a growing satisfaction.

"You're his kid, all right. This is just the way Black Jack
would of sat—cool as ice—with a gang under him talking
about stretching his neck. And now, bo, hark to me sing! I
got the job fixed and— But wait a minute. What you been
doing all these years? Black Jack was *known* when he was
your age!"

With a peculiar thrill of awe and of aversion Terry watched
the face of the man who had known his father so well. He
tried to make himself believe that twenty-four years ago
Denver might have been quite another type of man. But it
was impossible to re-create that face other than as a bulldog

in the human flesh. The craft and the courage of a fighter were written large in those features.

"I've been leading—a quiet life," he said gently.

The other grinned. "Sure—quiet," he chuckled. "And then you wake up and bust Minter for your first crack. You began late, son, but you may go far. Pretty tricky with the gat, eh?"

He nodded in anticipatory admiration.

"Old Minter had a name. Ain't I had my run-in with him? He was smooth with a cannon. And fast as a snake's tongue. But they say you beat him fair and square. Well, well, I call that a snappy start in the world!"

Terry was silent, but his companion refused to be chilled.

"That's Black Jack over again," he said. "No wind about what he'd done. No jabber about what he was going to do. But when you wanted something done, go to Black Jack. Bam! There it was done clean for you and no talk afterward. Oh, he was a bird, was your old man. And you take after him, right enough!"

A voice rose in Terry. He wanted to argue. He wanted to explain. It was not that he felt any consuming shame because he was the son of Black Jack Hollis. But there was a sort of foster parenthood to which he owed a clean-minded allegiance—the fiction of the Colby blood. He had worshipped that thought for twenty years. He cauld not discard it in an instant.

Denver was breezing on in his quick, husky voice, so carefully toned that it barely served to reach Terry.

"I been waiting for a pal like you, kid. And here's where we hit it off. You don't know much about the game, I guess? Neither did Black Jack. As a peterman he was a loud ha-ha; as a damper-getter he was just an amateur; as a heel or a houseman, well, them things were just outside him. When it come to the gorilla stuff, he was there a million, though. And when there was a call for fast, quick, soft work, Black Jack was the man. Kid, I can see that you're cut right on his pattern. And here's where you come in with me. Right off the bat there's going to be velvet. Later on I'll educate you. In three months you'll be worth your salt. Are you on?"

He hardly waited for Terry to reply. He rambled on.

"I got a plant that can't fail to blossom into the long

green, kid. The store safe. You know what's in it? I'll tell you. Ten thousand cold. Ten thousand bucks, boy. Well, well, and how did it get there? Because a lot of the boobs around here have put their spare cash in the safe for safekeeping!"

He tilted his chin and indulged in another of his yawning, silent bursts of laughter.

"And you never seen a peter like it. Tin, kid, tin. I could turn it inside out with a can opener. But I ain't long on a kit just now. I'm on the hog for fair, as a matter of fact. Well, I don't need a kit. I got some sawdust and I can make the soup as pretty as you ever seen. We'll blow the safe, kid, and then we'll float. Are you on?"

He paused, grinning with expectation, his face gradually becoming blank as he saw no response in Terry.

"As nearly as I can make out—because most of the slang is new to me," said Terry, "you want to dynamite the store safe and—"

"Who said sawdust? Soup, kid, soup! I want to blow the door off the peter, not the roof off the house. Say, who d'you think I am, a boob?"

"I understand, then. Nitroglycerin? Denver, I'm not with you. It's mighty good of you to ask me to join in—but that isn't my line of work."

The yegg raised an expostulatory hand, but Terry went on: "I'm going to keep straight, Denver."

It seemed as though this simple tiding took the breath from Denver.

"Ah!" he nodded at length. "You playing up a new line. No strong-arm stuff except when you got to use it. Going to try scratching, kid? Is that it, or some other kind of slick stuff?"

"I mean what I say, Denver. I'm going straight."

The yegg shook his head, bewildered. "Say," he burst out suddenly, "ain't you Black Jack's kid?"

"I'm his son," said Terry.

"All right. You'll come to it. It's in the blood, Black Jack. You can't get away from it."

Terry tugged his shirt open at the throat; he was stifling. "Perhaps," he said.

"It's the easy way," went on Denver. "Well, maybe you ain't ripe yet, but when you are, tip me off. Gimme a ring and I'll be with you."

"One more thing. You're broke, Denver. And I suppose you need what's in that safe. But if you take it, the widow will be ruined. She runs the hotel and the store, too, you know."

"Why, you poor boob," groaned Denver, "don't you know she's the old dame that's trying to get you mobbed?"

"I suppose so. But she was pretty fond of the sheriff, you know. I don't blame her for carrying a grudge. Now, about the money, Denver; I happen to have a little with me. Take what you want."

Denver took the proffered money without a word, counted it with a deftly stabbing forefinger, and shoved the wad into his hip pocket.

"All right," he said, "this'll sort of sweeten the pot. You don't need it?"

"I'll get along without it. And you won't break the safe?"

"Hell!" grunted Denver. "Does it hang on that?"

Terry leaned forward in his chair.

"Denver, don't break that safe!"

"You kind of say that as if you was boss, maybe," sneered Denver.

"I am," said Terry, "as far as this goes."

"How'll you stop me, kid? Sit up all night and nurse the safe?"

"No. But I'll follow you, Denver. And I'll get you. You understand? I'll stay on your trail till I have you."

Again there was a long moment of silence, then, "Black Jack!" muttered Denver. "You're like his ghost! I think you'd get me, right enough! Well, I'll call it off. This fifty will help me along a ways."

At the door he whirled sharply on Terence Hollis. "How much have you got left?" he asked.

"Enough," said Terry.

"Then lemme have another fifty, will you?"

"I'm sorry. I can't quite manage it."

"Make it twenty-five, then."

"Can't do that either, Denver. I'm very sorry."

"Hell, man! Are you a short sport? I got a long jump before me. Ain't you got any credit around this town?"

"I—not very much, I'm afraid."

"You're kidding me," scowled Denver. "That wasn't Black

Jack's way. From his shoes to his skin everything he had belonged to his partners. His ghost'll haunt you if you're turning me down, kid. Why, ain't you the heir of a rich rancher
over the hills? Ain't that what I been told?"

"I was," said Terry, "until today."

"Ah! You got turned out for beaning Minter?"

Terry remained silent.

"Without a cent?"

Suddenly the pudgy arm of Denver shot out and his finger
pointed into Terry's face.

"You damn fool! This fifty is the last cent you got in the
world!"

"Not at all," said Terry calmly.

"You lie!" Denver struck his knuckles across his forehead.
"And I was going to trim you. Black Jack, I didn't know
you was as white as this. Fifty? Pal, take it back!"

He forced the money into Terry's pocket.

"And take some more. Here; lemme stake you. I been pulling a sob story, but I'm in the clover, Black Jack. Gimme
your last cent, will you? Kid, here's a hundred, two hundred
—say what you want."

"Not a cent—nothing," said Terry, but he was deeply
moved.

Denver thoughtfully restored the money to his wallet.

"You're white," he said gently. "And you're straight as
they come. Keep it up if you can. I know damned well that
you can't. I've seen 'em try before. But they always slip. Keep
it up, Black Jack, but if you ever change your mind, lemme
know. I'll be handy. Here's luck!"

And he was gone as he had entered, with a whish of the
swiftly moved door in the air, and no click of the lock.

CHAPTER 19

THE DOOR HAD hardly closed on him when Terence wanted to run after him and call him back. There was a thrill still running in his blood since the time the yegg had leaned so close and said: "That wasn't Black Jack's way!"

He wanted to know more about Black Jack, and he wanted to hear the story from the lips of this man. A strange warmth had come over him. It had seemed for a moment that there was a third impalpable presence in the room—his father listening. And the thrill of it remained, a ghostly and yet a real thing.

But he checked his impulse. Let Denver go, and the thought of his father with him. For the influence of Black Jack, he felt, was quicksand pulling him down. The very fact that he was his father's son had made him shoot down one man. Again the shadow of Black Jack had fallen across his path today and tempted him to crime. How real the temptation had been, Terry did not know until he was alone. Half of ten thousand dollars would support him for many a month. One thing was certain. He must let his father remain simply a name.

Going to the window in his stocking feet, he listened again. There were more voices murmuring on the veranda of the hotel now, but within a few moments forms began to drift away down the street, and finally there was silence. Evidently the widow had not secured backing as strong as she could have desired. And Terry went to bed and to sleep.

He wakened with the first touch of dawn along the wall beside his bed and tumbled out to dress. It was early, even for a mountain town. The rattling at the kitchen stove commenced while he was on the way downstairs. And he had to waste time with a visit to El Sangre in the stable before his breakfast was ready.

Craterville was in the hollow behind him when the sun

rose, and El Sangre was taking up the miles with the tireless rhythm of his pace. He had intended searching for work of some sort near Craterville, but now he realized that it could not be. He must go farther. He must go where his name was not known.

For two days he held on through the broken country, climbing more than he dropped. Twice he came above the ragged timber line, with its wind-shaped army of stunted trees, and over the tiny flowers of the summit lands. At the end of the second day he came out on the edge of a precipitous descent to a prosperous grazing country below. There would be his goal.

A big mountain sheep rounded a corner with a little flock behind him. Terry dropped the leader with a snapshot and watched the flock scamper down what was almost the sheer face of a cliff—a beautiful bit of acrobatics. They found foothold on ridges a couple of inches deep, hardly visible to the eye from above. Plunging down a straight drop without a sign of a ledge for fifty feet below them, they broke the force of the fall and slowed themselves constantly by striking their hoofs from side to side against the face of the cliff. And so they landed, with bunched feet, on the first broad terrace below and again bounced over the ledge and so out of sight.

He dined on wild mutton that evening. In the morning he hunted along the edge of the cliffs until he came to a difficult route down to the valley. An ordinary horse would never have made it, but El Sangre was in his glory. If he had not the agility of the mountain sheep, he was well-nigh as level-headed in the face of tremendous heights. He knew how to pitch ten feet down to a terrace and strike on his bunched hoofs so that the force of the fall would not break his legs or unseat his rider. Again he understood how to drive in the toes of his hoofs and go up safely through loose gravel where most horses, even mustangs, would have skidded to the bottom of the slope. And he was wise in trails. Twice he rejected the courses which Terry picked, and the rider very wisely let him have his way. The result was that they took a more winding, but a far safer course, and arrived before midmorning in the bottomlands.

The first ranch house he applied to accepted him. And there he took up his work.

It was the ordinary outfit—the sun- and wind-racked shack

for a house, the stumbling outlying barns and sheds, and the maze of corral fences. They asked Terry no questions, accepted his first name without an addition, and let him go his way.

He was happy enough. He had not the leisure for thought or for remembering better times. If he had leisure here and there, he used it industriously in teaching El Sangre the "cow" business. The stallion learned swiftly. He began to take a joy in sitting down on a rope.

At the end of a week Terry won a bet when a team of draught horses hitched onto his line could not pull El Sangre over his mark, and broke the rope instead. There was much work, too, in teaching him to turn in the cow-pony fashion, dropping his head almost to the ground and bunching his feet altogether. For nothing of its size that lives is so deft in dodging as the cow-pony. That part of El Sangre's education was not completed, however, for only the actual work of a round-up could give him the faultless surety of a good cowpony. And, indeed, the ranchman declared him useless for real roundup work.

"A no-good, high-headed fool," he termed El Sangre, having sprained his bank account with an attempt to buy the stallion from Terry the day before.

At the end of a fortnight the first stranger passed, and ill-luck made it a man from Craterville. He knew Terry at a glance, and the next morning the rancher called Terry aside.

The work of that season, he declared, was going to be lighter than he had expected. Much as he regretted it, he would have to let his new hand go. Terry taxed him at once to get at the truth.

"You've found out my name. That's why you're turning me off. Is that the straight of it?"

The sudden pallor of the other was a confession.

"What's names to me?" he declared. "Nothing, partner. I take a man the way I find him. And I've found you all right. The reason I got to let go is what I said."

But Terry grinned mirthlessly.

"You know I'm the son of Black Jack Hollis," he insisted. "You think that if you keep me you'll wake up some morning to find your son's throat cut and your cattle gone. Am I right?"

"Listen to me," the rancher said uncertainly. "I know how

you feel about losing a job so suddenly when you figured it for a whole season. Suppose I give you a whole month's pay and—"

"Damn your money!" said Terry savagely. "I don't deny that Black Jack was my father. I'm proud of it. But listen to me, my friend. I'm living straight. I'm working hard. I don't object to losing this job. It's the attitude behind it that I object to. You'll not only send me away, but you'll spread the news around—Black Jack's son is here! Am I a plague because of that name?"

"Mr. Hollis," insisted the rancher in a trembling voice, "I don't mean to get you all excited. Far as your name goes, I'll keep your secret. I give you my word on it. Trust me, I'll do what's right by you."

He was in a panic. His glance wavered from Terry's eyes to the revolver at his side.

"Do you think so?" said Terry. "Here's one thing that you may not have thought of. If you and the rest like you refuse to give me honest work, there's only one thing left for me— and that's dishonest work. You turn me off because I'm the son of Black Jack; and that's the very thing that will make me the son of Black Jack in more than name. Did you ever stop to realize that?"

"Mr. Hollis," quavered the rancher, "I guess you're right. If you want to stay on here, stay and welcome, I'm sure."

And his eye hunted for help past the shoulder of Terry and toward the shed, where his eldest son was whistling. Terry turned away in mute disgust. By the time he came out of the bunkhouse with his blanket roll, there was neither father nor son in sight. The door of the shack was closed, and through the window he caught a glimpse of a rifle. Ten minutes later El Sangre was stepping away across the range at a pace that no mount in the cattle country could follow for ten miles.

CHAPTER 20

THERE WAS AN astonishing deal of life in the town, however. A large company had reopened some old diggings across the range to the north of Calkins, and some small fragments of business drifted the way of the little cattle town. Terry found a long line of a dozen horses waiting to be shod before the blacksmith shop. One great wagon was lumbering out at the farther end of the street, with the shrill yells of the teamster calling back as he picked up his horses one by one with his voice. Another freight-wagon stood at one side, blocking half the street. And a stir of busy life was everywhere in the town. The hotel and store combined was flooded with sound, and the gambling hall across the street was alive even at midday.

It was noon, and Terry found that the dining room was packed to the last chair. The sweating waiter improvised a table for him in the corner of the hall and kept him waiting twenty minutes before he was served with ham and eggs. He had barely worked his fork into the ham when a familiar voice hailed him.

"Got room for another at that table?"

He looked up into the grinning face of Denver. For some reason it was a shock to Terry. Of course, the second meeting was entirely coincidental, but a still small voice kept whispering to him that there was fate in it. He was so surprised that he could only nod. Denver at once appropriated a chair and seated himself in his usual noiseless way.

When he rearranged the silver which the waiter placed before him, there was not the faintest click of the metal. And Terry noted, too, a certain nice justness in every one of Denver's motions. He was never fiddling about with his hands; when they stirred, it was to do something, and when the thing was done, the hands became motionless again.

His eyes did not rove; they remained fixed for appreciable periods wherever they fell, as though Denver were finding something worth remembering in the wall, or in a spot on the table. When his glance touched on a face, it hung there in the same manner. After a moment one would forget all the rest of his face, brutal, muscular, shapeless, and see only the keen eyes.

Terry found it difficult to face the man. There was need to be excited about something, to talk with passion, in order to hold one's own in the presence of Denver, even when the chunky man was silent. He was not silent now; he seemed in a highly cheerful, amiable mood.

"Here's luck," he said. "I didn't know this God-forsaken country could raise as much as this!"

"Luck?" echoed Terry.

"Why not? D'you think I been tailing you?"

He chuckled in his noiseless way. It gave Terry a feeling of expectation. He kept waiting for the sound to come into that laughter, but it never did. Suddenly he was frank, because it seemed utterly futile to attempt to mask one's real thoughts from this fellow.

"I don't know," he said, "that it would surprise me if you *had* been tailing me. I imagine you're apt to do queer things, Denver."

Denver hissed, very softly and with such a cutting whistle to his breath that Terry's lips remained open over his last word.

"Forget that name!" Denver said in a half-articulate tone of voice.

He froze in his place, staring straight before him; but Terry gathered an impression of the most intense watchfulness—as though, while he stared straight before him, he had sent other and mysterious senses exploring for him. He seemed suddenly satisfied that all was well, and as he relaxed, Terry became aware of a faint gleam of perspiration on the brow of his companion.

"Why the devil did you tell me the name if you didn't want me to use it?" he asked.

"I thought you'd have some savvy; I thought you'd have some of your dad's horse sense," said Denver.

"No offense," answered Terry, with the utmost good nature.

"Call me Shorty if you want," said Denver. In the meantime he was regarding Terry more and more closely.

"Your old man would of made a fight out of it if I'd said as much to him as I've done to you," he remarked at length.

"Really?" murmured Terry.

And the portrait of his father swept back on him—the lean, imperious, handsome face, the boldness of the eyes. Surely a man all fire and powder, ready to explode. He probed his own nature. He had never been particularly quick of temper—until lately. But he began to wonder if his equable disposition might not rise from the fact that his life in Bear Valley had been so sheltered. He had been crossed rarely. In the outer world it was different. That very morning he had been tempted wickedly to take the tall rancher by the throat and grind his face into the sand.

"But maybe you're different," went on Denver. "Your old man used to flare up and be over it in a minute. Maybe you remember things and pack a grudge with you."

"Perhaps," said Terry, grown strangely meek. "I hardly know."

Indeed, he thought, how little he really knew of himself. Suddenly he said: "So you simply happened over this way, Shorty?"

"Sure. Why not? I got a right to trail around where I want. Besides, what would there be in it for me—following you?"

"I don't know," said Terry gravely. "But I expect to find out sooner or later. What else are you up to over here?"

"I have a little job in mind at the mine," said Denver. "Something that may give the sheriff a bit of trouble." He grinned.

"Isn't it a little—unprofessional," said Terry dryly, "for you to tell me these things?"

"Sure it is, bo—sure it is! Worst in the world. But I can always tell a gent that can keep his mouth shut. By the way, how many jobs you been fired from already?"

Terry started. "How do you know that?"

"I just guess at things."

"I started working for an infernal idiot," sighed Terry. When he learned my name, he seemed to be afraid I'd start shooting up his place one of these days."

"Well, he was a wise gent. You ain't cut out for working, son. Not a bit. It'd be a shame to let you go to waste simply raising calluses on your hands."

"You talk well," sighed Terry, "but you can't convince me."

"Convince you? Hell, I ain't trying to convince your father's son. You're like Black Jack. You got to find out yourself. We was with a Mick, once. Red-headed devil, he was. I says to Black Jack: 'Don't crack no jokes about the Irish around this guy!'

" 'Why not?' says your dad.

" 'Because there'd be an explosion,' says I.

" 'H'm,' says Black Jack, and lifts his eyebrows in a way he had of doing.

"And the first thing he does is to try a joke on the Irish right in front of the Mick. Well, there was an explosion, well enough."

"What happened?" asked Terry, carried way with curiosity.

"What generally happened, kid, when somebody acted up in front of your dad?" From the air he secured an imaginary morsel between stubby thumb and forefinger and then blew the imaginary particle into empty space.

"He killed him?" asked Terry hoarsely.

"No," said Denver, "he didn't do that. He just broke his heart for him. Kicked the gat out of the hand of the poor stiff and wrestled with him. Black Jack was a wildcat when it come to fighting with his hands. When he got through with the Irishman, there wasn't a sound place on the fool. Black Jack climbed back on his horse and threw the gun back at the guy on the ground and rode off. Next we heard, the guy was working for a Chinaman that run a restaurant. Black Jack had taken all the fight out of him."

That scene out of the past drifted vividly back before Terry's eyes. He saw the sneer on the lips of Black Jack; saw the Irishman go for his gun; saw the clash, with his father leaping in with tigerish speed; felt the shock of the two strong bodies, and saw the other turn to pulp under the grip of Black Jack.

By the time he had finished visualizing the scene, his jaw was set hard. It had been easy, very easy, to throw himself into the fierceness of his dead father's mood. During this moment of brooding he had been looking down, and he did not notice the glance of Denver fasten upon him with an almost hypnotic fervor, as though he were striving to reach to the very soul of the younger man and read what was written there. When Terry looked up, the face of his companion was as calm as ever.

"And you're like the old boy," declared Denver. "You got to find out for yourself. It'll be that way with this work idea of yours. You've lost one job. You'll lose the next one. But —I ain't advising you no more!"

CHAPTER 21

TERRY LEFT THE hotel more gloomy than he had been even when he departed from the ranch that morning. The certainty of Denver that he would find it impossible to stay by his program of honest work had made a strong impression upon his imaginative mind, as though the little safecracker really had the power to look into the future and into the minds of men. Where he should look for work next, he had no idea. And he balanced between a desire to stay near the town and work out his destiny there, or else drift far away. Distance, however, seemed to have no barrier against rumor. After two days of hard riding, he had placed a broad gap between himself and the Cornish ranch, yet in a short time rumor had overtaken him, casually, inevitably, and the force of his name was strong enough to take away his job.

Standing in the middle of the street he looked darkly over the squat roofs of the town to the ragged mountains that marched away against the horizon—a bleak outlook. Which way should he ride?

A loud outburst of curses roared behind him, a whip snapped above him, he stepped aside and barely from under the feet of the leaders as a long team wound by with the freight wagon creaking and swaying and rumbling behind it. The driver leaned from his seat in passing and volleyed a few crackling remarks in the very ear of Terry. It was strange that he did not resent it. Ordinarily he would have wanted to climb onto that seat and roll the driver down in the dust, but today he lacked ambition. Pain numbed him, a peculiar mental pain. And, with the world free before him to roam in, he felt imprisoned.

He turned. Someone was laughing at him from the veranda of the hotel and pointing him out to another, who laughed raucously in turn. Terry knew what was in their minds. A man who allowed himself to be cursed by a passing teamster was not worthy of the gun strapped at his thigh. He watched their faces as through a cloud, turned again, saw the door of the gambling hall open to allow someone to come out, and was invited by the cool, dim interior. He crossed the street and passed through the door.

He was glad, instantly. Inside there was a blanket of silence; beyond the window the sun was a white rain of heat, blinding and appalling. But inside his shoes took hold on a floor moist from a recent scrubbing and soft with the wear of rough boots; and all was dim, quiet, hushed.

There was not a great deal of business in the place, naturally, at this hour of the day. And the room seemed so large, the tables were so numerous, that Terry wondered how so small a town could support it. Then he remembered the mine and everything was explained. People who dug gold like dirt spent in the same spirit. Half a dozen men were here and there, playing in what seemed a listless manner, save when you looked close.

Terry slumped into a big chair in the darkest corner and relaxed until the coolness had worked through his skin and into his blood. Presently he looked about him to find something to do, and his eye dropped naturally on the first thing that made a noise—roulette. For a moment he watched the spinning disk. The man behind the table on his high stool was whirling the thing for his own amusement, it seemed. Terry walked over and looked on.

He hardly knew the game. But he was fascinated by the motions of the ball; one was never able to tell where it would stop, on one of the thirty-six numbers, on the red or on the black, on the odd or the even. He visualized a frantic, silent crowd around the wheel listening to the click of the ball.

And now he noted that the wheel had stopped the last four times on the odd. He jerked a five-dollar gold piece out of his pocket and placed it on the even. The wheel spun, clicked

to a stop, and the rake of the croupier slicked his five dollars
away across the smooth-worn top of the table.

How very simple! But certainly the wheel must stop on
the even this time, having struck the odd five times in a row.
He placed ten dollars on the even.

He did not feel that it was gambling. He had never gambled in his life, for Elizabeth Cornish had raised him to look
on gambling not as a sin, but as a crowning folly. However,
this was surely not gambling. There was no temptation. Not
a word had been spoken to him since he entered the place.
There was no excitement, no music, none of the drink and
song of which he had heard so much in robbing men of
their cooler senses. It was only his little system that tempted
him on.

He did not know that all gambling really begins with the
creation of a system that will beat the game. And when a
man follows a system, he is started on the most cold-blooded
gambling in the world.

Again the disk stopped, and the ball clicked softly and
the ten dollars slid away behind the rake of the man on the
stool. This would never do! Fifteen dollars gone out of a
total capital of fifty! He doubled with some trepidation again.
Thirty dollars wagered. The wheel spun—the money disappeared under the rake.

Terry felt like setting his teeth. Instead, he smiled. He
drew out his last five dollars and wagered it with a coldness
that seemed to make sure of loss, on a single number. The
wheel spun, clicked; he did not even watch, and was turning
away when a sound of a little musical shower of gold at-
tracted him. Gold was being piled before him. Five times
thirty-six made one hundred and eighty dollars he had won!
He came back to the table, scooped up his winnings carelessly and bent a kinder eye upon the wheel. He felt that
there was a sort of friendly entente between them.

It was time to go now, however. He sauntered to the door
with a guilty chill in the small of his back, half expecting re-
proaches to be shouted after him for leaving the game when
he was so far ahead of it. But apparently the machine which
won without remorse lost without complaint.

At the door he made half a pace into the white heat of
the sunlight. Then he paused, a cool edging of shadow fall-

ing across one shoulder while the heat burned through the
shirt of the other. Why go on?

Across the street the man on the veranda of the hotel began laughing again and pointing him out. Terry himself
looked the fellow over in an odd fashion, not with anger or
with irritation, but with a sort of cold calculation. The
fellow was trim enough in the legs. But his shoulders were
fat from lack of work, and the bulge of flesh around the
armpits would probably make him slow in drawing a gun.

He shrugged his own lithe shoulders in contempt and
turned. The man on the stool behind the roulette wheel was
yawning until his jaw muscles stood out in hard, pointed
ridges, and his cheeks fell in ridiculously. Terry went back.
He was not eager to win; but the gleam of colors on the
wheel fascinated him. He placed five dollars, saw the wheel
win, took in his winnings without emotion.

While he scooped the two coins up, he did not see the
croupier turn his head and shoot a single glance to a fat
squat man in the corner of the room, a glance to which the
fat man responded with the slightest of nods and smiles. He
was the owner. And he was not particularly happy at the
thought of some hundred and fifty dollars being taken out
of his treasury by some chance stranger.

Terry did not see the glance, and before long he was incapable of seeing anything saving the flash of the disk, the
blur of the alternate colors as they spun together. He paid
no heed to the path of the sunlight as it stretched along the
floor under the window and told of a westering sun. The first
Terry knew of it he was standing in a warm pool of gold,
but he gave the sun at his feet no more than a casual glance.
It was metallic gold that he was fascinated by and the whims
and fancies of that singular wheel. Twice that afternoon his
fortune had mounted above three thousand dollars—once
mounted to an even six thousand. He had stopped to count
his winnings at this point, and on the verge of leaving decided
to make it an even ten thousand before he went away. And
five minutes later he was gambling with five hundred in his
wallet.

When the sunlight grew yellow, other men began to enter
the room. Terry was still at his post. He did not see them.
There was no human face in the world for him except the
colorless face of the croupier, and the long, pale eyelash

that lifted now and then over greenish-orange eyes. And Terry did not heed when he was shouldered by the growing crowd around the wheel.

He only knew that other bets were being placed and that it was a nuisance, for the croupier took much longer in paying debts and collecting winnings, so that the wheel spun less often.

Meantime he was by no means unnoticed. A little whisper had gone the rounds that a real plunger was in town. And when men came into the hall, their attention was directed automatically by the turn of other eyes toward six feet of muscular manhood, heavy-shouldered and erect, with a flare of a red silk bandanna around his throat and a heavy sombrero worn tilted a little to one side and back on his head.

"He's playing a system," said someone. "Been standing there all afternoon and making poor Pedro—the thief!—sweat and shake in his boots."

In fact, the owner of the place had lost his complacence and his smile together. He approached near to the wheel and watched its spin with a face turned sallow and flat of cheek from anxiety. For with the setting of the sun it seemed that luck flooded upon Terry Hollis. He began to bet in chunks of five hundred, alternating between the red and the odd, and winning with startling regularity. His winnings were now shoved into an awkward canvas bag. Twenty thousand dollars! That had grown from the fifty.

No wonder the crowd had two looks for Terry. His face had lost its color and grown marvellously expressionless.

"The real gambler's look," they said.

His mouth was pinched at the corners, and otherwise his expression never varied.

Once he turned. A broad-faced man, laughing and obviously too self-contented to see what he was doing, trod heavily on the toes of Terry, stepping past the latter to get his winnings. He was caught by the shoulder and whirled around. The crowd saw the tall man draw his right foot back, balance, lift a trifle on his toes, and then a balled fist shot up, caught the broad-faced man under the chin and dumped him in a crumpled heap half a dozen feet away. They picked him up and took him away, a stunned wreck. Terry had turned back to his game, and in ten seconds had forgotten what he had done.

But the crowd remembered, and particularly he who had twice laughed at Terry from the veranda of the hotel.

The heap in the canvas sack diminished, shrank—he dumped the remainder of the contents into his pocket. He had been betting in solid lumps of a thousand for the past twenty minutes, and the crowd watched in amazement. This was drunken gambling, but the fellow was obviously sober. Then a hand touched the shoulder of Terry.

"Just a minute, partner."

He looked into the face of a big man, as tall as he and far heavier of build: a magnificent big head, heavily marked features, a short-cropped black beard that gave him dignity. A middle-aged man, about forty-five, and still in the prime of life.

"Lemme pass a few words with you."

Terry drew back to the side.

CHAPTER 22

"MY NAME's Pollard," said the older man. "Joe Pollard."

"Glad to know you, sir. My name—is Terry."

The other admitted this reticence with a faint smile.

"I got a name around here for keeping my mouth shut and not butting in on another gent's game. But I always noticed that when a gent is in a losing run, half the time he don't know it. Maybe that might be the way with you. I been watching and seen your winnings shrink considerable lately."

Terry weighed his money. "Yes, it's shrunk a good deal."

"Stand out of the game till later on. Come over and have a bite to eat with me."

He went willingly, suddenly aware of a raging appetite and a dinner long postponed. The man of the black beard was extremely friendly.

"One of the prettiest runs I ever see, that one you made,

he confided when they were at the table in the hotel. "You got a system, I figure."

A new one," said Terry. I've never played before."

The other blinked.

"Beginner's luck, I suppose," said Terry frankly. "I started with fifty, and now I suppose I have about eight hundred."

"Not bad, not bad," said the other. "Too bad you didn't stop half an hour before. Just passing through these parts?"

"I'm looking for a job," said Terry. "Can you tell me where to start hunting? Cows are my game."

The other paused a moment and surveyed his companion. There seemed just a shade of doubt in his eyes. They were remarkably large and yellowish gray, those eyes of Joe Pollard, and now and again when he grew thoughtful they became like clouded agate. They had that color now as he gazed at Terry. Eventually his glance cleared.

"I got a little work of my own," he declared. "My range is all clogged up with varmints. Any hand with a gun and traps?"

"Pretty fair hand," said Terry modestly.

And he was employed on the spot.

He felt one reassuring thing about his employer—that no echo out of his past or the past of his father would make the man discharge him. Indeed, taking him all in all, there was under the kindliness of Joe Pollard an indescribable basic firmness. His eyes, for example, in their habit of looking straight at one, reminded him of the eyes of Denver. His voice was steady and deep and mellow, and one felt that it might be expanded to an enormous volume. Such a man would not fly off into snap judgments and become alarmed because an employee had a past or a strange name.

They paid a short visit to the gambling hall after dinner, and then got their horses. Pollard was struck dumb with admiration at the sight of the blood-bay.

"Maybe you been up the Bear Creek way?" he asked Terry.

And when the latter admitted that he knew something of the Blue Mountain country, the rancher exclaimed: "By the Lord, partner, I'd say that hoss is a ringer for El Sangre."

"Pretty close to a ringer," said Terry. "This is El Sangre himself."

They were jogging out of town. The rancher turned in the saddle and crossed his companion with one of his search-

ing glances, but returned no reply. Presently, however, he
sent his own capable Steeldust into a sharp gallop; El Sangre
roused to a flowing pace and held the other even without the
slightest difficulty. At this Pollard drew rein with an exclamation.

"El Sangre as sure as I live!" he declared. "Ain't nothing
else in these parts that calls itself a hoss and slides over the
ground the way El Sangre does. Partner, what sort of a
price would you set on El Sangre, maybe?'

"His weight in gold," said Terry.

The rancher cursed softly, without seeming altogether
pleased. And thereafter during the ride his glánce continually
drifted toward the brilliant bay—brilliant even in the pallor
of the clear mountain starlight.

He explained this by saying after a time: "I been my whole
life in these parts without running across a hoss that could
pack me the way a man ought to be packed on a hoss. I
weigh two hundred and thirty, son, and it busts the back of
a horse in the mountains. Now, you ain't a flyweight yourself, and El Sangre takes you along like you was a feather."

Steeldust was already grunting at every sharp rise, and El
Sangre had not even broken out in perspiration.

A mile or so out of the town they left the road and struck
onto a mere semblance of a trail, broad enough, but practically as rough as nature chose to make it. This wound at
sharp and ever-changing angles into the hills, and presently
they were pressing through a dense growth of lodgepole pine.

It seemed strange to Terry that a prosperous rancher with
an outfit of any size should have a road no more beaten than
this one leading to his place. But he was thinking too busily
of other things to pay much heed to such surmises and small
events. He was brooding over the events of the afternoon. If
his exploits in the gaming hall should ever come to the ear of
Aunt Elizabeth, he was certain enough that he would be
finally damned in her judgment. Too often he had heard her
express an opinion of those who lived by "chance and their
wits," as she phrased it. And the thought of it irked him.

He roused himself out of his musing. They had come out
from the trees and were in sight of a solidly built house on the
hill. There was one thing which struck his mind at once.
No attempt had been made to find level for the foundation.
The log structure had been built apparently at random on the

slope. It conformed, at vast waste of labor, to the angle of the base and the irregularities of the soil. This, perhaps, made it seem smaller than it was. They caught the scent of wood smoke, and then saw a pale drift of the smoke itself.

A flurry of music escaped by the opening of a door and was shut out by the closing of it. It was a moment before Terry, startled, had analyzed the sound. Unquestionably it was a piano. But how in the world, and why in the world, had it been carted to the top of this mountain?

He glanced at his companion with a new respect and almost with a suspicion.

"Up to some damn doings again," growled the big man. "Never got no peace nor quiet up my way."

Another surprise was presently in store for Terry. Behind the house, which grew in proportions as they came closer, they reached a horse shed, and when they dismounted, a servant came out for the horses. Outside of the Cornish ranch he did not know of many who afforded such luxuries.

However, El Sangre could not be handled by another, and Terry put up his horse and found the rancher waiting for him when he came out. Inside the shed he had found ample bins of barley and oats and good grain hay. And in the stalls his practiced eye scanned the forms of a round dozen fine horses with points of blood and bone that startled him.

Coming to the open again, he probed the darkness as well as he could to gain some idea of the ranch which furnished and supported all these evidences of prosperity. But so far as he could make out, there was only a jumble of ragged hilltops behind the house, and before it the slope fell away steeply to the valley far below. He had not realized before that they had climbed so high or so far.

Joe Pollard was humming. Terry joined him on the way to the house with a deepened sense of awe; he was even beginning to feel that there was a touch or two of mystery in the make-up of the man.

Proof of the solidity with which the log house was built was furnished at once. Coming to the house, there was only a murmur of voices and of music. The moment they opened the door, a roar of singing voices and a jangle of piano music rushed into their ears.

Terry found himself in a very long room with a big table in the center and a piano at the farther end. The ceiling sloped down from the right to the left. At the left it descended toward the doors of the kitchen and storerooms; at the right it rose to the height of two full stories. One of these was occupied by a series of heavy posts on which hung saddles and bridles and riding equipment of all kinds, and the posts supported a balcony onto which opened several doors—of sleeping rooms, no doubt. As for the wall behind the posts, it, too, was pierced with several openings, but Terry could not guess at the contents of the rooms. But he was amazed by the size of the structure as it was revealed to him from within. The main room was like some baronial hall of the old days of war and plunder. A role, indeed, into which it was not difficult to fit the burly Pollard and the dignity of his beard.

Four men were around the piano, and a girl sat at the keys, splashing out syncopated music while the men roared the chorus of the song. But at the sound of the closing of the door all five turned toward the newcomers, the girl looking over her shoulder and keeping the soft burden of the song still running.

CHAPTER 23

So TURNED, Terry could not see her clearly. He caught a glimmer of red bronze hair, dark in shadow and brilliant in high lights, and a sheen of greenish eyes. Otherwise, he only noted the casual manner in which she acknowledged the introduction, unsmiling, indifferent, as Pollard said: "Here's my daughter Kate. This is Terry—a new hand."

It seemed to Terry that as he said this the rancher made a gesture as of warning, though this, no doubt, could be attributed to his wish to silently explain away the idosyncrasy of Terry in using his first name only. He was presented in turn to the four men, and thought them the oddest collection he had ever laid eyes on.

Slim Dugan was tall, but not so tall as he looked, owing to

his very small head and narrow shoulders. His hair was straw color, excessively silky, and thin as the hair of a year-old child. There were other points of interest in Slim Dugan; his feet, for instance, were small as the feet of a girl, accentuated by the long, narrow riding boots, and his hands seemed to be pulled out to a great and unnecessary length. They made up for it by their narrowness.

His exact opposite was Marty Cardiff, chunky, fat, it seemed, until one noted the roll and bulge of the muscles at the shoulders. His head was settled into his fat shoulders somewhat in the manner of Denver's, Terry thought.

Oregon Charlie looked the part of an Indian, with his broad nose and high cheekbones, flat face, slanted dark eyes; but his skin was a dead and peculiar white. He was a down-headed man, and one could rarely imagine him opening his lips to speak; he merely grunted as he shook hands with the stranger.

To finish the picture, there was a man as huge as Joe Pollard himself, and as powerful, to judge by appearances. His face was burned to a jovial red; his hair was red also, and there was red hair on the backs of his freckled hands.

All these men met Terry with cordial nods, but there was a carelessness about their demeanor which seemed strange to Terry. In his experience, the men of the mountains were a timid or a blustering lot before newcomers, uneasy, and anxious to establish their place. But these men acted as if meeting unknown men were a part of their common, daily experience. They were as much at their ease as social lions.

Pollard was explaining the presence of Terry.

"He's come up to clean out the varmints," he said to the others. "They been getting pretty thick on the range, you know."

"You came in just wrong," complained Kate, while the men turned four pairs of grave eyes upon Terry and seemed to be judging him. "I got Oregon singing at last, and he was doing fine. Got a real voice, Charlie has. Regular branded baritone, I'll tell a man."

"Strike up agin for us, Charlie," said Pollard good-naturedly. "You don't never make much more noise'n a grizzly."

But Charlie looked down at his hands and a faint spot of red appeared in his cheek. Obviously he was much embarrassed. And when he looked up, it was to fix a glance of cold suspicion upon Terry, as though warning him not to take this talk of social acquirements as an index to his real character.

"Get us some coffee, Kate," said Pollard. "Turned off cold coming up the hill."

She did not rise. She had turned around to her music again, and now she acknowledged the order by lifting her head and sending a shrill whistle through the room. Her father started violently.

"Damn it, Kate, don't do that!"

"The only thing that'll bring Johnny on the run," she responded carelessly.

And, indeed, the door on the left of the room flew open a moment later, and a wide-eyed Chinaman appeared with a long pigtail jerking about his head as he halted and looked about in alarm.

"Coffee for the boss and the new hand," said Kate, without turning her head, as soon as she heard the door open. "Pronto, Johnny."

Johnny snarled an indistinct something and withdrew muttering.

"You'll have Johnny quitting the job," complained Pollard, frowning. "You can't scare the poor devil out of his skin like that every time you want coffee. Besides, why didn't you get up and get it for us yoursef?"

Still she did not turn; but, covering a yawn, replied: "Rather sit here and play."

Her father swelled a moment in rage, but he subsided again without audible protest. Only he sent a scowl at Terry as though daring him to take notice of this insolence. As for the other men, they had scattered to various parts of the room and remained there, idly, while the boss and the new hand drank the scalding coffee of Johnny. All this time Pollard remained deep in thought. His meditations exploded as he banged the empty cup back on the table.

"Kate, this stuff has got to stop. Understand?"

The soft jingling of the piano continued without pause.

"Stop that damned noise!"

The music paused. Terry felt the long striking muscles leap into hard ridges along his arms, but glancing at the other four, he found that they were taking the violence of

Pollard quite as a matter of course. One was whittling, another rolled a cigarette, and all of them, if they took any visible notice of the argument, did so with the calmest of side glances.

"Turn around!" roared Pollard.

His daughter turned slowly and faced him. Not white-faced with fear, but to the unutterable astonishment of Terry she was quietly looking her father up and down. Pollard sprang to his feet and struck the table so that it quivered through all its massive length.

the big man. "Is that the scene?"

She flicked Terry Hollis with a glance. "I think he'll understand and make allowances."

It brought the heavy fist smashing on the table again. And an ugly feeling rose in Hollis that the big fellow might put hands on his daughter.

"And what d'you mean by that? What in hell d'you mean by that?"

In place of wincing, she in turn came to her feet gracefully. There had been such an easy dignity about her sitting at the piano that she had seemed tall to Terry. Now that she stood up, he was surprised to see that she was not a shade more than average height, beautifully and strongly made.

"You've gone about far enough with your little joke," said the girl, and her voice was low, but with an edge of vibrancy that went through Hollis. "And you're going to stop—pronto!"

There was a flash of teeth as she spoke, and a quiver through her body. Terry had never seen such passion, such unreasoning, wild passion, as that which had leaped on the girl. Though her face was not contorted, danger spoke from every line of it. He made himself tense, prepared for a similar outbreak from the father, but the latter relaxed as suddenly as his daughter had become furious.

"There you go," he complained, with a sort of heavy whine. "Always flying off the handle. Always turning into a wildcat when I try to reason with you!"

"Reason!" cried the girl. "Reason!"

Joe Pollard grew downcast under her scorn. And Terry, sensing that the crisis of the argument had passed, watched the other four men in the room. They had not paid the slightest attention to the debate during its later phases. And two of them—Slim and huge Phil Marvin—had begun to roll dice on a folded blanket, the little ivories winking in the light rapidly until they came to a rest at the farther end of the cloth. Possibly this family strife was a common thing in the Pollard household. At any rate, the father now passed off from accusation to abrupt apology.

"You always get me riled at the end of the day, Kate. Damn it! Can't you never bear with a gent?"

The tigerish alertness passed from Kate Pollard. She was filled all at once with a winning gentleness and, crossing to her father, took his heavy hands in hers.

"I reckon I'm a bad one," she accused herself. "I try to get over tantrums—but—I can't help it! Something—just sort of grabs me by the throat when I get mad. I—I see red."

"Hush up, honey," said the big man tenderly, and he ran his thick fingers over her hair. "You ain't so bad. And all that's bad in you comes out of me. You forget and I'll forget."

He waved across the table.

"Terry'll be thinking we're a bunch of wild Indians the way we been actin'."

"Oh!"

Plainly she was recalled to the presence of the stranger for the first time in many minutes and, dropping her chin in her hand, she studied the new arrival.

He found it difficult to meet her glance. The Lord had endowed Terry Hollis with a remarkable share of good looks, and it was not the first time that he had been investigated by the eyes of a woman. But in all his life he had never been subjected to an examination as minute, as insolently frank as this one. He felt himself taken part and parcel, examined in detail as to forehead, chin, and eyes and heft of shoulders, and then weighed altogether. In self-defense he looked boldly back at her, making himself examine her in equal detail. Seeing her so close, he was aware of a marvellously delicate olive-tanned skin with delightful tints of rose just beneath the surface. He found himself saying inwardly: "It's easy to look at her. It's very easy. By the Lord, she's beautiful!"

As for the girl, it seemed that she was not quite sure in her judgment. For now she turned to her father with a faint frown of wonder. And again it seemed to Terry that Joe Pollard made an imperceptible sign, such as he had made to the four men when he introduced Terry.

But now he broke into breezy talk.

"Met Terry down in Pedro's—"

The girl seemed to have dismissed Terry from her mind already, for she broke in: "Crooked game he's running, isn't it?"

"I thought so till today. Then I seen Terry, here, trim Pedro for a flat twenty thousand!"

"Oh," nodded the girl. Again her gaze reverted leisurely to the stranger and with a not unflattering interest.

"And then I seen him lose most of it back again. Roulette."

She nodded, keeping her eyes on Terry, and the boy found himself desiring mightily to discover just what was going on behind the changing green of her eyes. He was shocked when he discovered. It came like the break of high dawn in the mountains of the Big Bend. Suddenly she had smiled openly, frankly. "Hard luck, partner!"

A little shivering sense of pleasure ran through him. He knew that he had been admitted by her—accepted.

Her father had thrown up his head.

"Someone come in the back way. Oregon, go find out!"

Dark-eyed Oregon Charlie slipped up and through the door. Everyone in the room waited, a little tense, with lifted heads. Slim was studying the last throw that Phil Marvin had made. Terry could not but wonder what significance that "back way" had. Presently Oregon reappeared.

"Pete's come."

"The hell!"

"Went upstairs."

"Wants to be alone," interrupted the girl. "He'll come down and talk when he feels like it. That's Pete's way."

"Watching us, maybe," growled Joe Pollard, with a shade of uneasiness still. "Damned funny gent, Pete is. Watches a man like a cat; watches a gopher hole all day, maybe. And maybe the gent he watches is a friend he's known for ten years. Well—let Pete go. They ain't no explaining him."

Through the last part of his talk, and through the heaviness of his voice, cut another tone, lighter, sharper, venomous: "Phil, you gummed them dice that last time!"

Joe Pollard froze in place; the eyes of the girl widened. Terry, looking across the room, saw Phil Marvin scoop up the dice and start to his feet.

"You lie, Slim!"

Instinctively Terry slipped his hand onto his gun. It was what Phil Marvin had done, as a matter of fact. He stood swelling and glowering, staring down at Slim Dugan. Slim had not risen. His thin, lithe body was coiled, and he reminded Terry in ugly fashion of a snake ready to strike. His hand was not near his gun. It was the calm courage and self-confidence of a man who is sure of himself and of his enemy. Terry had heard of it before, but never seen it. As for Phil, it was plain that he was ill at ease in spite of his bulk and the advantage of his position. He was ready to fight. But he was not at all pleased with the prospect.

Terry again glanced at the witnesses. Every one of them was alert, but there was none of that fear which comes in the faces of ordinary men when strife between men is at hand. And suddenly Terry knew that every one of the five men in the room was an old familiar of danger, every one of them a past master of gun fighting!

CHAPTER 24

THE UNEASY WAIT continued for a moment or more. The whisper of Joe Pollard to his daughter barely reached the ear of Terry.

"Cut in between 'em, girl. You can handle 'em. I can't!"

She responded instantly, before Terry recovered from his shock of surprise.

"Slim, keep away from your gun!"

She spoke as she whirled from her chair to her feet. It was strange to see her direct all her attention to Slim, when Phil Marvin seemed the one about to draw.

"I ain't even nearin' my gun," asserted Slim truthfully. "It's Phil that's got a strangle hold on his."

"You're waiting for him to draw," said the girl calmly enough. "I know you, Slim. Phil, don't be a fool. Drop your hand away from that gat!"

He hesitated; she stepped directly between him and his enemy of the moment and jerked the gun from its holster. Then she faced Slim. Obviously Phil was not displeased to have the matter taken out of his hands; obviously Slim was not so pleased. He looked coldly up to the girl.

"This is between him and me," he protested. "I don't need none of your help, Kate."

"Don't you? You're going to get it, though. Gimme that gun, Slim Dugan!"

"I want a square deal," he complained. "I figure Phil has been crooking the dice on me."

"Bah! Besides, I'll give you a square deal."

She held out her hand for the weapon.

"Got any doubts about me being square, Slim?"

"Kate, leave this to me!"

"Why, Slim, I wouldn't let you run loose now for a million. You got that ugly look in your eyes. I know you, partner!"

And to the unutterable astonishment of Terry, the man pulled his gun from its holster and passed it up to her, his eyes fighting hers, his hand moving slowly. She stepped back, weighing the heavy weapons in her hands. Then she faced Phil Marvin with glittering eyes.

"It ain't the first time you been accused of queer stunts with the dice. What's the straight of it, Phil? Been doing anything to these dice?"

"Me? Sure I ain't!"

Her glance lingered on him the least part of a second.

"H'm!" said the girl. "Maybe not."

Slim was on his feet, eager. "Take a look at 'em, Kate. Take a look at them dice!"

She held them up to the light—then dropped them into a pocket of her skirt. "I'll look at 'em in the morning, Slim."

"The stuff'll be dry by that time!"

"Dry or not, that's what I'm going to do. I won't trust lamplight."

Slim turned on his heel and flung himself sulkily down on the blanket, fighting her with sullen eyes. She turned on Phil.

"How much d'you win?"

"Nothin'. Just a couple of hundred."

"Just a couple of hundred! You call that nothing?"

Phil grunted. The other men leaned forward in their interest

to watch the progress of the trial, all saving Joe Pollard, who
sat with his elbows braced in sprawling fashion on the table,
at ease, his eyes twinkling contentedly at the girl. Why she
refused to examine the dice at once was plain to Terry. If
they proved to have been gummed, it would mean a gun fight
with the men at a battling temperature. In the morning when
they had cooled down, it might be a different matter. Terry
watched her in wonder. His idea of an efficient woman was
based on Aunt Elizabeth, cold of eye and brain, practical in
methods on the ranch, keen with figures. The efficiency of
this slip of a girl was a different matter, a thing of passion,
of quick insight, of lightning guesses. He could see the play
of eager emotion in her face as she studied Phil Marvin. And
how could she do justice? Terry was baffled.

"How long you two been playing?"

"About twenty minutes."

"Not more'n five!" cut in Slim hotly.

"Shut up, Slim!" she commanded. "I'm running this here
game; Phil, how many straight passes did you make?"

"Me? Oh, I dunno. Maybe—five."

"Five straight passes!" said the girl. "Five straight passes!"

"You heard me say it," growled big Phil Marvin.

All at once she laughed.

"Phil, give that two hundred back to Slim!"

It came like a bolt from the blue, this decision. Marvin
hesitated, shook his head.

"Damned if I do. I don't back down. I won it square!"

"Listen to me," said the girl. Instead of threatening, as
Terry expected, she had suddenly become conciliatory. She
stepped close to him and dropped a slim hand on his burly
shoulder. "Ain't Slim a pal of yours? You and him, ain't you
stuck together through thick and thin? He thinks you didn't
win that coin square. Is Slim's friendship worth two hundred
to you, or ain't it? Besides, you ain't lying down to nobody.
Why, you big squarehead, Phil, don't we all know that you'd
fight a bull with your bare hands? Who'd call you yaller?
We'd simply say you was square, Phil, and you know it."

There was a pause. Phil was biting his lip, scowling at Slim.
Slim was sneering in return. It seemed that she had failed.
Even if she forced Phil to return the money, he and Slim
would hate each other as long as they lived. And Terry gained
a keen impression that if the hatred continued, one of them

would die very soon indeed. Her solution of the problem was a strange one. She faced them both.

"You two big sulky babies!" she exclaimed. "Slim, what did Phil do for you down in Tecomo? Phil, did Slim stand by you last April—you know the time? Why, boys, you're just being plain foolish. Get up, both of you, and take a walk outside where you'll get cooled down."

Slim rose. He and Phil walked slowly toward the door, at a little distance from each other, one eyeing the other shrewdly. At the door they hesitated. Finally, Phil lurched forward and went out first. Slim glided after.

"By heaven!" groaned Pollard as the door closed. "There goes two good men! Kate, what put this last fool idea into your head?"

She did not answer for a moment, but dropped into a chair as though suddenly exhausted.

"It'll work out," she said at length. "You wait for it!"

"Well," grumbled her father, "the mischief is working. Run along to bed, will you?"

She rose, wearily, and started across the room. But she turned before she passed out of their sight and leaned against one of the pillars.

"Dad, why you so anxious to get me out of the way?"

"What d'you mean by that? I got no reason. Run along and don't bother me!"

He turned his shoulder on her. As for the girl, she remained a moment, looking thoughtfully at the broad back of Pollard. Then her glance shifted and dwelt a moment on Terry—with pity, he wondered?

"Good night, boys!"

When the door closed on her, Joe Pollard turned his attention more fully on his new employee, and when Terry suggested that it was time for him to turn in, his suggestion was hospitably put to one side. Pollard began talking genially of the mountains, of the "varmints" he expected Terry to clean out, and while he talked, he took out a broad silver dollar and began flicking it in the air and catching it in the calloused palm of his hand.

"Call it," he interrupted himself to say to Terry.

"Heads," said Terry carelessly.

The coin spun up, flickered at the height of its rise, and rang loudly on the table.

"You win," said Pollard. "Well, you're a lucky gent, Terry, but I'll go you ten you can't call it again."

But again Terry called heads, and again the coin chimed, steadied, and showed the Grecian goddess. The rancher doubled his bet. He lost, doubled, lost again, doubled again, lost. A pile of money had appeared by magic before Terry.

"I came to work for money," laughed Terry, "not *take* it away."

"I always lose at this game," sighed Joe Pollard.

The door opened, and Phil Marvin and Slim Dugan came back, talking and laughing together.

"What d'you know about that?" Pollard exclaimed softly. "She guessed right. She always does! Oughta be a man, with a brain like she's got. Here we are again!"

He spun the coin; it winked, fell, a streak of light, and again Terry had won. He began to grow excited. On the next throw he lost. A moment later his little pile of winnings had disappeared. And now he had forgotten the face of Joe Pollard, forgotten the room, forgotten everything except the quick thumb that snapped the coin into the air. The cold, quiet passion of the gambler grew in him. He was losing steadily. Out of his wallet came in a steady stream the last of his winnings at Pedro's. And still he played. Suddenly the wallet squeezed flat between his fingers.

"Pollard," he said regretfully, "I'm broke."

The other waved away the idea.

"Break up a fine game like this because you're broke?" The cloudy agate eyes dwelt kindly on the face of Terry, and mysteriously as well. "That ain't nothing. Nothing between friends. You don't know the style of a man I am, Terry. Your word is as good as your money with me!"

"I've no security—"

"Don't talk security. Think I'm a moneylender? This is a game. Come on!"

Five minutes later Terry was three hundred behind. A mysterious providence seemed to send all the luck the way of the heavy, tanned thumb of Pollard.

"That's my limit," he announced abruptly, rising.

"No, no!" Pollard spread out his big hand on the table. "You got the red hoss, son. You can bet to a thousand. He's worth that—to me!"

"I won't bet a cent on him," said Terry firmly.

"Every damn cent I've won from you ag'in' the hoss, son. That's a lot of cash if you win. If you lose, you're just out that much hossflesh, and I'll give you a good enough cayuse to take El Sangre's place."

"A dozen wouldn't take his place," insisted Terry.

"That so?"

Pollard leaned back in his chair and put a hand behind his neck to support his head. It seemed to Terry that the big man made some odd motion with his hidden fingers. At any rate, the four men who lounged on the farther side of the room now rose and slowly drifted in different directions. Oregon Charlie wandered toward the door. Slim sauntered to the window behind the piano and stood idly looking out into the night. Phil Marvin began to examine a saddle hanging from a peg on one of the posts, and finally, chunky Marty Cardiff strolled to the kitchen door and appeared to study the hinges.

All these things were done casually, but Terry, his attention finally off the game, caught a meaning in them. Every exit was blocked for him. He was trapped at the will of Joe Pollard!

CHAPTER 25

LOOKING BACK, he could understand everything easily. The horse was the main objective of Pollard. He had won the money so as to tempt Terry to gamble with the value of the blood-bay. But by fair means or foul he intended to have El Sangre. And now, the moment his men were in place, a change came over Pollard. He straightened in the chair. A slight outthrust of his lower jaw made his face strangely brutal, conscienceless. And his cloudy agate eyes were unreadable.

"Look here, Terry," he argued calmly, but Terry could see that the voice was raised so that it would undubitably reach the ears of the farthest of the four men. "I don't mind letting a gambling debt ride when a gent ain't got anything more to put up for covering his money. But when a gent has got more, I figure he'd ought to cover with it."

Unreasoning anger swelled in the throat of Terry Hollis; the same blind passion which had surged in him before he started up at the Cornish table and revealed himself to the sheriff. And the similarity was what sobered him. It was the hunger to battle, to kill. And it seemed to him that Black Jack had stepped out of the old picture and now stood behind him, tempting him to strike.

Another covert signal from Pollard. Every one of the four turned toward him. The chances of Terry were diminished, nine out of ten, for each of those four, he shrewdly guessed, was a practiced gunman. Cold reason came to Terry's assistance.

"I told you when I was broke," he said gently. "I told you that I was through. You told me to go on."

"I figured you was kidding me," said Pollard harshly. "I knew you still had El Sangre back. Son, I'm a kind sort of a man, I am. I got a name for it."

In spite of himself a faint and cruel smile flickered at the corners of his mouth as he spoke. He became grave again.

"But they's some things I can't stand. They's some things that I hate worse'n I hate poison. I won't say what one of 'em is. I leave it to you. And I ask you to keep in the game. A thousand bucks ag'in' a hoss. Ain't that more'n fair?"

He no longer took pains to disguise his voice. It was hard and heavy and rang into the ear of Terry. And the latter, feeling that his hour had come, looked deliberately around the room and took note of every guarded exit, the four men now openly on watch for any action on his part. Pollard himself sat erect, on the edge of his chair, and his right hand had disappeared beneath the table.

"Suppose I throw the coin this time?" he suggested.

"By God!" thundered Pollard, springing to his feet and throwing off the mask completely. "You damned skunk, are you accusin' me of crooking the throw of a coin?"

Terry waited for the least moment—waited in a dull wonder to find himself unafraid. But there was no fear in him. There was only a cold, methodical calculation of chances. He told himself, deliberately, that no matter how fast Pollard might be, he would prove the faster. He would kill Pollard.

And he would undoubtedly kill one of the others. And they, beyond a shadow of a doubt, would kill him. He saw all this as in a picture.

"Pollard," he said, more gently than before, "you'll have to eat that talk!"

A flash of bewilderment crossed the face of Pollard—then rage—then that slight contraction of the features which in some men precedes a violent effort.

But the effort did not come. While Terry literally wavered on tiptoe, his nerves straining for the pull of his gun and the leap to one side as he sent his bullet home, a deep, unmusical voice cut in on them:

"Just hold yourself up a minute, will you, Joe?"

Terry looked up. On the balcony in front of the sleeping rooms of the second story, his legs spread apart, his hands shoved deep into his trouser pockets, his shapeless black hat crushed on the back of his head, and a broad smile on his ugly face, stood his nemesis—Denver the yegg!

Pollard sprang back from the table and spoke with his face still turned to Terry.

"Pete!" he called. "Come in!"

But Denver, alias Shorty, alias Pete, merely laughed.

"Come in nothing, you fool! Joe, you're about half a second from hell, and so's a couple more of you. D'you know who the kid is? Eh? I'll tell you, boys. It's the kid that dropped old Minter. It's the kid that beat foxy Joe Minter to the draw. It's young Hollis. Why, you damned blind men, look at his face! It's the son of Black Jack. It's Black Jack himself come back to us!"

Joe Pollard had let his hand fall away from his gun. He gaped at Terry as though he were seeing a ghost. He came a long pace nearer and let his arms fall on the table, where they supported his weight.

"Black Jack," he kept whispering. "Black Jack! God above, are you Black Jack's son?"

And the bewildered Terry answered:

"I'm his son. Whatever you think, and be damned to you all! I'm his son and I'm proud of it. Now get your gun!"

But Joe Pollard became a great catapult that shot across the table and landed beside Terry. Two vast hands swallowed the hands of the younger man and crushed them to numbness.

"Proud of it? God a'mighty, boy, why wouldn't you be? Black Jack's son! Pete, thank God you come in time!"

"In time to save your head for you, Joe."

"I believe it," said the big man humbly. "I b'lieve he would of cleaned up on me. Maybe on all of us. Black Jack would of come close to doing it. But you come in time, Pete. And I'll never forget it."

While he spoke, he was still wringing the hands of Terry. Now he dragged the stunned Terry around the table and forced him down in his own huge, padded armchair, his sign of power. But it was only to drag him up from the chair again.

"Lemme look at you! Black Jack's boy! As like Black Jack as ever I seen, too. But a shade taller. Eh, Pete? A shade taller. And a shade heavier in the shoulders. But you got the look. I might of knowed you by the look in your eyes. Hey, Slim, damn your good-for-nothing hide, drag Johnny here pronto by the back of the neck!"

Johnny, the Chinaman, appeared, blinking at the lights. Joe Pollard clapped him on the shoulder with staggering force.

"Johnny, you see!" a broad gesture to Terry. "Old friend. Just find out. Velly old friend. Like pretty much a whole damned lot. Get down in the cellar, you yaller old sinner, and get out the oldest bourbon I got there. You savvy? Pretty damned pronto—hurry up—quick—old keg. Git out!"

Johnny was literally hurled out of the room toward the kitchen, trailing a crackle of strange-sounding but unmistakable profanity behind him. And Joe Pollard, perching his bulk on the edge of the table, introduced Terry to the boys again, for Oregon had come back with word that Kate would be out soon.

"Here's Denver Pete. You know him already, and he's worth his weight in any man's company. Here's Slim Dugan, that could scent a big coin shipment a thousand miles away. Phil Marvin ain't any slouch at stalling a gent with a fat wallet and leading him up to be plucked. Marty Cardiff ain't half so tame as he looks, and he's the best trailer that ever squinted at a buzzard in the sky; he knows this whole country like a book. And Oregon Charlie is the best all-around man you ever seen, from railroads to stages. And me—I'm sort of a handyman. Well, Black Jack, your old man himself never got a finer crew together than this, eh?"

Denver Pete had waited until his big friend finished. Then he remarked quietly: "All very pretty, partner, but Terry figures he walks the straight and narrow path. Savvy?"

"Just a kid's fool hunch!" snorted Joe Pollard. "Didn't your dad show me the ropes? Wasn't it him that taught me all I ever knew? Sure it was, and I'm going to do the same for you, Terry. Damn my eyes if I ain't! And here I been sitting, trimming you! Son, take back the coin. I was sure playing a cheap game—and I apologize, man to man."

But Terry shook his head.

"You won it," he said quietly. "And you'll keep it."

"Won nothing. I can call every coin I throw. I was stealing, not gambling. I was gold-digging! Take back the stuff!"

"If I was fool enough to lose it that way, it'll stay lost," answered Terry.

"But I won't keep it, son."

"Then give it away. But not to me."

"Black Jack—" began Pollard.

But he received a signal from Denver Pete and abruptly changed the subject.

"Let it go, then. They's plenty of loose coin rolling about this day. If you got a thin purse today, I'll make it fat for you in a week. But think of me stumbling on to you!"

It was the first time that Terry had a fair opportunity to speak, and he made the best of it.

"It's very pleasant to meet you—on this basis," he said. "But as for taking up—er—road life—"

The lifted hand of Joe Pollard made it impossible for him to complete his sentence.

"I know. You got scruples, son. Sure you got 'em. I used to have 'em, too, till your old man got 'em out of my head."

Terry winced. But Joe Pollard rambled on, ignorant that he had struck a blow in the dark: "When I met up with the original Black Jack, I was slavin' my life away with a pick trying to turn ordinary quartz into pay dirt. Making a fool of myself, that's what I was doing. Along comes Black Jack. He needed a man. He picks me up and takes me along with him. I tried to talk Bible talk. He showed me where I was a fool.

" 'All you got to do,' he says to me, 'is to make sure that

you ain't stealing from an honest man. And they's about one gent in three with money that's come by it honest, in this part of the world. The rest is just plain thieves, but they been clever enough to cover it up. Pick on that crew, Pollard, and squeeze 'em till they run money into your hand. I'll show you how to do it!'

"Well, it come pretty hard to me at first. I didn't see how it was done. But he showed me. He'd sent a scout around to a mining camp. If they was a crooked wheel in the gambling house that was making a lot of coin, Black Jack would slide in some night, stick up the works, and clean out with the loot. If they was some dirty dog that had jumped a claim and was making a pile of coin out of it, Black Jack would drop out of the sky onto him and take the gold."

Terry listened, fascinated. He was having the workings of his father's mind re-created for him and spread plainly before his eyes. And there was a certain terror and also a certain attractiveness about what he discovered.

"It sounds, maybe, like an easy thing to do, to just stick on the trail of them that you know are worse crooks than you. But it ain't. I've tried it. I've seen Black Jack pass up ten thousand like it was nothing, because the gent that had it come by it honest. But I can't do it, speaking in general. But I'll tell you more about the old man."

"Thank you," said Terry, "but—"

"And when you're with us—"

"You see," said Terry firmly, "I plan to do the work you asked me to do—kill what you wanted killed on the range. And when I've worked off the money I owe you—"

Before he could complete his sentence, a door opened on the far side of the room, and Kate Pollard entered again. She had risen from her bed in some haste to answer the summons of her father. Her bright hair poured across her shoulders, a heavy, greenish-blue dressing gown was drawn about her and held close with one hand at her breast. She came slowly toward them. And she seemed to Terry to have changed. There was less of the masculine about her than there had been earlier in the evening. Her walk was slow, her eyes were wide as though she had no idea what might await her, and the light glinted white on the untanned portion of her throat, and on her arm where the loose sleeve of the dressing gown fell back from it.

"Kate," said her father, "I had to get you up to tell you the big news—biggest news you ever heard of! Girl, who've I always told you was the greatest gent that ever come into my life?"

"Jack Hollis—Black Jack," she said, without hesitation. "According to *your* way of thinking, Dad!"

Plainly her own conclusions might be very different.

"According to anybody's way of thinking, as long as they was thinking right. And you'd know who we've got here with us now? Could you guess it in a thousand years? Why, the kid that come tonight. Black Jack as sure as if he was a picture out of a book, and me a blind fool that didn't know him. Kate, here's the second Black Jack. Terry Hollis. Give him your hand again and say you're glad to have him for his dad's sake and for his own! Kate, he's done a man's job already. It's him that dropped old foxy Minter!"

The last of these words faded out of the hearing of Terry. He felt the lowered eyes of the girl rise and fall gravely on his face, and her glance rested there a long moment with a new and solemn questioning. Then her hand went slowly out to him, a cold hand that barely touched his with its fingertips and then dropped away.

But what Terry felt was that it was the same glance she had turned to him when she stood leaning against the post earlier that evening. There was a pity in it, and a sort of despair which he could not understand.

And without saying a word she turned her back on them and went out of the room as slowly as she had come into it.

CHAPTER 26

"IT DON'T MEAN nothing," Pollard hastened to assure Terry. "It don't mean a thing in the world except that she's a fool girl. The queerest, orneriest, kindest, strangest, wildest thing in the shape of calico that ever come into these parts since her mother died before her. But the more you see of her, the more you'll value her. She can ride like a man—no wear out to her—and she's got the courage of a man. Besides which she can sling a gun like it would do your heart good to see her! Don't take nothing she does to heart. She don't mean no harm. But she sure does tangle up a gent's ideas. Here I been living with her nigh onto twenty years and I don't savvy her none yet. Eh, boys?"

"I'm not offended in the least," said Terry quietly.

And he was not, but he was more interested than he had ever been before by man, woman, or child. And for the past few seconds his mind had been following her through the door behind which she had disappeared.

"And if I were to see more of her, no doubt—" He broke off with: "But I'm not apt to see much more of any of you, Mr. Pollard. If I can't stay here and work off that three-hundred-dollar debt—"

"Work, hell! No son of Black Jack Hollis can work for me. But he can live with me as a partner, son, and he can have everything I got, half and half, and the bigger half to him if he asks for it. That's straight!"

Terry raised a protesting hand. Yet he was touched—intimately touched. He had tried hard to fit in his place among the honest people of the mountains by hard and patient work. They would have none of him. His own kind turned him out. Among these men—men who had no law, as he had every reason to believe—he was instantly taken in and made one of them.

"But no more talk tonight," said Pollard. "I can see you're played out. I'll show you the room."

He caught a lantern from the wall as he spoke and began to lead the way up the stairs to the balcony. He pointed out the advantages of the house as he spoke.

"Not half bad—this house, eh?" he said proudly. "And who d'you think planned it? Your old man, kid. It was Black Jack Hollis himself that done it! He was took off sudden before he'd had a chance to work it out and build it. But I used his ideas in this the same's I've done in other things. His idea was a house like a ship.

"They build a ship in compartments, eh? Ship hits a rock, water comes in. But it only fills one compartment, and the old ship still floats. Same with this house. You seen them walls. And the walls on the outside ain't the only thing. Every partition is the same thing, pretty near; and a gent could stand behind these doors safe as if he was a mile away from a gun. Why? Because they's a nice little lining of the best steel you ever seen in the middle of 'em.

"Cost a lot. Sure. But look at us now. Suppose a posse was to rush the house. They bust into the kitchen side. Where are they? Just the same as if they hadn't got in at all. I bolt the doors from the inside of the big room, and they're shut out agin. Or suppose they take the big room? Then a couple of us slide out on this balcony and spray 'em with lead. This house ain't going to be took till the last room is filled full of the sheriff's men!"

He paused on the balcony and looked proudly over the big, baronial room below them. It seemed huger than ever from this viewpoint, and the men below them were dwarfed. The light of the lanterns did not extend all the way across it, but fell in pools here and there, gleaming faintly on the men below.

"But doesn't it make people suspicious to have a fort like this built on the hill?" asked Terry.

"Of course. If they knew. But they don't know, son, and they ain't going to find out the lining of this house till they try it out with lead."

He brought Terry into one of the bedrooms and lighted a lamp. As the flare steadied in the big circular oil burner and the light spread, Terry made out a surprisingly comfortable apartment. There was not a bunk, but a civilized bed, beside which was a huge, tawny mountain-lion skin softening the floor. The window was curtained in some pleasant blue stuff, and there were a few spots of color on the wall—only calendars, some of them, but helping to give a livable impression for the place.

"Kate's work," grinned Pollard proudly. "She's been fixing these rooms up all out of her own head. Never got no ideas out of me. Anything you might lack, son?"

Terry told him he would be very comfortable, and the big man wrung his hand again as he bade him good night.

"The best work that Denver ever done was bringing you to me," he declared. "Which you'll find it out before I'm through. I'm going to give you a home!" And he strode away before Terry could answer.

The rather rare consciousness of having done a good deed swelled in the heart of Joe Pollard on his way down from the balcony. When he reached the floor below, he found that the four men had gone to bed and left Denver alone, drawn back from the light into a shadowy corner, where he was flanked by the gleam of a bottle of whisky on the one side and a shimmering glass on the other. Although Pollard was the nominal leader, he was in secret awe of the yegg. For Denver was an "in-and-outer." Sometimes he joined them in the West; sometimes he "worked" an Eastern territory. He came and went as he pleased, and was more or less a law to himself. Moreover, he had certain qualities of silence and brooding that usually disturbed the leader. They troubled him now as he approached the squat, shapeless figure in the corner chair.

"What you think of him?" said Denver.

"A good kid and a clean-cut kid," decided Joe Pollard judicially. "Maybe he ain't another Black Jack, but he's tolerable cool for a youngster. Stood up and looked me in the eye like a man when I had him cornered a while back. Good thing for him you come out when you did!"

"A good thing for you, Joe," replied Denver Pete. "He'd of turned you into fertilizer, bo!"

"Maybe; maybe not. Maybe they's some things I could teach him about gun-slinging, Pete."

"Maybe; maybe not," parodied Denver. "You've learned a good deal about guns, Joe—quite a bit. But there's some things about gun fighting that nobody can learn. It's got to be born into 'em. Remember how Black Jack used to slide out his gat?"

"Yep. There was a man!"

"And Minter, too. There's a born gunman."

"Sure. We all know Uncle Joe—damn his soul!"

"But the kid beat Uncle Joe fair and square from an even break—and beat him bad. Made his draw, held it so's Joe could partway catch up with him, and then drilled him clean!"

Pollard scratched his chin.

"I'd believe that if I seen it," he declared.

"Pal, it wasn't Terry that done the talking; it was Gainor. He's seen a good deal of gunplay, and said that Terry's was the coolest he ever watched."

"All right for that part of it," said Joe Pollard. "Suppose he's fast—but can I use him? I like him well enough; I'll give him a good deal; but is he going to mean charity all the time he hangs out with me?"

"Maybe; maybe not," chuckled Denver again. "Use him the way he can be used, and he'll be the best bargain you ever turned. Black Jack started you in business; Black Jack the Second will make you rich if you handle him right—and ruin you if you make a slip."

"How come? He talks this 'honesty' talk pretty strong."

"Gimme a chance to talk," said Denver contemptuously. "Takes a gent that's used to reading the secrets of a safe to read the secrets of a gent's head. And I've read the secret of young Black Jack Hollis. He's a pile of dry powder, Joe. Throw in the spark and he'll explode so damned loud they'll hear him go off all over the country."

"How?"

"First, you got to keep him here."

"How?"

Joe Pollard sat back with the air of one who will be convinced through no mental effort of his own. But Denver was equal to the demand.

"*I'm* going to show you. He thinks he owes you three hundred."

"That's foolish. I cheated the kid out of it. I'll give it back to him and all the rest I won."

Denver paused and studied the other as one amazed by such stupidity.

"Pal, did you ever try, in the old days, to *give* anything to the old Black Jack?"

"H'm. Well, he sure hated charity. But this ain't charity."

"It ain't in your eyes. It is in Terry's. If you insist, he'll get sore. No, Joe. Let him think he owes you that money. Let him start in working it off for you—honest work. You ain't got any ranch work. Well, set him to cutting down trees, or anything. That'll help to hold him. If he makes some gambling play—and he's got the born gambler in him—you got one last thing that'll be apt to keep him here."

"What's that?"

"Kate."

Pollard stirred in his chair.

"How d'you mean that?" he asked gruffly.

"I mean what I said," retorted Denver. "I watched young Black Jack looking at her. He had his heart in his eyes, the kid did. He likes her, in spite of the frosty mitt she handed him. Oh, he's falling for her, pal—and he'll keep on falling. Just slip the word to Kate to kid him along. Will you? And after we got him glued to the place here, we'll figure out the way to turn Terry into a copy of his dad. We'll figure out how to shoot the spark into the powder, and then stand clear for the explosion."

Denver came silently and swiftly out of the chair, his pudgy hand spread on the table and his eyes gleaming close to the face of Pollard.

"Joe," he said softly, "if that kid goes wrong, he'll be as much as his father ever was—and maybe more. He'll rake in the money like it was dirt. How do I know? Because I've talked to him. I've watched him and trailed him. He's trying hard to go straight. He's failed twice; the third time he'll bust and throw in with us. And if he does, he'll clean up the coin—and we'll get our share. Why ain't you made more money yourself, Joe? You got as many men as Black Jack ever had. It's because you ain't got the fire in you. Neither have I. We're nothing but tools ready for another man to use the way Black Jack used us. Nurse this kid along a little while, and he'll show us how to pry open the places where the real coin is cached away. And he'll lead us in and out with no danger to us and all the real risk on his own head. That's his way—that was his dad's way before him."

Pollard nodded slowly. "Maybe you're right."

"I know I am. He's a gold mine, this kid is. But we got to buy him with something more than gold. And I know what that something is. I'm going to show him that the good, lawabiding citizens have made up their minds that he's no good; that they're all ag'in' him; and when he finds that out, he'll go wild. They ain't no doubt of it. He'll show his teeth! And when he shows his teeth, he'll taste blood—they ain't no doubt of it."

"Going to make him—kill?" asked Pollard very softly.

"Why not? He'll do it sooner or later anyway. It's in his blood."

"I suppose it is."

"I got an idea. There's a young gent in town named Larrimer, ain't there?"

"Sure. A rough kid, too. It was him that killed Kennedy last spring."

"And he's proud of his reputation?"

"Sure. He'd go a hundred miles to have a fight with a gent with a good name for gunplay."

"Then hark to me sing, Joe! Send Terry into town to get something for you. I'll drop in ahead of him and find Larrimer, and tell Larrimer that Black Jack's son is around—the man that dropped Sheriff Minter. Then I'll bring 'em together and give 'em a running start."

"And risk Terry getting his head blown off?"

"If he can't beat Larrimer, he's no use to us; if he kills Larrimer, it's good riddance. The kid is going to get bumped off sometime, anyway. He's bad—all the way through."

Pollard looked with a sort of wonder on his companion.

"You're a nice, kind sort of a gent, ain't you, Denver?"

"I'm a moneymaker," asserted Denver coldly. "And, just now, Terry Hollis is my gold mine. Watch me work him!"

CHAPTER 27

IT WAS SOME TIME before Terry could sleep, though it was now very late. When he put out the light and slipped into the bed, the darkness brought a bright flood of memories of the day before him. It seemed to him that half a lifetime had been crowded into the brief hours since he was fired on the ranch that morning. Behind everything stirred the ugly face of Denver as a sort of controlling nemesis. It seemed to him that the chunky little man had been pulling the wires all the time while he, Terry Hollis, danced in response. Not a flattering thought.

Nervously, Terry got out of bed and went to the window. The night was cool, cut crisp rather than chilling. His eye went over the velvet blackness of the mountain slope above him to the ragged line of the crest—then a dizzy plunge to the brightness of the stars beyond. The very sense of distance was soothing; it washed the gloom and the troubles away from him. He breathed deep of the fragrance of the pines and then went back to his bed.

He had hardly taken his place in it when the sleep began to well up over his brain—waves of shadows running out of corners of his mind. And then suddenly he was wide awake, alert.

Someone had opened the door. There had been no sound; merely a change in the air currents of the room, but there was also the sense of another presence so clearly that Terry almost imagined he could hear the breathing.

He was beginning to shrug the thought away and smile at his own nervousness, when he heard that unmistakable sound of a foot pressing the floor. And then he remembered that he had left his gun belt far from the bed. In a burning moment that lesson was printed in his mind, and would never be forgotten. Slowly as possible and without sound, he drew up his feet little by little, spread his arms gently on either side of him, and made himself tense for the effort. Whoever it was that entered, they might be taken by surprise. He dared not lift his head to look; and he was on the verge of leaping up and at the approaching noise, when a whisper came to him softly: "Black Jack!"

The soft voice, the name itself, thrilled him. He sat erect in the bed and made out, dimly, the form of Kate Pollard in the blackness. She would have been quite invisible, save that the square of the window was almost exactly behind her. He made out the faint whiteness of the hand which held her dressing robe at the breast.

She did not start back, though she showed that she was startled by the suddenness of his movement by growing the faintest shade taller and lifting her head a little. Terry watched her, bewildered.

"I been waiting to see you," said Kate. "I want to—I mean —to—talk to you."

He could think of nothing except to blurt with sublime stupidity: "It's good of you. Won't you sit down?"

The girl brought him to his senses with a sharp "Easy! Don't talk out. Do you know what'd happen if Dad found me here?"

"I—" began Terry.

But she helped him smoothly to the logical conclusion. "He'd blow your head off, Black Jack; and he'd do it— pronto. If you are going to talk, talk soft—like me."

She sat down on the side of the bed so gently that there was no creaking. They peered at each other through the darkness for a time.

She was not whispering, but her voice was pitched almost as low, and he wandered at the variety of expression she was able to pack in the small range of that murmur. "I suppose I'm a fool for coming. But I was born to love chances. Born for it!"

She lifted her head and laughed.

It amazed Terry to hear the shaken flow of her breath and catch the glinting outline of her face. He found himself leaning forward a little; and he began to wish for a light, though perhaps it was an unconscious wish.

"First," she said "what d'you know about Dad—and Denver Pete?"

"Practically nothing."

She was silent for a moment, and he saw her hand go up and prop her chin while she considered what she could say next.

"They's so much to tell," she confessed, "that I can't put it short. I'll tell you this much, Black Jack—"

"That isn't my name, if you please."

"It'll be your name if you stay around these parts with Dad very long," she replied, with an odd emphasis. "But where you been raised, Terry? And what you been doing with yourself?"

He felt the blood tingle in his cheeks, and a real anger some subtle manner. It enabled him, for instance, to call her Kate, and he decided with a thrill that he would do so at the first opportunity. He reverted to her question.

"I suppose," he admitted gloomily, "that I've been raised to do pretty much as I please—and the money I've spent has been given to me."

The girl shook her head with conviction.

"It ain't possible," she declacred.

"Why not?"

"No son of Black Jack would live off somebody's charity." He felt the blood tingle in his cheeks, and a real anger against her rose. Yet he found himself explaining humbly.

"You see, I was taken when I wasn't old enough to decide for myself. I was only a baby. And I was raised to depend upon Elizabeth Cornish. I—I didn't even know the name of my father until a few days ago."

The girl gasped. "You didn't know your father—not your own father?" She laughed again scornfully. "Terry, I ain't green enough to believe that!"

He fell into a dignified silence, and presently the girl leaned closer, as though she were peering to make out his face. Indeed, it was now possible to dimly make out objects in the room. The window was filled with an increasing brightness, and presently a shaft of pale light began to slide across the floor, little by little. The moon had pushed up above the crest of the mountain.

"Did that make you mad?" queried the girl. "Why?"

"You seemed to doubt what I said," he remarked stiffly.

"Why not? You ain't under oath, or anything, are you?"

Then she laughed again. "You're a queer one all the way through. This Elizabeth Cornish—got anything to do with the Cornish ranch?"

"I presume she owns it, very largely."

The girl nodded. "You talk like a book. You must of studied a terrible pile."

"Not so much, really."

"H'm," said the girl, and seemed to reserve judgment.

Then she asked with a return of her former sharpness: "How come you gambled today at Pedro's?"

"I don't know. It seemed the thing to do—to kill time, you know."

"Kill time! At Pedro's? Well—you *are* green, Terry!"

"I suppose I am, Kate."

He made a little pause before her name, and when he spoke it, in spite of himself, his voice changed, became softer. The girl straightened somewhat, and the light was now increased to such a point that he could make out that she was frowning at him through the dimness.

"First, you been adopted, then you been raised on a great big place with everything you want, mostly, and now you're out—playing at Pedro's. How come, Terry?"

"I was sent away," said Terry faintly, as all the pain of that farewell came flooding back over him.

"Why?"

"I shot a man."

"Ah!" said Kate. "You shot a man?" It seemed to silence her. "Why, Terry?"

"He had killed my father," he explained, more softly than ever.

"I know. It was Minter. And they turned you out for that?"

There was a trembling intake of her breath. He could catch the sparkle of her eyes, and knew that she had flown into one of her sudden, fiery passions. And it warmed his heart to hear her.

"I'd like to know what kind of people they are, anyway! I'd like to meet up with that Elizabeth Cornish, the—"

"She's the finest woman that ever breathed," said Terry simply.

"You say that," she pondered slowly, "after she sent you away?"

"She did only what she thought was right. She's a little hard, but very just, Kate."

She was shaking her head; the hair had become a dull and wonderful gold in the faint moonshine.

"I dunno what kind of a man you are, Terry. I didn't ever know a man could stick by—folks—after they'd been hurt by 'em. I couldn't do it. I ain't got much Bible stuff in me, Terry. Why, when somebody does me a wrong, I hate 'em—I hate 'em! And I never forgive 'em till I get back at 'em." She sighed. "But you're different, I guess. I begin to figure that you're pretty white, Terry Hollis."

There was something so direct about her talk he could not answer. It seemed to him that there was in her a cross between a boy and a man—the simplicity of a child and the straightforward strength of a grown man, and all this tempered and made strangely delightful by her own unique personality.

"But I guessed it the first time I looked at you," she was murmuring. "I guessed that you was different from the rest."

She had her elbow on her knee now, and, with her chin cupped in the graceful hand, she leaned toward him and studied him.

"When they're clean-cut on the outside, they're spoiled on the inside. They're crooks, hard ones, out for themselves, never giving a rap about the next gent in line. But mostly they ain't even clean on the outside, and you can see what they are the first time you look at 'em.

"Oh, I've liked some of the boys now and then; but I had to make myself like 'em. But you're different. I seen that when you started talking. You didn't sulk; and you didn't look proud like you wanted to show us what you could do; and you didn't boast none. I kept wondering at you while I was at the piano. And—you made an awful hit with me, Terry."

Again he was too staggered to reply. And before he could gather his wits, the girl went on:

"Now, is they any real reason why you shouldn't get out of here tomorrow morning?"

It was a blow of quite another sort.

"But why should I go?"

She grew very solemn, with a trace of sadness in her voice.

"I'll tell you why, Terry. Because if you stay around here too long, they'll make you what you don't want to be—another Black Jack. Don't you see that that's why they like you? Because you're his son, and because they want you to be another like him. Not that I have anything against him. I guess he was a fine fellow in his way." She paused and stared directly at him in a way he found hard to bear. "He must of been! But that isn't the sort of a man you want to make out of yourself. I know. You're trying to go straight. Well, Terry, nobody that ever stepped could stay straight long when they had around 'em Denver Pete and—my father." She said the last with a sob of grief. He tried to protest, but she waved him away.

"I know. And it's true. He'd do anything for me, except change himself. Believe me, Terry, you got to get out of here —pronto. Is they anything to hold you here?"

"A great deal. Three hundred dollars I owe your father."

She considered him again with that mute shake of the head. Then: "Do you mean it? I see you do. I don't suppose it does any good for me to tell you that he cheated you out of that money?"

"If I was fool enough to lose it that way, I won't take it back."

"I knew that, too—I guessed it. Oh, Terry, I know a pile more about the inside of your head than you'd ever guess! Well, I knew that—and I come with the money so's you can pay back Dad in the morning. Here it is—and they's just a mite more to help you on your way."

She laid the little handful of gold on the table beside the bed and rose.

"Don't go," said Terry, when he could speak. "Don't go, Kate! I'm not that low. I can't take your money!"

She stood by the bed and stamped lightly. "Are you going to be a fool about this, too?"

"Your father offered to give me back all the money I'd won. I can't do it, Kate."

He could see her grow angry, beautifully angry.

"Is they no difference between Kate Pollard and Joe Pollard?"

Something leaped into his throat. He wanted to tell her in a thousand ways just how vast that difference was.

"Man, you'd make a saint swear, and I ain't a saint by some miles. You take that money and pay Dad, and get on your way. This ain't no place for you, Terry Hollis."

"I—" he began.

She broke in: "Don't say it. You'll have me mad in a minute. Don't say it."

"I have to. I can't take money from you."

"Then take a loan."

He shook his head.

"Ain't I good enough to even loan you money?" she cried fiercely.

The shaft of moonlight had poured past her feet; she stood in a pool of it.

"Good enough?" said Terry. "Good enough?" Something that had been accumulating in him now swelled to bursting, flooded from his heart to his throat. He hardly knew his own voice, it was so transformed with sudden emotion.

"There's more good in you than in any man or woman I've ever known."

"Terry, are you trying to make me feel foolish?"

"I mean it—and it's true. You're kinder, more gentle—"

"Gentle? Me? Oh, Terry!"

But she sat down on the bed, and she listened to him with her face raised, as though music were falling on her, a thing barely heard at a perilous distance.

"They've told you other things, but they don't know. I know, Kate. The moment I saw you I knew, and it stopped

my heart for a beat—the knowing of it. That you're beautiful
—and true as steel; that you're worthy of honor—and that I
honor you with all my heart. That I love your kindness,
your frankness, your beautiful willingness to help people,
Kate. I've lived with a woman who taught me what was true.
You've taught me what's glorious and worth living for. Do
you understand, Kate?"

And no answer; but a change in her face that stopped him.

"I shouldn't of come," she whispered at length, "and I
—I shouldn't have let you—talk the way you've done. But,
oh, Terry—when you come to forget what you've said—
don't forget it all the way—keep some of the things—tucked
away in you—somewhere—"

She rose from the bed and slipped across the white bril-
liance of the shaft of moonlight. It made a red-gold fire of
her hair. Then she flickered into the shadow. Then she was
swallowed by the darkness.

CHAPTER 28

THERE WAS NO Kate at breakfast the next morning. She had
left the house at dawn with her horse.

"May be night before she comes back," said her father.
"No telling how far she'll go. May be tomorrow before she
shows up."

It made Terry thoughtful for reasons which he himself did
not understand. He had a peculiar desire to climb into the
saddle on El Sangre and trail her across the hills. But he was
very quickly brought to the reality that if he chose to make
himself a laboring man and work out the three hundred dollars he would not take back from Joe Pollard, the big man
was now disposed to make him live up to his word.

He was sent out with an ax and ordered to attack a stout
grove of the pines for firewood. But he quickly resigned himself to the work. Whatever gloom he felt disappeared with

the first stroke that sunk the edge deep into the soft wood. The next stroke broke out a great chip, and a resinous, fresh smell came up to him.

He made quick work of the first tree, working the morning chill out of his body, and as he warmed to his labor, the long muscles of arms and shoulders limbering, the blows fell in a shower. The sturdy pines fell one by one, and he stripped them of branches with long, sweeping blows of the ax, shearing off several at a stroke. He was not an expert axman, but he knew enough about that cunning craft to make his blows tell, and a continual desire to sing welled up in him.

Once, to breathe after the heavy labor, he stepped to the edge of the little grove. The sun was sparkling in the tops of the trees; the valley dropped far away below him. He felt as one who stands on the top of the world. There was flash and gleam of red; there stood El Sangre in the corral below him; the stallion raised his head and whinnied in reply to the master's whistle.

A great, sweet peace dropped on the heart of Terry Hollis. Now he felt he was at home. He went back to his work.

But in the midmorning Joe Pollard came to him and grunted at the swath Terry had driven into the heart of the lodgepole pines.

"I wanted junk for the fire," he protested; "not enough to build a house. But I got a little errand for you in town, Terry. You can give El Sangre a stretching down the road?"

"Of course."

It gave Terry a little prickling feeling of resentment to be ordered about. But he swallowed the resentment. After all, this was labor of his own choosing, though he could not but wonder a little, because Joe Pollard no longer pressed him to take back the money had lost. And he reverted to the talk of Kate the night before. That three hundred dollars was now an anchor holding him to the service of her father. And he remembered, with a touch of dismay, that it might take a year of ordinary wages to save three hundred dollars. Or more than a year.

It was impossible to be downhearted long, however. The morning was a fresh as a rose, and the four men came out of the house with Pollard to see El Sangre dancing under the saddle. Terry received the commission for a box of shotgun cartridges and the money to pay for them.

"And the change," said Pollard liberally, "don't worry me none. Step around and make yourself to home in town. About coming back—well, when I send a man into town, I figure on him making a day of it. S'long, Terry!"

"Hey," called Slim, "is El Sangre gun-shy?"

"I suppose so."

The stallion quivered with eagerness to be off.

"Here's to try him."

The gun flashed into Slim's hand and boomed. El Sangre bolted straight into the air and landed on legs of jack-rabbit qualities that flung him sidewise. The hand and voice of Terry quieted him, while the others stood around grinning with delight at the fun and at the beautiful horsemanship.

"But what'll he do if you pull a gun yourself?" asked Joe Pollard, showing a sudden concern.

"He'll stand for it—long enough," said Terry. "Try him!"

There was a devil in Slim that morning. He snatched up a shining bit of quartz and hurled it—straight at El Sangre! There was no warning—just a jerk of the arm and the stone came flashing.

"Try your gun—on that!"

The words were torn off short. The heavy gun had twitched into the hand of Terry, exploded, and the gleaming quartz puffed into a shower of bright particles that danced toward the earth. El Sangre flew into a paroxysm of educated bucking of the most advanced school. The steady voice of Terry Hollis brought him at last to a quivering stop. The rider was stiff in the saddle, his mouth a white, straight line.

He shoved his revolver deliberately back into the holster.

The four men had drawn together, still muttering with wonder. Luck may have had something to do with the success of that snapshot, but it was such a feat of marksmanship as would be remembered and talked about.

"Dugan!" said Terry huskily.

Slim lunged forward, but he was ill at ease.

"Well, kid?"

"It seemed to me," said Terry, "that you threw that stone *at* El Sangre. I hope I'm wrong?"

"Maybe," growled Slim. He flashed a glance at his companions, not at all eager to push this quarrel forward to a conclusion in spite of his known prowess. He had been a little irritated by the adulation which had been shown to the son of Black Jack the night before. He was still more irritated by the display of fine riding. For horsemanship and clever gunplay were the two main feathers in the cap of Slim Dugan. He had thrown the stone simply to test the qualities of this new member of the gang; the snapshot had stunned him. So he glanced at his companions. If they smiled, it meant that they took the matter lightly. But they were not smiling; they met his glance with expressions of uniform gravity. To torment a nervous horse is something which does not fit with the ways of the men of the mountain desert, even at their roughest. Besides, there was an edgy irritability about Slim Dugan which had more than once won him black looks. They wanted to see him tested now by a foeman who seemed worthy of his mettle. And Slim saw that common desire in his flickering side glance. He turned a cold eye on Terry.

"Maybe," he repeated. "But maybe I meant to see what you could do with a gun."

"I thought so," said Terry through his teeth. "Steady, boy!"

El Sangre became a rock for firmness. There was not a quiver in one of his long, racing muscles. It was a fine tribute to the power of the rider.

"I thought you might be trying out my gun," repeated Terry. "Are you entirely satisfied?"

He leaned a little in the saddle. Slim moistened his lips. It was a hard question to answer. The man in the saddle had become a quivering bundle of nerves; Slim could see the twitching of the lips, and he knew what it meant. Instinctively he fingered one of the broad bright buttons of his shirt. A man who could hit a glittering thrown stone would undoubtedly be able to hit that stationary button. The thought had elements in it that were decidedly unpleasant. But he had gone too far. He dared not recede now if he wished to hold up his head again among his fellows—and fear of death had never yet controlled the actions of Slim Dugan.

"I dunno," he remarked carelessly. "I'm a sort of curious gent. It takes more than one lucky shot to make me see the light."

The lips of Terry worked a moment. The companions of Slim Dugan scattered of one accord to either side. There was no doubting the gravity of the crisis which had so suddenly sprung up. As for Joe Pollard, he stood in the doorway in the direct line projected from Terry to Slim and beyond. There was very little sentiment in the body of Joe Pollard. Slim had always been a disturbing factor in the gang. Why not? He bit his lips thoughtfully.

"Dugan," said Terry at length, "curiosity is a very fine quality, and I admire a man who has it. Greatly. Now, you may notice that my gun is in the holster again. Suppose you try me again and see how fast I can get it out of the leather —and hit a target."

The challenge was entirely direct. There was a perceptible tightening in the muscles of the men. They were nerving themselves to hear the crack of a gun at any instant. Slim Dugan, gathering his nerve power, fenced for a moment more of time. His narrowing eyes were centering on one spot on Terry's body—the spot at which he would attempt to drive his bullet, and he chose the pocket of Terry's shirt. It steadied him, gave him his old self-confidence to have found that target. His hand and his brain grew steady, and the thrill of the fighter's love of battle entered him.

"What sort of a target d'you want?" he asked.

"I'm not particular," said Hollis. "Anything will do for me—even a button!"

It jarred home to Slim—the very thought he had had a moment before. He felt his certainty waver, slip from him. Then the voice of Pollard boomed out at them:

"Keep them guns in their houses! You hear me talk? The first man that makes a move I'm going to drill! Slim, get back into the house. Terry, you damn meateater, git on down that hill!"

Terry did not move, but Slim Dugan stirred uneasily, turned, and said: "It's up to you, chief. But I'll see this through sooner or later!"

And not until then did Terry turn his horse and go down the hill without a backward look.

CHAPTER 29

THERE HAD BEEN a profound reason behind the sudden turning of Terry Hollis's horse and his riding down the hill. For as he sat the saddle, quivering, he felt rising in him an all-controlling impulse that was new to him, a fierce and sudden passion.

It was joyous, free, terrible in its force—that wish to slay. The emotion had grown, held back by the very force of a mental thread of reason, until, at the very moment when the thread was about to fray and snap, and he would be flung into sudden action, the booming voice of Joe Pollard had cleared his mind as an acid clears a cloudy precipitate. He saw himself for the first time in several moments, and what he saw made him shudder.

And still in fear of himself he swung El Sangre and put him down the slope recklessly. Never in his life had he ridden as he rode in those first five minutes down the pitch of the hill. He gave El Sangre his head to pick his own way, and he confined his efforts to urging the great stallion along. The blood-bay went like the wind, passing up-jutting boulders with a swish of gravel knocked from his plunging hoofs against the rock.

Even in Terry's passion of self-dread he dimly appreciated the prowess of the horse, and when they shot onto the level going of the valley road, he called El Sangre out of the mad gallop and back to the natural pace, a gait as swinging and smooth as running water—yet still the road poured beneath them at the speed of an ordinary gallop. It was music to Terry Hollis, that matchless gait. He leaned and murmured to the pricking ears with that soft, gentle voice which horses love. The glorious head of El Sangre went up a little, his tail flaunted somewhat more proudly; from the quiver of his nostrils to the ringing beat of his black hoofs he bespoke his confidence that he bore the king of men on his back.

141

And the pride of the great horse brought back some of Terry's own waning self-confidence. His father had been up in him as he faced Slim Dugan, he knew. Once more he had escaped from the commission of a crime. But for how long would he succeed in dodging that imp of the perverse which haunted him?

It was like the temptation of a drug—to strike just once, and thereafter to be raised above himself, take to himself the power of evil which is greater than the power of good. The blow he struck at the sheriff had merely served to launch him on his way. To strike down was not what he wanted, but to kill! To feel that once he had accomplished the destiny of some strong man, to turn a creature of mind and soul, ambition and hope, at a single stroke into so many pounds of flesh, useless, done for. What could be more glorious? What could be more terrible? And the desire to strike, as he had looked into the sneering face of Slim Dugan, had been almost overmastering.

Sooner or later he would strike that blow. Sooner or later he would commit the great and controlling crime. And the rest of his life would be a continual evasion of the law.

If they would only take him into their midst, the good and the law-abiding men of the mountains! If they would only accept him by word or deed and give him a chance to prove that he was honest! Even then the battle would be hard, against temptation; but they were too smugly sure that his downfall was certain. Twice they had rejected him without cause. How long would it be before they actually raised their hands against him? How long would it be before they violently put him in the class of his father?

Grinding his teeth, he swore that if that time ever came when they took his destiny into their own hands, he would make it a day to be marked in red all through the mountains!

The cool, fresh wind against his face blew the sullen anger away. And when he came close to the town, he was his old self.

A man on a tall gray, with the legs of speed and plenty of girth at the cinches, where girth means lung power, twisted out of a side trail and swung past El Sangre at a fast gallop. The blood-bay snorted and came hard against the bit in a desire to follow. On the range, when he led his wild band, no horse had ever passed El Sangre and hardly the voice of the master could keep him back now. Terry loosed him. He did not break into a gallop, but fled down the road like an arrow, and the gray came back to him slowly and surely until the rider twisted around and swore in surprise.

He touched his mount with the spurs; there was a fresh start from the gray, a lunge that kicked a little spurt of dust into the nostrils of El Sangre. He snorted it out. Terry released his head completely, and now, as though in scorn refusing to break into his sweeping gallop, El Sangre flung himself ahead to the full of his natural pace.

And the gray came back steadily. The town was shoving up at them at the end of the road more and more clearly. The rider of the gray began to curse. He was leaning forward, jockeying his horse, but still El Sangre hurled himself forward powerfully, smoothly. They passed the first shanty on the outskirts of the town with the red head of the stallion at the hip of the other. Before they straightened into the main sreet, El Sangre had shoved his nose past the outstretched head of the gray. Then the other rider jerked back on his reins with a resounding oath. Terry imitated; one call to El Sangre brought him back to a gentle amble.

"Going to sell this damned skate," declared the stranger, a lean-faced man of middle age with big, patient, kindly eyes. "If he can't make another hoss break out of a pace, he ain't worth keeping! But I'll tell a man that you got quite a hoss there, partner!"

"Not bad," admitted Terry modestly. "And the gray has pretty good points, it seems to me."

They drew the horses back to a walk.

"Ought to have. Been breeding for him fifteen years—and here I get him beat by a hoss that don't break out of a pace."

He swore again, but less violently and with less disappointment. He was beginning to run his eyes appreciatively over the superb lines of El Sangre. There were horses and horses, and he began to see that this was one in a thousand—or more.

"What's the strain in that stallion?" he asked.

"Mustang," answered Terry.

"Mustang? Man, man, he's close to sixteen hands!"

"Nearer fifteen three. Yes, he stands pretty high. Might call him a freak mustang, I guess. He reverts to the old source stock."

"I've heard something about that," nodded the other. "Once in a generation they say a mustang turns up somewhere on the range that breeds back to the old Arab. And that red hoss is sure one of 'em."

They dismounted at the hotel, the common hitching rack for the town, and the elder man held out his hand.

"I'm Jack Baldwin."

"Terry'll do for me, Mr. Baldwin. Glad to know you."

Baldwin considered his companion with a slight narrowing of the eyes. Distinctly this "Terry" was not the type to be wandering about the country known by his first name alone. There were reasons and reasons why men chose to conceal their family names in the mountains, however, and not all of them were bad. He decided to reserve judgment. Particularly since he noted a touch of similarity between the high head and the glorious lines of El Sangre and the young pride and strength of Terry himself. There was something reassuringly clean and frank about both horse and rider, and it pleased Baldwin.

They made their purchases together in the store.

"Where might you be working?" asked Baldwin.

"For Joe Pollard."

"Him?" There was a lifting of the eyebrows of Jack Baldwin. "What line?"

"Cutting wood, just now."

Baldwin shook his head.

"How Pollard uses so much help is more'n I can see. He's got a range back of the hills, I know, and some cattle on it; but he's sure a waster of good labor. Take me, now. I need a hand right bad to help me with the cows."

"I'm more or less under contract with Pollard," said Terry. He added: "You talk as if Pollard might be a queer sort."

Baldwin seemed to be disarmed by this frankness.

"Ain't you noticed anything queer up there? No? Well, maybe Pollard is all right. He's sort of a newcomer around here. That big house of his ain't more'n four or five years old. But most usually a man buys land and cattle around here before he builds him a big house. Well—Pollard is an open-handed cuss, I'll say that for him, and maybe they ain't anything in the talk that goes around."

What that talk was Terry attempted to discover, but he could not. Jack Baldwin was a cautious gossip.

Since they had finished buying, the storekeeper perched on the edge of his selling counter and began to pass the time of the day. It began with the usual preliminaries, invariable in the mountains.

"What's the news out your way?"

"Nothing much to talk about. How's things with you and your family?"

"Fair to middlin' and better. Patty had the croup and we sat up two nights firing up the croup kettle. Now he's better, but he still coughs terrible bad."

And so on until all family affairs had been exhausted. This is a formality. One must not rush to the heart of his news or he will mortally offend the sensitive Westerner.

This is the approved method. The storekeeper exemplified it, and having talked about nothing for ten minutes, quietly remarked that young Larrimer was out hunting a scalp, had been drinking most of the morning, and was now about the town boasting of what he intended to do.

"And what's more, he's apt to do it."

"Larrimer is a no-good young skunk," said Baldwin, with deliberate heat. "It's sure a crime when a boy that ain't got enough brains to fill a peanut shell can run over men just because he's spent his life learning how to handle firearms. He'll meet up with his finish one of these days."

"Maybe he will, maybe he won't," said the storekeeper, and spat with precision and remarkable power through the window beside him. "That's what they been saying for the last two years. Dawson come right down here to get him; but it was Dawson that was got. And Kennedy was called a good man with a gun—but Larrimer beat him to the draw and filled him plumb full of lead."

"I know," growled Baldwin. "Kept on shooting after Kennedy was down and had the gun shot out of his hand and was helpless. And yet they call that self-defense."

"We can't afford to be too particular about shootings," said the storekeeper. "Speaking personal, I figure that a shooting now and then lets the blood of the youngsters and gives 'em a new start. Kind of like to see it."

"But who's Larrimer after now?"

"A wild-goose chase, most likely. He says he's heard that the son of old Black Jack is around these parts, and that he's going to bury the outlaw's son after he's salted him away with lead."

"Black Jack's son! Is he around town?"

The tone sent a chill through Terry; it contained a breathless horror from which there was no appeal. In the eye of Jack Baldwin, fair-minded man though he was, Black Jack's son was judged and condemned as worthless before his case had been heard.

"I dunno," said the storekeeper; "but if Larrimer put one of Black Jack's breed under the ground, I'd call him some use to the town."

Jack Baldwin was agreeing fervently when the storekeeper made a violent signal.

"There's Larrimer now, and he looks all fired up."

Terry turned and saw a tall fellow standing in the doorway. He had been prepared for a youth; he saw before him a hardened man of thirty and more, gaunt-faced, bristling with the rough beard of some five or six days' growth, a thin, cruel, hawlike face.

CHAPTER 30

A MOMENT LATER, from the side door which led from the store into the main body of the hotel, stepped the chunky form of Denver Pete, quick and light of foot as ever. He went straight to the counter and asked for matches, and as the storekeeper, still keeping half an eye upon the formidable figure of Larrimer, turned for the matches, Denver spoke softly from the side of his mouth to Terry—only in the lockstep line of the prison do they learn to talk in this manner—gauging the carrying power of the whisper with nice accuracy.

"That bird's after you. Crazy with booze in the head, but steady in the hand. One of two things. Clear out right now, or else say the word and I'll stay and help you get rid of him."

For the first time in his life fear swept over Terry—fear of himself compared with which the qualm he had felt after turning from Slim Dugan that morning had been nothing. For the second time in one day he was being tempted, and the certainty came to him that he would kill Larrimer. And what made that certainty more sure was the appearance of his nemesis, Denver Pete, in this crisis. As though, with sure scent for evil, Denver had come to be present and watch the launching of Terry into a career of crime. But it was not the public that Terry feared. It was himself. His moral determination was a dam which blocked fierce currents in him that were struggling to get free. And a bullet fired at Larrimer would be the thing that burst the dam and let the flood waters of self-will free. Thereafter what stood in his path would be crushed and swept aside.

He said to Denver: "This is my affair, not yours. Stand away, Denver. And pray for me."

A strange request. It shattered even the indomitable self-control of Denver and left him gaping.

Larrimer, having completed his survey of the dim interior of the store, stalked down upon them. He saw Terry for the first time, paused, and his bloodshot little eyes ran up and down the body of the stranger. He turned to the storekeeper, but still half of his attention was fixed upon Terry.

"Bill," he said, "you seen anything of a spavined, long-horned, no-good skunk named Hollis around town today?"

And Terry could see him wait, quivering, half in hopes that the stranger would show some anger at this denunciation.

"Ain't seen nobody by that name," said Bill mildly. "Maybe you're chasing a wild goose? Who told you they was a gent named Hollis around?"

"Black Jack's son," insisted Larrimer. "Wild-goose chase, hell! I was told he was around by a gent named—"

"These ain't the kind of matches I want!" cried Denver Pete, with a strangely loud-voiced wrath. "I don't want painted wood. How can a gent whittle one of these damned matches down to toothpick size? Gimme plain wood, will you?"

The storekeeper, wondering, made the exchange. Drunken Larrimer had roved on, forgetful of his unfinished sentence. For the very purpose of keeping that sentence unfinished,

Denver Pete remained on the scene, edging toward the outskirts. Now was to come, in a single moment, both the temptation and the test of Terry Hollis, and well Denver knew
that if Larrimer fell with a bullet in his body there would
be an end of Terry Hollis in the world and the birth of a
new soul—the true son of Black Jack!

"It's him that plugged Sheriff Minter," went on Larrimer.
"I hear tell as how he got the sheriff from behind and
plugged him. This town ain't a place for a man-killing houn'
dog like young Black Jack, and I'm here to let him know it!"

The torrent of abuse died out in a crackle of curses. Terry
Hollis stood as one stunned. Yet his hand stayed free of his
gun.

"Suppose we go on to the hotel and eat?" he asked Jack
Baldwin softly. "No use staying and letting that fellow deafen
us with his oaths, is there?"

"Better than a circus," declared Baldwin. "Wouldn't miss
it. Since old man Harkness died, I ain't heard cussing to
match up with Larrimer's. Didn't know that he had that
much brains."

It seemed that the fates were surely against Terry this day.
Yet still he determined to dodge the issue. He started toward
the door, taking care not to walk hastily enough to draw suspicion on him because of his withdrawal, but to the heated
brain of Larrimer all things were suspicious. His long arm
darted out as Terry passed him; he jerked the smaller man
violently back.

"Wait a minute. I don't know you, kid. Maybe you got
the information I want?"

"I'm afraid not."

Terry blinked. It seemed to him that if he looked again
at that vicious, contracted face, his gun would slip into his
hand of its own volition.

"Who are you?"

"A stranger in these parts," said Terry slowly, and he
looked down at the floor.

He heard a murmur from the men at the other end of the
room. He knew that small, buzzing sound. They were wondering at the calmness with which he "took water."

"So's Hollis a stranger in these parts," said Larrimer, facing his victim more fully. "What I want to know is about the

gent that owns the red hoss in front of the store. Ever hear of him?"

Terry was silent. By a vast effort he was able to shake his head. It was hard, bitterly hard, but every good influence that had ever come into his life now stood beside him and fought with and for him—Elizabeth Cornish, the long and fictitious line of his Colby ancestors, Kate Pollard with her clear-seeing eyes. He saw her last of all. When the men were scorning him for the way he had avoided this battle, she, at least, would understand, and her understanding would be a mercy.

"Hollis is somewhere around," declared Larrimer, drawing back and biting his lip. "I know it, damn well. His hoss is standing out yonder. I know what'll fetch him. I'll shoot that hoss of his, and that'll bring him—if young Black Jack is half the man they say he is! I ain't out to shoot cowards— I want men!"

He strode to the door.

"Don't do it!" shouted Bill, the storekeeper.

"Shut up!" snapped Baldwin. "I know something. Shut up!"

That fierce, low voice reached the ear of Terry, and he understood that it meant Baldwin had judged him as the whole world judged him. After all, what difference did it make whether he killed or not? He was already damned as a slayer of men by the name of his father before him.

Larrimer had turned with a roar.

"What d'you mean by stopping me, Bill? What in hell d'you mean by it?"

With the brightness of the door behind him, his bearded face was wolfish.

"Nothing," quavered Bill, this torrent of danger pouring about him. "Except—that it ain't very popular around here —shooting hosses, Larrimer."

"Damn you and your ideas," said Larrimer. "I'm going to go my own way. I know what's best."

He reached the door, his hand went back to the butt of his revolver.

And then it snapped in Terry, that last restraint which had been at the breaking-point all this time. He felt a warmth run through him—the warmth of strength and the cold of a mysterious and evil happiness.

"Wait, Larrimer!"

The big man whirled as though he had heard a gun; there was a ring in the voice of Terry like the ring down the barrel of a shotgun after it has been cocked.

"You agin?" barked Larrimer.

"Me again. Larrimer, don't shoot the horse."

"Why not?"

"For the sake of your soul, my friend."

"Boys, ain't this funny? This gent is a sky-pilot, maybe?" He made a long stride back.

"Stop where you are!" cried Terry.

He stood like a soldier with his heels together, straight, trembling. And Larrimer stopped as though a blow had checked him.

"I may be your sky-pilot, Larrimer. But listen to sense. Do you really mean you'd shoot that red horse in front of the hotel?"

"Ain't you heard me say it?"

"Then the Lord pity you, Larrimer!"

Ordinarily Larrimer's gun would have been out long before, but the change from this man's humility of the moment before, his almost cringing meekness, to his present defiance was so startling that Larrimer was momentarily at sea.

"Damn my eyes," he remarked furiously, "this is funny, this is. Are you preaching at me, kid? What d'you mean by that? Eh?"

"I'll tell you why. Face me squarely, will you? Your head up, and your hands ready."

In spite of his rage and wonder, Larrimer instinctively obeyed, for the words came snapping out like military commands.

"Now I'll tell you. You manhunting cur, I'm going to send you to hell with your sins on your head. I'm going to kill you, Larrimer!"

It was so unexpected, so totally startling, that Larrimer blinked, raised his head, and laughed.

But the son of Black Jack tore away all thought of laughter.

"Larrimer, I'm Terry Hollis. Get your gun!"

The wide mouth of Larrimer writhed silently from mirth to astonishment, and then sinister rage. And though he was in the shadow against the door, Terry saw the slow gleam in the face of the tall man—then his hand whipped for the gun. It came cleanly out. There was no flap to his holster, and the sight had been filed away to give more oiled and perfect freedom to the draw. Years of patient practice had taught his muscles to reflex in this one motion with a speed that baffled the eye. Fast as light that draw seemed to those who watched, and the draw of Terry Hollis appeared to hang in midair. His hand wavered, then clutched suddenly, and they saw a flash of metal, not the actual motion of drawing the gun. Just that gleam of the barrel at his hip, hardly clear of the holster, and then in the dimness of the big room a spurt of flame and the boom of the gun.

There was a clangor of metal at the farthest end of the room. Larrimer's gun had rattled on the boards, unfired. He tossed up his great gaunt arms as though he were appealing for help, leaped into the air, and fell heavily, with a force that vibrated the floor where Terry stood.

There was one heartbeat of silence.

Then Terry shoved the gun slowly back into his holster and walked to the body of Larrimer.

To these things Bill, the storekeeper, and Jack Baldwin, the rancher, afterward swore. That young Black Jack leaned a little over the corpse and then straightened and touched the fallen hand with the toe of his boot. Then he turned upon them a perfectly calm, unemotional look.

"I seem to have been elected to do the scavenger work in this town," he said. "But I'm going to leave it to you gentlemen to take the carrion away. Shorty, I'm going back to the house. Are you ready to ride that way?"

When they went to the body of Larrimer afterward, they found a neat, circular splotch of purple exactly placed between the eyes.

CHAPTER 31

THE FIRST THING the people in Pollard's big house knew of the return of the two was a voice singing faintly and far off in the stable—they could hear it because the door to the big living room was opened. And Kate Pollard, who had been sitting idly at the piano, stood up suddenly and looked around her. It did not interrupt the crap game of the four at one side of the room, where they kneeled in a close circle. But it brought big Pollard himself to the door in time to meet Denver Pete as the latter hurried in.

When Denver was excited he talked very nearly as softly as he walked. And his voice tonight was like a contented humming.

"It worked," was all he said aside to Pollard as he came through the door. They exchanged silent grips of the hands. Then Kate drew down on them; as if a mysterious signal had been passed to them by the subdued entrance of Denver, the four rose at the side of the room.

It was Pollard who forced him to talk.

"What happened?"

"A pretty little party," said Denver. His purring voice was so soft that to hear him the others instantly drew close. Kate Pollard stood suddenly before him.

"Terry Hollis has done something," she said. "Denver, what has he done?"

"Him? Nothing much. To put it in his own words, he's just played scavenger for the town—and he's done it in a way they won't be forgetting for a good long day."

"Denver!"

"Well? No need of acting up, Kate."

"Who was it?"

"Ever meet young Larrimer?"

She shuddered. "Yes. A—beast of a man."

152

"Sure. Worse'n a beast, maybe. Well, he's carrion now, to use Terry's words again."

"Wait a minute," cut in big blond Phil Marvin. "Don't spoil the story for Terry. But did he really do for Larrimer? Larrimer was a neat one with a gun—no good otherwise."

"Did he do for Larrimer?" echoed Denver in his purring voice. "Oh, man, man! Did he do for Larrimer? And I ain't spoiling his story. He won't talk about it. Wouldn't open his face about it all the way home. A pretty neat play, boys. Larrimer was looking for a rep, and he wanted to make it on Black Jack's son. Came tearing in.

"At first Terry tried to sidestep him. Made me weak inside for a minute because I thought he was going to take water. Then he got riled a bit and then—whang! It was all over. Not a body shot. No, boys, nothing clumsy and amateurish like that, because a man may live to empty his gun at you after he's been shot through the body. This young Hollis, pals, just ups and drills Larrimer clean between the eyes. If you'd measured it off with a ruler, you couldn't have hit exact center any better'n he done. Then he walks up and stirs Larrimer with his toe to make sure he was dead. Cool as hell."

"You lie!" cried the girl suddenly.

They whirled at her, and found her standing and flaming at them.

"You hear me say it, Kate," said Denver, losing a little of his calm.

"He wasn't as cool as that—after killing a man. He wasn't."

"All right, honey. Don't you hear him singing out there in the stable? Does that sound as if he was cut up much?"

"Then you've made him a murderer—you, Denver, and you, Dad. Oh, if they's a hell, you're going to travel there for this! Both of you!"

"As if we had anything to do with it!" exclaimed Denver innocently. "Besides, it wasn't murder. It was plain self-defense. Nothing but that. Three witnesses to swear to it. But, my, my—you should hear that town rave. They thought nobody could beat Larrimer."

The girl slipped back into her chair again and sat with her chin in her hand, brooding. It was all impossible—it could not be. Yet there was Denver telling his story, and far away the clear baritone of Terry Hollis singing as he cared for El Sangre.

She waited to make sure, waited to see his face and hear him speak close at hand. Presently the singing rang out more clearly. He had stepped out of the barn.

> Oh, I am a friar of orders gray,
> Through hill and valley I take my way.
> My long bead roll I merrily chant;
> Wherever I wander no money I want!

And as the last word rang through the room, Terry Hollis stood in the doorway, with his saddle and bridle hanging over one strong arm and his gun and gun belt in the other hand. And his voice came cheerily to them in greeting. It was impossible—more impossible than ever.

He crossed the room, hung up his saddle, and found her sitting near. What should he say? How would his color change? In what way could he face her with that stain in his soul?

And this was what Terry said to her: "I'm going to teach El Sangre to let you ride him, Kate. By the Lord, I wish you'd been with us going down the hill this morning!"

No shame, no downward head, no remorse. And he was subtly and strangely changed. She could not put the difference into words. But his eye seemed larger and brighter—it was no longer possible for her to look deeply into it, as she had done so easily the night before. And there were other differences.

He held his head in a more lordly fashion. About every movement there was a singular ease and precision. He walked with a lighter step and with a catlike softness almost as odd as that of Denver. His step had been light before, but it was not like this. But through him and about him there was an air of uneasy, alert happiness—as of one who steals a few perfect moments, knowing that they will not be many. A great pity welled in her, and a great anger. It was the anger which showed.

"Terry Hollis, what have you done? You're lookin' me in the eye, but you ought to be hangin' your head. You've done murder! Murder! Murder!"

She let the three words ring through the room like three blows, cutting the talk to silence. And all save Terry seemed moved.

He was laughing down at her—actually laughing, and there was no doubt as to the sincerity of that mirth. His presence drew her and repelled her; she became afraid for the first time in her life.

"A little formality with a gun," he said calmly. "A dog got in my way, Kate—a mad dog. I shot the beast to keep it from doing harm."

"Ah, Terry, I know everything. I've heard Denver tell it. I know it was a man, Terry."

He insisted carelessly. "By the Lord, Kate, only a dog—and a mad dog at that. Perhaps there was the body of a man, but there was the soul of a dog inside the skin. Tut! It isn't worth talking about."

She drew away from him. "Terry, God pity you. I pity you," she went on hurriedly and faintly. "But you ain't the same any more, Terry. I—I'm almost afraid of you!"

He tried laughingly to stop her, and in a sudden burst of hysterical terror she fled from him. Out of the corner of her eye she saw him come after her, light as a shadow. And the shadow leaped between her and the door; the force of her rush drove her into his arms.

In the distance she could hear the others laughing—they understood such a game as this, and enjoyed it with all their hearts. Ah, the fools!

He held her lightly, his fingertips under her elbows. For all the delicacy of that touch, she knew that if she attempted to flee, the grip would be iron. He would hold her where she was until he was through talking to her.

"Don't you see what I've done?" he was saying rapidly. "You wanted to drive me out last night. You said I didn't fit—that I didn't belong up here. Well, Kate, I started out today to make myself fit to belong to this company of fine fellows."

He laughed a little; if it were not real mirth, at least there was a fierce quality of joy in his voice.

"You see, I decided that if I went away I'd be lonely. Particularly, I'd be lonely as the devil, Kate, for you!"

"You've murdered to make yourself one—of us?"

"Tush, Kate. You exaggerate entirely. Do you know what I've really done? Why, I've wakened; I've come to my senses. After all, there was no other place for me to go. I tried the world of good, ordinary working people. I asked them to let me come in and prove my right to be one of them. They discharged me when I worked honestly on the range. They sent their professional gunmen and bullies after me. And then—I reached the limit of my endurance, Kate, and I struck back. And the mockery of it all is this—that though they have struck me repeatedly and I have endured it, I—having struck back a single time—am barred from among them forever. Let it be so!"

"Hush, Terry. I—I'm going to think of ways!"

"You couldn't. Last night—yes. Today I'm a man—and I'm free. And freedom is the sweetest thing in the world. There's no place else for me to go. This is my world. You're my queen. I've won my spurs; I'll use them in your service, Kate."

"Stop, Terry!"

"By the Lord, I will, though! I'm happy—don't you see? And I'm going to be happier. I'm going to work my way along until I can tell you—that I love you, Kate—that you're the daintiest body of fire and beauty and temper and gentleness and wisdom and fun that was ever crowned with the name of a woman. And—"

But under the rapid fire of his words there was a touch of hardness—mockery, perhaps. She drew back, and he stepped instantly aside. She went by him through the door with bowed head. And Terry, closing it after her, heard the first sob.

CHAPTER 32

IT WAS AS IF a gate which had hitherto been closed against him in the Pollard house were now opened. They no longer held back from Terry, but admitted him freely to their counsels. But the first person to whom he spoke was Slim Dugan. There was a certain nervousness about Slim this evening, and a certain shame. For he felt that in the morning, to an extent, he had backed down from the quarrel with young Black Jack.

The killing of Larrimer now made that reticence of the morning even more pointed than it had been before. With all these things taken into consideration, Slim Dugan was in the mood to fight and die; for he felt that his honor was concerned. A single slighting remark to Terry, a single sneering side glance, would have been a signal for gunplay. And everyone knew it.

The moment there was silence the son of Black Jack went straight to Slim Dugan.

"Slim," he said, just loud enough for everyone to hear, "a fellow isn't himself before noon. I've been thinking over that little trouble we had this morning, and I've made up my mind that if there were any fault it was mine for taking a joke too seriously. At any rate, if it's agreeable to you, Slim, I'd like to shake hands and call everything square. But if there's going to be any ill will, let's have it out right now."

Slim Dugan wrung the hand of Terry without hesitation.

"If you put it that way," he said cordially, "I don't mind saying that I was damned wrong to heave that stone at the hoss. And I apologize, Terry."

And so everything was forgotten. Indeed, where there had been enmity before, there was now friendship. And there was a breath of relief drawn by every member of the gang. The peacemaking tendency of Hollis had more effect on the others than a dozen killings. They already granted that he was formidable. They now saw that he was highly desirable also.

Dinner that night was a friendly affair, except that Kate stayed in her room with a headache. Johnny the Chinaman smuggled a tray to her. Oregon Charlie went to the heart of matters with one of his rare speeches:

"You hear me talk, Hollis. She's mad because you've stepped off. She'll get over it all right."

Oregon Charlie had a right to talk. It was an open secret that he had loved Kate faithfully ever since he joined the gang. But apparently Terry Hollis cared little about the moods of the girl. He was the center of festivities that evening until an interruption from the outside formed a diversion. It came in the form of a hard rider; the mutter of his hoofs swept to the door, and Phil Marvin, having examined the stranger from the shuttered loophole beside the entrance, opened the door to him at once.

"It's Sandy," he fired over his shoulder in explanation.

A weary-looking fellow came into the room, swinging his hat to knock the dust off it, and loosening the bandanna at his throat. The drooping, pale mustache explained his name. Two words were spoken, and no more.

"News?" said Pollard.

"News," grunted Sandy, and took a place at the table.

Terry had noted before that there were always one or two extra places laid; he had always liked the suggestion of hospitality, but he was rather in doubt about this guest. He ate with marvellous expedition, keeping his lean face close to the table and bolting his food like a hungry dog. Presently he drained his coffee cup, arranged his mustache with painful care, and seemed prepared to talk.

"First thing," he said now—and utter silence spread around the table as he began to talk—"first thing is that McGuire is coming. I seen him on the trail, cut to the left and took the short way. He ought to be loping in almost any minute."

Terry saw the others looking straight at Pollard; the leader was thoughtful for a moment.

"Is he coming with a gang, Sandy?"

"Nope—alone."

"He was always a nervy cuss. Someday—"

He left the sentence unfinished. Denver had risen noiselessly.

"I'm going to beat it for my bunk," he announced. "Let me know when the sheriff is gone."

"Sit where you are, Denver. McGuire ain't going to lay hands on you."

"Sure he ain't," agreed Denver. "But I ain't partial to having guys lay eyes on me, neither. Some of you can go out and beat up trouble. I like to stay put."

And he glided out of the room with no more noise than a sliding shadow. He had hardly disappeared when a heavy hand beat at the door.

"That's McGuire," announced Pollard. "Let him in, Phil."

So saying, he twitched his gun out of the holster, spun the cylinder, and dropped it back.

"Don't try nothing till you see me put my hand into my beard, boys. He don't mean much so long as he's come alone."

Marvin drew back the door. Terry saw a man with shoulders of martial squareness enter. And there was a touch of the military in his brisk step and the curt nod he sent at

Marvin as he passed the latter. He had not taken off his sombrero. It cast a heavy shadow across the upper part of his worn, sad face.

"Evening, sheriff," came from Pollard, and a muttered chorus from the others repeated the greeting. The sheriff cast his glance over them like a schoolteacher about to deliver a lecture.

"Evening, boys."

"Sit down, McGuire."

"I'm only staying a minute. I'll talk standing." It was a declaration of war.

"I guess this is the first time I been up here, Pollard?"

"The very first, sheriff."

"Well, if I been kind of neglectful, it ain't that I'm not interested in you-all a heap!"

He brought it out with a faint smile; there was no response to that mirth.

"Matter of fact, I been keeping my eye on you fellows right along. Now, I ain't up here to do no accusing. I'm up here to talk to you man to man. They's been a good many queer things happen. None of 'em in my county, mind you, or I might have done some talking to you before now. But they's been a lot of queer things happen right around in the mountains; and some of 'em has traced back kind of close to Joe Pollard's house as a starting point. I ain't going to go any further. If I'm wrong, they ain't any harm done; if I'm right, you know what I mean. But I tell you this, boys—we're a long-sufferin' lot around these parts, but they's some things that we don't stand for, and one of 'em that riles us particular much is when a gent that lays out to be a regular hard-working rancher—even if he ain't got much of a ranch to talk about and work about—takes mankillers under their wings. It ain't regular, and it ain't popular around these parts. I guess you know what I mean."

Terry expected Pollard to jump to his feet. But there was no such response. The other men stared down at the table, their lips working. Pollard alone met the eye of the sheriff.

The sheriff changed the direction of his glance. Instantly, it fell on Terry and stayed there.

"You're the man I mean; you're Terry Hollis, Black Jack's son?"

Terry imitated the others and did not reply.

"Oh, they ain't any use beating about the bush. You got Black Jack's blood in you. That's plain. I remember your old man well enough."

Terry rose slowly from his chair.

"I think I'm not disputing that, sheriff. As a matter of fact, I'm very proud of my father."

"I think you are," said the sheriff gravely. "I think you are —damned proud of him. So proud you might even figure on imitating what he done in the old days."

"Perhaps," said Terry. The imp of the perverse was up in him now, urging him on.

"Step soft, sheriff," cried Pollard suddenly, as though he sensed a crisis of which the others were unaware. "Terry, keep hold on yourself!"

The sheriff waved the cautionary advice away.

"My nerves are tolerable good, Pollard," he said coldly. "The kid ain't scaring me none. And now hark to me, Black Jack. You've got away with two gents already—two that's known, I mean. Minter was one and Larrimer was two. Both times it was a square break. But I know your kind like a book. You're going to step over the line pretty damn pronto, and when you do, I'm going to get you, friend, as sure as the sky is blue! You ain't going to do what your dad done before you. I'll tell you why. In the old days the law was a joke. But it's tolerable strong now. You hear me talk—get out of these here parts and stay out. We don't want none of your kind."

There was a flinching of the men about the table. They had seen the tigerish suddenness with which Terry's temper could flare—they had received an object lesson that morning. But to their amazement he remained perfectly cool under fire. He sauntered a little closer to the sheriff.

"I'll tell you, McGuire," he said gently. "Your great mistake is in talking too much. You've had a good deal of success, my friend. So much that your head is turned. You're quite confident that no one will invade your special territory; and you keep your sympathy for neighboring counties. You pity the sheriffs around you. Now listen to me. You've branded me as a criminal in advance. And I'm not going to disappoint you. I'm going to try to live up to your high hopes. And what I do will be done right in your county, my

friend. I'm going to make the sheriffs pity *you*, McGuire. I'm
going to make your life a small bit of hell. I'm going to keep
you busy. And now—get out! And before you judge the next
man that crosses your path, wait for the advice of twelve
good men and true. You need advice, McGuire. You need it
to beat hell! Start on your way!"

His calmness was shaken a little toward the end of this
speech and his voice, at the close, rang sharply at McGuire.
The latter considered him from beneath frowning brows for
a moment and then, without another word, without a glance
to the others and a syllable of adieu, turned and walked
slowly, thoughtfully, out of the room. Terry walked back to
his place. As he sat down, he noticed that every eye was upon
him, worried.

"I'm sorry that I've had to do so much talking," he said.
"And I particularly apologize to you, Pollard. But I'm tired
of being hounded. As a matter of fact, I'm now going to try
to play the part of the hound myself. Action, boys; action is
what we must have, and action right in this county under the
nose of the complacent McGuire!"

CHAPTER 33

THERE WAS NO exuberant joy to meet this suggestion. Mc-
Guire had, as a matter of fact, made his territory practically
crime-proof for so long that men had lost interest in planning
adventures within the sphere of his authority. It seemed to
the four men of Pollard's gang a peculiar folly to cast a challenge in the teeth of the formidable sheriff himself. Even
Pollard was shaken and looked to Denver. But that worthy,
who had returned from the door where he was stationed
during the presence of the sheriff, remained in his place
smiling down at his hands. He, for one, seemed oddly pleased.

In the meantime Sandy was setting forth his second and
particularly interesting news item.

"You-all know Lewison?" he asked.

"The sour old grouch," affirmed Phil Marvin. "Sure, we know him."

"I know him, too," said Sandy. "I worked for the tender-foot that he skinned out of the ranch. And then I worked for Lewison. If they's anything good about Lewison, you'd need a spyglass to find it, and then it wouldn't be fit to see. His wife couldn't live with him; he drove his son off and turned him into a drunk; and he's lived his life for his coin."

"Which he ain't got much to show for it," remarked Marvin. "He lives like a starved dog."

"And that's just why he's got the coin," said Sandy. "He lives on what would make a dog sick and his whole life he's been saving every cent he's made. He gives his wife one dress every three years till she died. That's how tight he is. But he's sure got the money. Told everybody his kid run off with all his savings. That's a lie. His kid didn't have the guts or the sense to steal even what was coming to him for the work he done for the old miser. Matter of fact, he's got enough coin saved—all gold—to break the back of a mule. That's a fact! Never did no investing, but turned everything he made into gold and put it away."

"How do you know?" This from Denver.

"How does a buzzard smell a dead cow?" said Sandy inelegantly. "I ain't going to tell you how I smell out the facts about money. Wouldn't be any use to you if you knew the trick. The facts is these: he sold his ranch. You know that?"

"Sure, we know that."

"And you know he wouldn't take nothing but gold coin paid down at the house?"

"That so?"

"It sure is! Now the point's this. He had all his gold in his own private safe at home."

Denver groaned.

"I know, Denver," nodded Sandy. "Easy pickings for you; but I didn't find all this out till the other day. Never even knew he had a safe in his house. Not till he has 'em bring out a truck from town and he ships the safe and everything in it to the bank. You see, he sold out his own place and he's going to another that he bought down the river. Well, boys, here's the dodge. That safe of his is in the bank tonight, guarded by old Lewison himself and two gunmen he's hired for the job. Tomorrow he starts out down the river with the safe on a big wagon, and he'll have half a dozen guards along with him. Boys, they's going to be forty thousand dollars in that safe! And the minute she gets out of the county—because old McGuire will guard it to the boundary line—we can lay back in the hills and—"

"You done enough planning, Sandy," broke in Joe Pollard. "You've smelled out the loot. Leave it to us to get it. Did you say forty thousand?"

And on every face around the table Terry saw the same hunger and the same yellow glint of the eyes. It would be a big haul, one of the biggest, if not the very biggest, Pollard had ever attempted.

Of the talk that followed, Terry heard little, because he was paying scant attention. He saw Joe Pollard lie back in his chair with squinted eyes and run over a swift description of the country through which the trail of the money would lead. The leader knew every inch of the mountains, it seemed. His memory was better than a map; in it was jotted down every fallen log, every boulder, it seemed. And when his mind was fixed on the best spot for the holdup, he sketched his plan briefly.

To this man and to that, parts were assigned in brief. There would be more to say in the morning about the details. And every man offered suggestions. On only one point were they agreed. This was a sum of money for which they could well afford to spill blood. For such a prize as this they could well risk making the countryside so hot for themselves that they would have to leave Pollard's house and establish headquarters elsewhere. Two shares to Pollard and one to each of his men, including Sandy, would make the total loot some four thousand dollars and more per man. And in the event that someone fell in the attempt, which was more than probable, the share for the rest would be raised to ten thousand for Pollard and five thousand for each of the rest. Terry saw cold glances pass the rounds, and more than one dwelt upon him. He was the last to join; if there were to be a death in this affair, he would be the least missed of all.

A sharp order from Pollard terminated the conference and

sent his men to bed, with Pollard setting the example. But
Terry lingered behind and called back Denver.

"There is one point," he said when they were alone, "that
it seems to me the chief has overlooked."

"Talk up, kid," grinned Denver Pete. "I seen you was
thinking. It sure does me good to hear you talk. What's on
your mind? Where was Joe wrong?"

"Not wrong, perhaps. But he overlooked this fact: tonight
the safe is guarded by three men only; tomorrow it will be
guarded by six."

Denver stared, and then blinked.

"You mean, try the safe right in town, inside the old bank?
Son, you don't know the gents in this town. They sleep with
a gat under every head and ears that hear a pin drop in the
next room—right while they're snoring. They dream about
fighting and they wake up ready to shoot."

Terry smiled at this outburst.

"How long has it been since there was a raid on McGuire's
town?"

"Dunno. Don't remember anybody being that foolish."

"Then it's been so long that it'll give us a chance. It's been
so long that the three men on guard tonight will be half
asleep."

"I dunno but you're right. Why didn't you speak up in
company? I'll call the chief and—"

"Wait," said Terry, laying a hand on the round, hard-
muscled shoulder of the yegg. "I had a purpose in waiting.
Seven men are too many to take into a town."

"Eh?"

"Two men might surprise three. But seven men are more
apt to be surprised."

"Two ag'in' three ain't such bad odds, pal. But—the first
gun that pops, we'll have the whole town on our backs."

"Then we'll have to do it without shooting. You understand, Denver?"

Denver scratched his head. Plainly he was uneasy; plainly,
also, he was more and more fascinated by the idea.

"You and me to turn the trick alone?" he whispered out
of the side of his mouth in a peculiar, confidentially guilty
way that was his when he was excited. "Kid, I begin to hear
the old Black Jack talk in you! I begin to hear him talk! I
knew it would come!"

CHAPTER 34

AN HOUR'S RIDE brought them to the environs of the little town. But it was already nearly the middle of night and the village was black; whatever life waked at that hour had been drawn into the vortex of Pedro's. And Pedro's was a place of silence. Terry and Denver skirted down the back of the town and saw the broad windows of Pedro's, against which passed a moving silhouette now and again, but never a voice floated out to them.

Otherwise the town was dead. They rode until they were at the other extremity of the main street. Here, according to Denver, was the bank which had never in its entire history been the scene of an attempted raid. They threw the reins of their horses after drawing almost perilously close.

"Because if we get what we want," said Terry, "it will be too heavy to carry far."

And Denver agreed, though they had come so close that from the back of the bank it must have been possible to make out the outlines of the horses. The bank itself was a broad, dumpy building with adobe walls, whose corners had been washed and rounded by time to shapelessness. The walls angled in as they rose; the roof was flat. As for the position, it could not have been worse. A dwelling abutted on either side of the bank. The second stories of those dwellings commanded the roof of the bank; and the front and back porches commanded the front and back entrances of the building.

The moment they had dismounted, Terry and Denver stood a while motionless. There was no doubt, even before they approached nearer, about the activity and watchfulness of the guards who took care of the new deposit in the bank. Across the back wall of the building drifted a shadowy outline—a guard marching steadily back and forth and keeping sentry watch.

"A stiff job, son," muttered Denver. "I told you these birds wouldn't sleep with more'n one eye; and they's a few that's got 'em both open."

But there was no wavering in Terry. The black stillness of the night; the soundless, slowly moving figure across the wall of the building; the hush, the stars, and the sense of something to be done stimulated him, filled him with a giddy happiness such as he had never known before. Crime? It was no crime to Terry Hollis, but a great and delightful game.

Suddenly he regretted the very presence of Denver Pete. He wanted to be alone with this adventure, match his cunning and his strength against whoever guarded the money or old Lewison, the miser.

"Stay here," he whispered in the ear of Denver. "Keep quiet. I'm going to slip over there and see what's what. Be patient. It may take a long time."

Denver nodded.

"Better let me come along. In case—"

"Your job is opening that safe; my job is to get you to it in safety and get you away again with the stuff."

Denver shrugged his shoulders. It was much in the method of famous old Black Jack himself. There were so many features of similarity between the methods of the boy and his father that it seemed to Denver that the ghost of the former man had stepped into the body of his son.

In the meantime Terry faded into the dark. His plan of approach was perfectly simple. The house to the right of the bank was painted blue. Against that dark background no figure stood out clearly. Instead of creeping close to the ground to get past the guard at the rear of the building, he chose his time when the watcher had turned from the nearest end of his beat and was walking in the opposite direction. The moment that happened, Terry strode forward as lightly and rapidly as possible.

Luckily the ground was quite firm. It had once been planted with grass, and though the grass had died, its roots remained densely enough to form a firm matting, and there was no telltale crunching of the sand underfoot. Even so, some slight sound made the guard pause abruptly in the middle of his walk and whirl toward Terry. Instead of attempting to hide by dropping down to the ground, it came to Terry that the least motion in the dark would serve to make him visible. He simply halted at the same moment that the guard halted and trusted to the dark background of the house which was now beside him to make him invisible. Apparently he was justified. After a moment the guard turned and resumed his pacing, and Terry slipped on into the narrow walk between the bank and the adjoining house on the right.

He had hoped for a side window. There was no sign of one. Nothing but the sheer, sloping adobe wall, probably of great thickness, and burned to the density of soft stone. So he came to the front of the building, and so doing, almost ran into a second guard, who paced down the front of the bank just as the first kept watch over the rear entrance. Terry flattened himself against the side wall and held his breath. But the guard had seen nothing and, turning again at the end of his beat, went back in the opposite direction, a tall, gaunt man—so much Terry could make out even in the dark, and his heel fell with the heaviness of age. Perhaps this was Lewison himself.

The moment he was turned, Terry peered around the corner at the front of the building. There were two windows, one close to his corner and one on the farther side of the door. Both were lighted, but the farther one so dimly that it was apparent the light came from one source, and that source directly behind the window nearest Terry. He ventured one long, stealthy pace, and peered into the window.

As he had suspected, the interior of the bank was one large room. Half of it was fenced off with steel bars that terminated in spikes at the top as though, ludicrously, they were meant to keep one from climbing over. Behind this steel fencing were the safes of the bank. Outside the fence at a table, with a lamp between them, two men were playing cards. And the lamplight glinted on the rusty old safe which stood a little at one side.

Certainly old Lewison was guarding his money well. The hopes of Terry disappeared, and as Lewison was now approaching the far end of his beat, Terry glided back into the walk between the buildings and crouched there. He needed time and thought sadly.

As far as he could make out, the only two approaches to the bank, front and rear, were thoroughly guarded. Not only that, but once inside the bank, one would encounter the main obstacle, which consisted of two heavily armed men sitting in readiness at the table. If there were any solution to the problem, it must be found in another examination of the room.

Again the tall old man reached the end of his beat nearest Terry, turned with military precision and went back. Terry slipped out and was instantly at the window again. All was as before. One of the guards had laid down his cards to light a cigarette, and dense clouds of smoke floated above his head. That partial obscurity annoyed Terry. It seemed as if the luck were playing directly against him. However, the smoke began to clear rapidly. When it had mounted almost beyond the strongest inner circle of the lantern light, it rose with a sudden impetus, as though drawn up by an electric fan. Terry wondered at it, and squinted toward the ceiling, but the ceiling was lost in shadow.

He returned to his harborage between the two buildings for a fresh session of thought. And then his idea came to him. Only one thing could have sucked that straight upward so rapidly, and that was either a fan—which was ridiculous —or else a draught of air passing through an opening in the ceiling.

Unquestionably that was the case. Two windows, small as they were, would never serve adequately to ventilate the big single room of the bank. No doubt there was a skylight in the roof of the building and another aperture in the floor of the loft.

At least that was the supposition upon which he must act, or else not act at all. He went back as he had come, passed the rear guard easily, and found Denver unmoved beside the heads of the horses.

"Denver," he said, "we've got to get to the roof of that bank, and the only way we can reach it is through the skylight."

"Skylight?" echoed Denver. "Didn't know there was one."

"There has to be," said Terry, with surety. "Can you force a door in one of those houses so we can get to the second story of one of 'em and drop to the roof?"

"Force nothing," whispered Denver. "They don't know what locks on doors mean around here."

And he was right.

They circled in a broad detour and slipped onto the back

porch of the blue house; the guard at the rear of the bank was whistling softly as he walked.

"Instead of watchdogs they keep doors with rusty hinges," said Denver as he turned the knob, and the door gave an inch inward. "And I dunno which is worst. But watch this, bo!"

And he began to push the door slowly inward. There was never a slackening or an increase in the speed with which his hand travelled. It took him a full five minutes to open the door a foot and a half. They slipped inside, but Denver called Terry back as the latter began to feel his way across the kitchen.

"Wait till I close this door."

"But why?" whispered Terry.

"Might make a draught—might wake up one of these birds. And there you are. That's the one rule of politeness for a burglar, Terry. Close the doors after you!"

And the door was closed with fully as much caution and slowness as had been used when it was opened. Then Denver took the lead again. He went across the kitchen as though he could see in the dark, and then among the tangle of chairs in the dining room beyond. Terry followed in his wake, taking care to step, as nearly as possible, in the same places. But for all that, Denver continually turned in an agony of anger and whispered curses at the noisy clumsiness of his companion—yet to Terry it seemed as though both of them were not making a sound.

The stairs to the second story presented a difficult climb. Denver showed him how to walk close to the wall, for there the weight of their bodies would act with less leverage on the boards and there would be far less chance of causing squeaks. Even then the ascent was not noiseless. The dry air had warped the timber sadly, and there was a continual procession of murmurs underfoot as they stole to the top of the stairs.

To Terry, his senses growing superhumanly acute as they entered more and more into the heart of their danger, it seemed that those whispers of the stairs might serve to waken a hundred men out of sound sleep; in reality they were barely audible.

In the hall a fresh danger met them. A lamp hung from the ceiling, the flame turned down for the night. And by that uneasy light Terry made out the face of Denver, white, strained, eager, and the little bright eyes forever glinting back and forth. He passed a side mirror and his own face was dimly visible. It brought him erect with a squeak of the flooring that made Denver whirl and shake his fist.

For what Terry had seen was the same expression that had been on the face of his companion—the same animal alertness, the same hungry eagerness. But the fierce gesture of Denver brought him back to the work at hand.

There were three rooms on the side of the hall nearest the bank. And every door was closed. Denver tried the nearest door first, and the opening was done with the same caution and slowness which had marked the opening of the back door of the house. He did not even put his head through the opening, but presently the door was closed and Denver returned.

"Two," he whispered.

He could only have told by hearing the sounds of two breathing; Terry wondered quietly. The man seemed possessed of abnormal senses. It was strange to see that bulky, burly, awkward body become now a sensitive organism, possessed of a dangerous grace in the darkness.

The second door was opened in the same manner. Then the third, and in the midst of the last operation a man coughed. Instinctively Terry reached for the handle of his gun, but Denver went on gradually closing the door as if nothing had happened. He came back to Terry.

"Every room got sleepers in it," he said. "And the middle room has got a man who's awake. We'll have to beat it."

"We'll stay where we are," said Terry calmly, "for thirty minutes—by guess. That'll give him time to go asleep. Then we'll go through one of those rooms and drop to the roof of the bank."

The yegg cursed softly. "Are you trying to hang me?" he gasped.

"Sit down," said Terry. "It's easier to wait that way."

And they sat cross-legged on the floor of the hall. Once the springs of a bed creaked as someone turned in it heavily. Once there was a voice—one of the sleepers must have spoken without waking. Those two noises, and no more, and yet they remained for what seemed two hours to Terry, but what he knew could not be more than twenty minutes.

"Now," he said to Denver, "we start."

"Through one of them rooms and out the windows—without waking anybody up?"

"You can do it. And I'll do it because I have to. Go on."

He heard the teeth of Denver grit, as though the yegg were being driven on into this madcap venture merely by a pride which would not allow him to show less courage—even rash courage—than his companion.

The door opened—Denver went inside and was soaked up—a shadow among shadows. Terry followed and stepped instantly into the presence of the sleeper. He could tell it plainly. There was no sound of breathing, though no doubt that was plain to the keen ear of Denver—but it was something more than sound or sight. It was like feeling a soul—that impalpable presence in the night. A ghostly and a thrilling thing to Terry Hollis.

Now, against the window on the farther side of the room, he made out the dim outline of Denver's chunky shoulders and shapeless hat. Luckily the window was open to its full height. Presently Terry stood beside Denver and they looked down. The roof of the bank was only some four feet below them, but it was also a full three feet in distance from the side of the house. Terry motioned the yegg back and began to slip through the window. It was a long and painful process, for at any moment a button might catch or his gun scrape—and the least whisper would ruin everything. At length, he hung from his arms at full length. Glancing down, he faintly saw Lewison turn at the end of his beat. Why did not the fool look up?

With that thought he drew up his feet, secured a firm purchase against the side of the house, raised himself by the ledge, and then flung himself out into the air with the united effort of arms and legs.

He let himself go loose and relax in the air, shot down, and felt the roof take his weight lightly, landing on his toes. He had not only made the leap, but he had landed a full foot and a half in from the edge of the roof.

Compared with the darkness of the interior of the house, everything on the outside was remarkably light now. He could see Denver at the window shaking his head. Then the professional slipped over the sill with praticed ease, dangled at arm's length, and flung himself out with a quick thrust of his feet against the wall.

The result was that while his feet were flung away far enough and to spare, the body of Denver inclined forward. He seemed bound to strike the roof with his feet and then drop head first into the alley below. Terry set his teeth with a groan, but as he did so, Denver whirled in the air like a cat. His body straightened, his feet barely secured a toehold on the edge of the roof. The strong arm of Terry jerked him in to safety.

For a moment they stood close together, Denver panting. He was saying over and over again: "Never again. I ain't any acrobat, Black Jack!"

That name came easily on his lips now.

Once on the roof it was simple enough to find what they wanted. There was a broad skylight of dark green glass propped up a foot or more above the level of the rest of the flat roof. Beside it Terry dropped upon his knees and pushed his head under the glass. All below was pitchy-back, but he distinctly caught the odor of Durham tobacco smoke.

CHAPTER 35

THAT SCENT OF smoke was a clear proof that there was an open way through the loft to the room of the bank below them. But would the opening be large enough to admit the body of a man? Only exploring could show that. He sat back on the roof and put on the mask with which the all-thoughtful Denver had provided him. A door banged somewhere far down the street, loudly. Someone might be making a hurried and disgusted exit from Pedro's. He looked quietly around him. After his immersion in the thick darkness of the house, the outer night seemed clear and the stars burned low through the thin mountain air. Denver's face was black under the shadow of his hat.

"How are you, kid—shaky?" he whispered.

Shaky? It surprised Terry to feel that he had forgotten about fear. He had been wrapped in a happiness keener than anything he had known before. Yet the scheme was far from accomplished. The real danger was barely beginning. Listening keenly, he could hear the sand crunch underfoot of the watcher who paced in front of the building; one of the cardplayers laughed from the room below—a faint, distant sound.

"Don't worry about me," he told Denver, and, securing a strong fingerhold on the edge of the ledge, he dropped his full length into the darkness under the skylight.

His tiptoes grazed the floor beneath, and letting his fingers slide off their purchase, he lowered himself with painful care so that his heels might not jar on the flooring. Then he held his breath—but there was no creaking on the loft floor.

That made the adventure more possible. An ill-laid floor would have set up a ruinous screeching as he moved, however carefully, across it. Now he whispered up to Denver. The latter instantly slid down and Terry caught the solid bulk of the man under the armpits and lowered him carefully.

"A rotten rathole," snarled Denver to his companion in that inimitable, guarded whisper. "How we ever coming back this way—in a hurry?"

It thrilled Terry to hear that appeal—an indirect surrendering of the leadership to him. Again he led the way, stealing toward a ghost of light that issued upward from the center of the floor. Presently he could look down through it.

It was an ample square, a full three feet across. Below, and a little more than a pace to the side, was the table of the cardplayers. As nearly as he could measure, through the misleading wisps and drifts of cigarette smoke, the distance to the floor was not more than ten feet—an easy drop for a man hanging by his fingers.

Denver came to his side, silent as a snake.

"Listen," whispered Terry, cupping a hand around his lips and leaning close to the ear of Denver so that the least thread of sound would be sufficient. "I'm going to cover those two from this place. When I have them covered, you slip through the opening and drop to the floor. Don't stand still, but softfoot it over to the wall. Then cover them with your gun while I come down. The idea is this. Outside that window there's a second guard walking up and down. He can look through and see the table where they're playing, but he can't see the safe against the wall. As long as he sees those two sitting there playing their cards, he'll be sure that everything is all right. Well, Denver, he's going to keep on seeing them sitting at their game—but in the meantime you're going to make your preparations for blowing the safe. Can you do it? Is your nerve up to it?"

Even the indomitable Denver paused before answering. The chances of success in this novel game were about one in ten. Only shame to be outbraved by his younger companion and pupil made him nod and mutter his assent.

That mutter, strangely, was loud enough to reach to the room below. Terry saw one of the men look up sharply, and at the same moment he pulled his gun and shoved it far enough through the gap for the light to catch on its barrel.

"Sit tight!" he ordered them in a cutting whisper. "Not a move, my friends!"

There was a convulsive movement toward a gun on the part of the first man, but the gesture was frozen midway; the second man looked up, gaping, ludicrous in astonishment. But Terry was in no mood to see the ridiculous.

"Look down again!" he ordered brusquely. "Keep on with that game. And the moment one of you goes for a gun—the minute one of you makes a sign or a sound to reach the man in front of the house, I drill you both. Is that clear?"

The neck of the man who was nearest to him swelled as though he were lifting a great weight with his head; no doubt he was battling with shrewd temptations to spring to one side and drive a bullet at the robbers above him. But prudence conquered. He began to deal, laying out the cards with mechanical, stiff motions.

"Now," said Terry to Denver.

Denver was through the opening in a flash and dropped to the floor below with a thud. Then he leaped away toward the wall out of sight of Terry. Suddenly a loud, nasal voice spoke through one of the front windows:

"What was that, boys?"

Terry caught his breath. He dared not whisper advice to those men at the table for fear his voice might carry to the guard who was apparently leaning at the window outside. But the dealer jerked his head for an instant toward the direction in which Denver had disappeared. Evidently the yegg was silently communicating imperious instructions, for presently the dealer said, in a voice natural enough: "Nothing happened, Lewison. I just moved my chair; that was all, I figure."

"I dunno," growled Lewison. "I been waiting for something to happen for so long that I begin to hear things and suspect things where they ain't nothing at all."

And, still mumbling, his voice passed away.

Terry followed Denver's example, dropping through the opening; but, more cautious, he relaxed his leg muscles, so that he landed in a bunched heap, without sound, and instantly joined Denver on the farther side of the room. Lewison's gaunt outline swept past the window at the same moment.

He found that he had estimated viewpoints accurately enough. From only the right-hand window could Lewison see into the interior of the room and make out his two guards at the table. And it was only by actually leaning through the window that he would be able to see the safe beside which Terry and Denver stood.

"Start!" said Terry, and Denver deftly laid out a little kit and two small packages. With incredible speed he began to make his molding of soft soap around the crack of the safe door. Terry turned his back on his companion and gave his undivided attention to the two at the table.

Their faces were odd studies in suppressed shame and rage. The muscles were taut; their hands shook with the cards.

"You seem kind of glum, boys!" broke in the voice of Lewison at the window.

Terry flattened himself against the wall and jerked up his gun—a warning flash which seemed to be reflected by the glint in the eyes of the red-headed man facing him. The latter turned slowly to the window.

"Oh, we're all right," he drawled. "Kind of getting wearying, this watch."

"Mind you," crackled the uncertain voice of Lewison, "five dollars if you keep on the job till morning. No, six dollars, boys!"

He brought out the last words in the ringing voice of one making a generous sacrifice, and Terry smiled behind his mask. Lewison passed on again. Forcing all his nerve power into the faculty of listening, Terry could tell by the crunching of the sand how the owner of the safe went far from the window and turned again toward it.

"Start talking," he commanded softly of the men at the table.

"About what?" answered the red-haired man through his teeth. "About what, damn you!"

"Tell a joke," ordered Terry.

The other scowled down at his hand of cards—and then obeyed.

"Ever hear about how Rooney—"

The voice was hard at the beginning; then, in spite of the levelled gun which covered him, the red-haired man became absorbed in the interest of the tale. He began to labor to win a smile from his companion. That would be something worthwhile—something to tell about afterward; how he made Pat laugh while a pair of bandits stood in a corner with guns on them!

In his heart Terry admired that red-haired man's nerve. The next time Lewison passed the window, he darted out and swiftly went the rounds of the table, relieving each man of his weapon. He returned to his place. Pat had broken into hearty laughter.

"That's it!" cried Lewison, passing the window again. "Laughin' keeps a gent awake. That's the stuff, Red!"

A time of silence came, with only the faint noises of Denver at his rapid work.

"Suppose they was to rush the bank, even?" said Lewison on his next trip past the window.

"Who's they?" asked Red, and looked steadily into the mouth of Terry's gun.

"Why, them that wants my money. Money that I slaved and worked for all my life! Oh, I know they's a lot of crooked thieves that would like to lay hands on it. But I'm going to fool 'em, Red. Never lost a cent of money in all my born days, and I ain't going to form the habit this late in life. I got too much to live for!"

And he went on his way muttering.

"Ready!" said Denver.

"Red," whispered Terry, "how's the money put into the safe?"

The big, red-haired fellow fought him silently with his eyes.

"I dunno!"

"Red," said Terry swiftly, "you and your friend are a dead weight on us just now. And there's one quick, convenient way of getting rid of you. Talk out, my friend. Tell us how that money is stowed."

Red flushed, the veins in the center of his forehead swelling under a rush of blood to the head. He was silent.

It was Pat who weakened, shuddering.

"Stowed in canvas sacks, boys. And some paper money."

The news of the greenbacks was welcome, for a large sum of gold would be an elephant's burden to them in their flight.

"Wait," Terry directed Denver. The latter kneeled by his fuse until Lewison passed far down the end of his beat. Terry stepped to the door and dropped the bolt.

"Now!" he commanded.

He had planned his work carefully. The loose strips of cords which Denver had put into his pocket—"nothing so handy as strong twine," he had said—were already drawn out. And the minute he had given the signal, he sprang for the men at the table, backed them into a corner, and tied their hands behind their backs.

The fuse was sputtering.

"Put out the light!" whispered Denver. It was done—a leap and a puff of breath, and then Terry had joined the huddled group of men at the farther end of the room.

"Hey!" called Lewison. "What's happened to the light? What the hell—"

His voice boomed out loudly at them as he thrust his head through the window into the darkness. He caught sight of the red, flickering end of the fuse.

His voice, grown shrill and sharp, was chopped off by the explosion. It was a noise such as Terry had never heard before—like a tremendously condensed and powerful puff of wind. There was not a sharp jar, but he felt an invisible pressure against his body, taking his breath. The sound of the explosion was dull, muffled, thick. The door of the safe crushed into the flooring.

Terry had nerved himself for two points of attack—Lewison from the front of the building, and the guard at the rear. But Lewison did not yell for help. He had been dangerously close to the explosion and the shock to his nerves, per-

haps some dislodged missile, had flung him senseless on the
sand outside the bank.

But from the rear of the building came a dull shout; then
the door beside which Terry stood was dragged open—he
struck with all his weight, driving his fist fairly into the face
of the man, and feeling the knuckles cut through flesh and
lodge against the cheekbone. The guard went down in the
middle of a cry and did not stir. Terry leaned to shake his
arm—the man was thoroughly stunned. He paused only to
scoop up the fallen revolver which the fellow had been carrying, and fling it into the night. Then he turned back into the
dark bank, with Red and Pat cursing in frightened unison as
they cowered against the wall behind him.

The air was thick with an ill-smelling smoke, like that of
a partially snuffed candle. Then he saw a circle of light spring
out from the electric lantern of Denver and fall on the partially wrecked safe. And it glinted on yellow. One of the
sacks had been slit and the contents were running out onto
the floor like golden water.

Over it stooped the shadow of Denver, and Terry was
instantly beside him. They were limp little sacks, marvellously
ponderous, and the chill of the metal struck through the
canvas to the hand. The searchlight flickered here and there
—it found the little drawer which was wrenched open and
Denver's stubby hand came out, choked with greenbacks.

"Now away!" snarled Denver. And his voice shook and
quaked; it reminded Terry of the whine of a dog half-starved
and come upon meat—a savage, subdued sound.

There was another sound from the street where old Lewison
was coming to his senses—a gasping sound, and then a
choked cry: "Help!"

His senses and his voice seemed to return to him with a
rush. His shriek split through the darkness of the room like
a ray of light probing to find the guilty: "Thieves! Help!"

The yell gave strength to Terry. He caught some of the
burden that was staggering Denver into his own arms and
floundered through the rear door into the blessed openness
of the night. His left arm carried the crushing burden of the
canvas sacks—in his right hand was the gun—but no form
showed behind him.

But there were voices beginning. The yells of Lewison had
struck out echoes up and down the street. Terry could hear

shouts begin inside houses in answer, and bark out with sudden clearness as a door or a window was opened.

They reached the horses, dumped the precious burdens into the saddlebags, and mounted.

"Which way?" gasped Denver.

A light flickered in the bank; half a dozen men spilled out of the back door, cursing and shouting.

"Walk your horse," said Terry. "Walk it—you fool!"

Denver had let his horse break into a trot. He drew it back to a walk at this hushed command.

"They won't see us unless we start at a hard gallop," continued Terry. "They won't watch for slowly moving objects now. Besides, it'll be ten minutes before the sheriff has a posse organized. And that's the only thing we have to fear."

CHAPTER 36

THEY DRIFTED past the town, quickening to a soft trot after a moment, and then to a faster trot—El Sangre was gliding along at a steady pace.

"Not back to the house!" said Denver with an oath, when they straightened back to the house of Pollard. "That's the first place McGuire will look, after what you said to him the other night."

"That's where I want him to look," answered Terry, "and that's where he'll find me. Pollard will hide the coin and we'll get one of the boys to take our sweaty horses over the hills. We can tell McGuire that the two horses have been put out to pasture, if he asks. But he mustn't find hot horses in the stable. Certainly McGuire will strike for the house. But what will he find?"

He laughed joyously.

Suddenly the voice of Denver cut in softly, insinuatingly.

"You dope it that he'll cut for the house of Pollard? So do I. Now, kid, why not go another direction—and keep on going? What right have Pollard and the others to cut in on this coin? You and me, kid, can—"

"I don't hear you, Denver," interrupted Terry. "I don't hear you. We wouldn't have known where to find the stuff if it hadn't been for Pollard's friend Sandy. They get their share—but you can have my part, Denver. I'm not doing this for money; it's only an object lesson to that fat-headed sheriff. I'd pay twice this price for the sake of the little talk I'm going to have with him later on tonight."

"All right—Black Jack," muttered Denver. For it seemed to him that the voice of the lost leader had spoken. "Play the fool, then, kid. But—let's feed these skates the spur! The town's boiling!"

Indeed, there was a dull roar behind them.

"No danger," chuckled Terry. "McGuire knows perfectly well that I've done this. And because he knows that, and he knows that I know it, he'll strike in the opposite direction to Pollard's house. He'll never dream that I would go right back to Pollard and sit down under the famous nose of McGuire!"

The dawn was brightening over the mountains above them, and the skyline was ragged with forest. A free country for free men—like the old Black Jack and the new. A short life, perhaps, but a full one.

The coming of the day showed Denver's face weary and drawn. Those moments in the bank, surrounded by danger, had been nerve-racking even to his experience. But to him it was a business, and to Terry it was a game. He felt a qualm of pity for Lewison—but, after all, the man was a wolf, selfish, accumulating money to no purpose, useless to the world. He shrugged the thought of Lewison away.

It was close to sunrise when they reached the house, and having put up the horses, staggered in and called to Johnny to bring them coffee; he was already rattling at the kitchen stove. Then, with a shout, they brought Pollard himself stumbling down from the balcony rubbing the sleep out of his eyes. They threw the money down before him.

He was stupefied, and then his big lion's voice went booming with the call for his men. Terry did not wait; he stretched himself with a great yawn and made for his bed, and passed Phil Marvin and the others hurrying downstairs to answer the summons. Kate Pollard came also. She paused as he went by her and he saw her eyes go down to his dusty boots, with the leather polished where the stirrup had chafed, then flashed back to his face.

"You, Terry!" she whispered.

But he went by her with a wave of the hand.

The girl went on down to the big room. They were gathered already, a bright-eyed, hungry-faced crew of men. Gold was piled across the table in front of them. Slim Dugan had been ordered to go to the highest window of the house and keep watch for the coming of the expected posse. In the meantime the others counted the money, ranging it in bright little stacks; and Denver told the tale.

He took a little more credit to himself than was his due. But it was his part to pay a tribute to Terry. For was it not he who had brought the son of Black Jack among them?

"And of all the close squeezes I ever been in," concluded Denver, "that was the closest. And of all the nervy, cold-eyed guys I ever see, Black Jack's kid takes the cake. Never a quiver all the time. And when he whispered, them two guys at the table jumped. He meant business, and they knew it."

The girl listened. Her eye alone was not upon the money, but fixed far off, at thin distance.

"Thirty-five thousand gold," announced Pollard, with a break of excitement in his voice, "and seventeen thousand three hundred and eighty-two in paper. Boys, the richest haul we ever made! And the coolest deal all the way through. Which I say, Denver and Terry—Terry particular—gets extra shares for what they done!"

And there was a chorus of hearty approval. The voice of Denver cut it short.

"Terry don't want none. No, boys, knock me dead if he does. Can you beat it? 'I did it to keep my word,' he says, 'with the sheriff. You can have my share, Denver.'

"And he sticks on it. It's a game with him, boys. He plays at it like a big kid!"

In the hush of astonishment, the eyes of Kate misted. Something in that last speech had stung her cruelly. Something had to be done, and quickly, to save young Terry Hollis. But what power could influence him?

It was that thought which brought her to the hope for a solution. A very vague and faraway hope to which she clung and which unravelled slowly in her imagination. Before she left the kitchen, her plan was made, and immediately after breakfast, she went to her room and dressed for a long journey.

"I'm going over the hills to visit the Stockton girls," she told her father. "Be gone a few days."

His mind was too filled with hope for the future to understand her. He nodded idly, and she was gone.

She roped the toughest mustang of her "string" in the corral, and ten minutes later she was jogging down the trail. Halfway down a confused group of riders—some dozen in all—swarmed up out of the lower trail. Sheriff McGuire rode out on a sweating horse that told of fierce and long riding and stopped her.

His salutation was brief; he plunged into the heart of his questions. Had she noticed anything unusual this morning? Which of the men had been absent from the house last night? Particularly, who went out with Black Jack's kid?

"Nobody left the house," she said steadily. "Not a soul."

And she kept a blank eye on the sheriff while he bit his lip and studied her.

"Kate," he said at length, "I don't blame you for not talking. I don't suppose I would in your place. But your dad has about reached the end of the rope with us. If you got any influence, try to change him, because if he don't do it by his own will, he's going to be changed by force!"

And he rode on up the trail, followed by the silent string of riders on their grunting, tired horses. She gave them only a careless glance. Joe Pollard had baffled officers of the law before, and he would do it again. That was not her great concern on this day.

Down the trail she sent her mustang again, and broke him out into a stiff gallop on the level ground below. She headed straight through the town, and found a large group collected in and around the bank building. They turned and looked after her, but no one spoke a greeting. Plainly the sheriff's suspicions were shared by others.

She shook that shadow out of her head and devoted her entire attention to the trail which roughened and grew narrow on the other side of the town. Far away across the mountains lay her goal—the Cornish ranch.

CHAPTER 37

WHEN SHE FIRST glimpsed Bear Valley from the summits of the Blue Mountains, it seemed to her a small paradise. And as she rode lower and lower among the hills, the impression gathered strength. So she came out onto the road and trotted her cow-pony slowly under the beautiful branches of the silver spruce, and saw the bright tree shadows reflected in Bear Creek. Surely here was a place of infinite quiet, made for happiness. A peculiar ache and sense of emptiness entered her heart, and the ghost of Terry Hollis galloped soundlessly beside her on flaming El Sangre through the shadow. It seemed to her that she could understand him more easily. His had been a sheltered and pleasant life here, half dreamy; and when he wakened into a world of stern reality and stern men, he was still playing at a game like a boy—as Denver Pete had said.

She came out into view of the house. And again she paused. It was like a palace to Kate, that great white façade and the Doric columns of the veranda. She had always thought that the house of her father was a big and stable house; compared with this, it was a shack, a lean-to, a veritable hovel. And the confidence which had been hers during the hard ride of two days across the mountains grew weaker. How could she talk to the woman who owned such an establishment as this? How could she even gain access to her?

On a broad, level terrace below the house men were busy with plows and scrapers smoothing the ground; she circled around them, and brought her horse to a stop before the veranda. Two men sat on it, one white-haired, hawk-faced, spreading a broad blueprint before the other; and this man was middle-aged, with a sleek, young face. A very good-looking fellow, she thought.

"Maybe you-all could tell me," said Kate Pollard, lounging

183

in the saddle, "where I'll find the lady that owns this here place?"

It seemed to her that the sleek-faced man flushed a little.

"If you wish to talk to the owner," he said crisply, and barely touching his hat to her, "I'll do your business. What is it? Cattle lost over the Blue Mountains again? No strays have come down into the valley."

"I'm not here about cattle," she answered curtly enough. "I'm here about a man."

"H'm," said the other. "A man?" His attention quickened. "What man?"

"Terry Hollis."

She could see him start. She could also see that he endeavored to conceal it. And she did not know whether she liked or disliked that quick start and flush. There was something either of guilt or of surprise remarkably strong in it. He rose from his chair, leaving the blueprint fluttering in the hands of his companion alone.

"I am Vance Cornish," he told her. She could feel his eyes prying at her as though he were trying to get at her more accurately. "What's Hollis been up to now?"

He turned and explained carelessly to his companion: "That's the young scapegrace I told you about, Waters. Been raising Cain again, I suppose." He faced the girl again.

"A good deal of it," she answered. "Yes, he's been making quite a bit of trouble."

"I'm sorry for that, really," said Vance. "But we are not responsible for him."

"I suppose you ain't," said Kate Pollard slowly. "But I'd like to talk to the lady of the house."

"Very sorry," and again he looked in his sharp way—like a fox, she thought—and then glanced away as though there were no interest in her or her topic. "Very sorry, but my sister is in—er—critically declining health. I'm afraid she cannot see you."

This repulse made Kate thoughtful. She was not used to such bluff talk from men, however smooth or rough the exterior might be. And under the quiet of Vance she sensed an opposition like a stone wall.

"I guess you ain't a friend of Terry's?"

"I'd hardly like to put it strongly one way or the other. I know the boy, if that's what you mean."

"It ain't." She considered him again. And again she was secretly pleased to see him stir under the cool probe of her eyes. "How long did you live with Terry?"

"He was with us twenty-four years." He turned and explained casually to Waters. "He was taken in as a foundling, you know. Quite against my advice. And then, at the end of the twenty-four years, the bad blood of his father came out, and he showed himself in his true colors. Fearful waste of time to us all—of course, we had to turn him out."

"Of course," nodded Waters sympathetically, and he looked wistfully down at his blueprint.

"Twenty-four years you lived with Terry," said the girl softly, "and you don't like him, I see."

Instantly and forever he was damned in her eyes. Anyone who could live twenty-four years with Terry Hollis and not discover his fineness was beneath contempt.

"I'll tell you," she said. "I've *got* to see Miss Elizabeth Cornish."

"H'm!" said Vance. "I'm afraid not. But—just what have you to tell her?"

The girl smiled.

"If I could tell you that, I wouldn't have to see her."

He rubbed his chin with his knuckles, staring at the floor of the veranda, and now and then raising quick glances at her. Plainly he was suspicious. Plainly, also, he was tempted in some manner.

"Something he's done, eh? Some yarn about Terry?"

It was quite plain that this man actually wanted her to have something unpleasant to say about Terry. Instantly she suited herself to his mood; for he was the door through which she must pass to see Elizabeth Cornish.

"Bad?" she said, hardening her expression as much as possible. "Well, bad enough. A killing to begin with."

There was a gleam in his eyes—a gleam of positive joy, she was sure, though he banished it at once and shook his head in deprecation.

"Well, well! As bad as that? I suppose you may see my sister. For a moment. Just a moment. She is not well. I wish I could understand your purpose!"

The last was more to himself than to her. But she was already off her horse. The man with the blueprint glared at her, and she passed across the veranda and into the house, where Vance showed her up the big stairs. At the door of his sister's room he paused again and scrutinized.

"A killing—by Jove!" he murmured to himself, and then knocked.

A dull voice called from within, and he opened. Kate found herself in a big, solemn room, in one corner of which sat an old woman wrapped to the chin in a shawl. The face was thin and bleak, and the eyes that looked at Kate were dull.

"This girl—" said Vance. "By Jove, I haven't asked your name, I'm afraid."

"Kate Pollard."

"Miss Pollard has some news of Terry. I thought it might —interest you, Elizabeth."

Kate saw the brief struggle on the face of the old woman. When it passed, her eyes were as dull as ever, but her voice had become husky.

"I'm surprised, Vance. I thought you understood—his name is not to be spoken, if you please."

"Of course not. Yet I thought—never mind. If you'll step downstairs with me, Miss Pollard, and tell me what—"

"Not a step," answered the girl firmly, and she had not moved her eyes from the face of the elder woman. "Not a step with you. What I have to say has got to be told to someone who loves Terry Hollis. I've found that someone. I stick here till I've done talking."

Vance Cornish gasped. But Elizabeth opened her eyes, and they brightened—but coldly, it seemed to Kate.

"I think I understand," said Elizabeth Cornish gravely. "He has entangled the interest of this poor girl—and sent her to plead for him. Is that so? If it's money he wants, let her have what she asks for, Vance. But I can't talk to her of the boy."

"Very well," said Vance, without enthusiasm. He stepped before her. "Will you step this way, Miss Pollard?"

"Not a step," she repeated, and deliberately sat down in a chair. "You'd better leave," she told Vance.

He considered her in open anger. "If you've come to make a scene, I'll have to let you know that on account of my sister I cannot endure it. Really—"

"I'm going to stay here," she echoed, "until I've done talking. I've found the right person. I know that. Tell you what I want? Why, you hate Terry Hollis!"

"Hate—him?" murmured Elizabeth.

"Nonsense!" cried Vance.

"Look at his face, Miss Cornish," said the girl.

"Vance, by everything that's sacred, your eyes were positively shrinking. *Do* you hate—him?"

"My dear Elizabeth, if this unknown—"

"You'd better leave," interrupted the girl. "Miss Cornish is going to hear me talk."

Before he could answer, his sister said calmly: "I think I shall, Vance. I begin to be intrigued."

"In the first place," he blurted angrily, "it's something you shouldn't hear—some talk about a murder—"

Elizabeth sank back in her chair and closed her eyes.

"Ah, coward!" cried Kate Pollard, now on her feet.

"Vance, will you leave me for a moment?"

For a moment he was white with malice, staring at the girl, then suddenly submitting to the inevitable, turned on his heel and left the room.

"Now," said Elizabeth, sitting erect again, "what is it? Why do you insist on talking to me of—him? And—what has he done?"

In spite of her calm, a quiver of emotion was behind the last words, and nothing of it escaped Kate Pollard.

"I knew," she said gently, "that *two* people couldn't live with Terry for twenty-four years and both hate him, as your brother does. I can tell you very quickly why I'm here, Miss Cornish."

"But first—what has he done?"

Kate hesitated. Under the iron self-control of the older woman she saw the hungry heart, and it stirred her. Yet she was by no means sure of a triumph. She recognized the most formidable of all foes—pride. After all, she wanted to humble that pride. She felt that all the danger in which Terry Hollis now stood, both moral and physical, was indirectly the result of this woman's attitude. And she struck her, deliberately, cruelly.

"He's taken up with a gang of hard ones, Miss Cornish. That's one thing."

The face of Elizabeth was like stone.

"Professional—thieves, robbers!"

And still Elizabeth refused to wince. She forced a cold, polite smile of attention.

"He went into a town and killed the best fighter they had."

And even this blow did not tell.

"And then he defied the sheriff, went back to the town, and broke into a bank and stole fifty thousand dollars."

The smile wavered and went out, but still the dull eyes of Elizabeth were steady enough. Though perhaps that dullness was from pain. And Kate, waiting eagerly, was chagrined to see that she had not broken through to any softness of emotion. One sign of grief and trembling was all she wanted before she made her appeal; but there was no weakness in Elizabeth Cornish, it seemed.

"You see I am listening," she said gravely and almost gently. "Although I am really not well. And I hardly see the point of this long recital of crimes. It was because I foresaw what he would become that I sent him away."

"Miss Cornish, why'd you take him in in the first place?"

"It's a long story," said Elizabeth.

"I'm a pretty good listener," said Kate.

Elizabeth Cornish looked away, as though she hesitated to touch on the subject, or as though it were too unimportant to be referred to at length.

"In brief, I saw from a hotel window Black Jack, his father, shot down in the street; heard about the infant son he left, and adopted the child—on a bet with my brother. To see if blood would tell or if I could make him a fine man."

She paused.

"My brother won the bet!"

And her smile was a wonderful thing, so perfectly did it mask her pain.

"And, of course, I sent Terry away. I have forgotten him, really. Just a bad experiment."

Kate Pollard flushed.

"You'll never forget him," she said firmly. "You think of him every day!"

The elder woman started and looked sharply at her visitor. Then she dismissed the idea with a shrug.

"That's absurd. Why should I think of him?"

There is a spirit of prophecy in most women, old or young; and especially they have a way of looking through the flesh of their kind and seeing the heart. Kate Pollard came a little closer to her hostess.

"You saw Black Jack die in the street," she queried, "fighting for his life?"

Elizabeth dreamed into the vague distance.

"Riding down the street with his hair blowing—long black hair, you know," she reminisced. "And holding the crowd back as one would hold back a crowd of curs. Then—he was shot from the side by a man in concealment. That was how he fell!"

"I knew," murmured the girl, nodding. "Miss Cornish, I know now why you took in Terry."

"Ah?"

"Not because of a bet—but because you—you loved Black Jack Hollis!"

It brought an indrawn gasp from Elizabeth. Rather of horror than surprise. But the girl went on steadily:

"I know. You saw him with his hair blowing, fighting his way—he rode into your heart. I know, I tell you! Maybe you've never guessed it all these years. But has a single day gone when you haven't thought of the picture?"

The scornful, indignant denial died on the lips of Elizabeth Cornish. She stared at Kate as though she were seeing a ghost.

"Not one day!" cried Kate. "And so you took in Terry, and you raised him and loved him—not for a bet, but because he was Black Jack's son!"

Elizabeth Cornish had grown paler than before. "I mustn't listen to such talk," she said.

"Ah," cried the girl, "don't you see that I have a right to talk? Because I love him also, and I know that you love him, too."

Elizabeth Cornish came to her feet, and there was a faint flush in her cheeks.

"You love Terry? Ah, I see. And he has sent you!"

"He'd die sooner than send me to you."

"And yet—you came?"

"Don't you see?" pleaded Kate. "He's in a corner. He's about to go—bad!"

"Miss Pollard, how do you know these things?"

"Because I'm the daughter of the leader of the gang!"

She said it without shame, proudly.

"I've tried to keep him from the life he intends leading,"

said Kate. "I can't turn him. He laughs at me. I'm nothing to him, you see? And he loves the new life. He loves the freedom. Besides, he thinks that there's no hope. That he has to be what his father was before him. Do you know why he thinks that? Because you turned him out. *You* thought he would turn bad. And he respects you. He still turns to you. Ah, if you could hear him speak of you! He loves you still!"

Elizabeth Cornish dropped back into her chair, grown suddenly weak, and Kate fell on her knees beside her.

"Don't you see," she said softly, "that no strength can turn Terry back now? He's done nothing wrong. He shot down the man who killed his father. He has killed another man who was a professional bully and mankiller. And he's broken into a bank and taken money from a man who deserved to lose it—a wolf of a man everybody hates. He's done nothing really wrong yet, but he will before long. Just because he's stronger than other men. And he doesn't know his strength. And he's fine, Miss Cornish. Isn't he always gentle and—"

"Hush!" said Elizabeth Cornish.

"He's just a boy; you can't bend him with strength, but you can win him with love."

"What," gasped Elizabeth, "do you want me to do?"

"Bring him back. Bring him back, Miss Cornish!"

Elizabeth Cornish was trembling.

"But I—if you can't influence him, how can I? You with your beautiful—you are very beautiful, dear child. Ah, very lovely!"

She barely touched the bright hair.

"He doesn't even think of me," said the girl sadly. "But I have no shame. I have let you know everything. It isn't for me. It's for Terry, Miss Cornish. And you'll come? You'll come as quickly as you can? You'll come to my father's house? You'll ask Terry to come back? One word will do it! And I'll hurry back and—keep him there till you come. God give me strength! I'll keep him till you come!"

Outside the door, his ear pressed to the crack, Vance Cornish did not wait to hear more. He knew the answer of Elizabeth before she spoke. And all his high-built schemes he saw topple about his ears. Grief had been breaking the heart of his sister, he knew. Grief had been bringing her close to the grave. With Terry back, she would regain ten years of life. With Terry back, the old life would begin again.

He straightened and staggered down the stairs like a drunken man, clinging to the banister. It was an old-faced man who came out onto the veranda, where Waters was chewing his cigar angrily. At sight of his host he started up. He was a keen man, was Waters. He could sense money a thousand miles away. And it was this buzzard keenness which had brought him to the Cornish ranch and made him Vance's right-hand man. There was much money to be spent; Waters would direct and plan the spending, and his commission would not be small.

In the face of Vance he saw his own doom.

"Waters," said Vance Cornish, "everything is going up in smoke. That damned girl— Waters, we're ruined."

"Tush!" said Waters, smiling, though he had grown gray. "No one girl can ruin two middle-aged men with our senses developed. Sit down, man, and we'll figure a way out of this."

CHAPTER 38

THE FINE GRAY head, the hawklike, aristocratic face, and the superior manner of Waters procured him admission to many places where the ordinary man was barred. It secured him admission on this day to the office of Sheriff McGuire, though McGuire had refused to see his best friends.

A proof of the perturbed state of his mind was that he accepted the proffered fresh cigar of Waters without comment or thanks. His mental troubles made him crisp to the point of rudeness.

"I'm a tolerable busy man, Mr.—Waters, I think they said your name was. Tell me what you want, and make it short, if you don't mind."

"Not a bit, sir. I rarely waste many words. But I think on this occasion we have a subject in common that will interest you."

Waters had come on what he felt was more or less of a wild-goose chase. The great object was to keep young Hollis from coming in contact with Elizabeth Cornish again. One such interview, as Vance Cornish had assured him, would restore the boy to the ranch, make him the heir to the estate, and turn Vance and his high ambitions out of doors. Also, the high commission of Mr. Waters would cease. With no plan in mind, he had rushed to the point of contact, and hoped to find some scheme after he arrived there. As for Vance, the latter would promise money; otherwise he was a shaken wreck of a man and of no use. But with money, Mr. Waters felt that he had the key to this world and he was not without hope.

Three hours in the hotel of the town gave him many clues. Three hours of casual gossip on the veranda of the same hotel had placed him in possession of about every fact, true or presumably true, that could be learned, and with the knowledge a plan sprang into his fertile brain. The worn, worried face of the sheriff had been like water on a dry field; he felt that the seed of his plan would immediately spring up and bear fruit.

"And that thing we got in common?" said the sheriff tersely.

"It's this—young Terry Hollis."

He let that shot go home without a follow-up and was pleased to see the sheriff's forehead wrinkle with pain.

"He's like a ghost hauntin' me," declared McGuire, with an attempted laugh that failed flatly. "Every time I turn around, somebody throws this Hollis in my face. What is it now?"

"Do you mind if I run over the situation briefly, as I understand it?"

"Fire away!"

The sheriff settled back; he had forgotten his rush of business.

"As I understand it, you, Mr. McGuire, have the reputation of keeping your county clean of crime and scenes of violence."

"Huh!" grunted the sheriff.

"Everyone says," went on Waters, "that no one except a man named Minter has done such work in meeting the criminal element on their own ground. You have kept your county peaceful. I believe that is true?"

"Huh," repeated McGuire. "Kind of soft-soapy, but it ain't all wrong. They ain't been much doing in these parts since I started to clean things up."

"Until recently," suggested Waters.

The face of the sheriff darkened. "Well?" he asked aggressively.

"And then two crimes in a row. First, a gun brawl in broad daylight—young Hollis shot a fellow named—er—"

"Larrimer," snapped the sheriff viciously. "It was a square fight. Larrimer forced the scrap."

"I suppose so. Nevertheless, it was a gunfight. And next, two men raid the bank in the middle of your town, and in spite of you and of special guards, blow the door off a safe and gut the safe of its contents. Am I right?"

The sheriff merely scowled.

"It ain't clear to me yet," he declared, "how you and me get together on any topic we got in common. Looks sort of like we was just hearing one old yarn over and over again."

"My dear sir," smiled Waters, "you have not allowed me to come to the crux of my story. Which is: that you and I have one great object in common—to dispose of this Terry Hollis, for I take it for granted that if you were to get rid of him the people who criticize now would do nothing but cheer you. Am I right?"

"*If* I could get him," sighed the sheriff. "Mr. Waters, gimme time and I'll get him, right enough. But the trouble with the gents around these parts is that they been spoiled. I cleaned up all the bad ones so damn quick that they think I can do the same with every crook that comes along. But this Hollis is a slick one, I tell you. He covers his tracks. Laughs in my face, and admits what he done, when he talks to me, like he done the other day. But as far as evidence goes, I ain't got anything on him—yet. But I'll get it!"

"And in the meantime," said Waters brutally, "they say that you're getting old."

The sheriff became a brilliant purple.

"Do they say that?" he muttered. "That's gratitude for you, Mr. Waters! After what I've done for 'em—they say I'm getting old just because I can't get anything on this slippery kid right off!"

He changed from purple to gray. To fail now and lose his position meant a ruined life. And Waters knew what was in his mind.

"But if you got Terry Hollis, they'd be stronger behind you than ever."

"Ah, wouldn't they, though? Tell me what a great gent I was quick as a flash."

He sneered at the thought of public opinion.

"And you see," said Waters, "where I come in is that I have a plan for getting this Hollis you desire so much."

"You do?" He rose and grasped the arm of Waters. "You do?"

Waters nodded.

"It's this way. I understand that he killed Larrimer, and Larrimer's older brother is the one who is rousing public opinion against you. Am I right?"

"The dog! Yes, you're right."

"Then get Larrimer to send Terry Hollis an invitation to come down into town and meet him face to face in a gun fight. I understand this Hollis is a daredevil sort and wouldn't refuse an invitation of that nature. He'd have to respond or else lose his growing reputation as a maneater."

"Maneater? Why, Bud Larrimer wouldn't be more'n a mouthful for him. Sure he'd come to town. And he'd clean up quick. But Larrimer ain't fool enough to send such an invite."

"You don't understand me," persisted Waters patiently. "What I mean is this. Larrimer sends the challenge, if you wish to call it that. He takes up a certain position. Say in a public place. You and your men, if you wish, are posted nearby, but out of view when young Hollis comes. When Terry Hollis arrives, the moment he touches a gun butt, you fill him full of lead and accuse him of using unfair play against Larrimer. Any excuse will do. The public want an end of young Hollis. They won't be particular with their questions."

He found it difficult to meet the narrowed eyes of the sheriff.

"What you want me to do," said the sheriff, with slow effort, "is to set a trap, get Hollis into it, and then—murder him?"

"A brutal way of putting it, my dear fellow."

"A true way," said the sheriff.

But he was thinking, and Waters waited.

When he spoke, his voice was soft enough to blend with the sheriff's thoughts without actually interrupting them.

"You're not a youngster any more, sheriff, and if you lose out here, your reputation is gone for good. You'll not have the time to rebuild it. Here is a chance for you not only to stop the evil rumors, but to fortify your past record with a new bit of work that will make people talk of you. They don't really care how you do it. They won't split hairs about method. They want Hollis put out of the way. I say, cache yourself away. Let Hollis come to meet Larrimer in a private room. You can arrange it with Larrimer yourself later on. You shoot from concealment the moment Hollis shows his face. It can be said that Larrimer did the shooting, and beat Hollis to the draw. The glory of it will bribe Larrimer."

The sheriff shook his head. Waters leaned forward.

"My friend," he said. "I represent in this matter a wealthy man to whom the removal of Terry Hollis will be worth money. Five thousand dollars cash, sheriff!"

The sheriff moistened his lips and his eyes grew wild. He had lived long and worked hard and saved little. Yet he shook his head.

"Ten thousand dollars," whispered Waters. "Cash!"

The sheriff groaned, rose, paced the room, and then slumped into a chair.

"Tell Bud Larrimer I want to see him," he said. The following letter, which was received at the house of Joe Pollard, was indeed a gem of English:

MR. TERRY BLACK JACK:

Sir, I got this to say. Since you done my brother dirt I bin looking for a chans to get even and I ain't seen any chanses coming my way so Ime going to make one which I mean that Ile be waiting for you in town today and if you dont come Ile let the boys know that you

aint only an ornery mean skunt but your a yaller
hearted dog also which I beg to remain

Yours very truly,
Bud Larrimer.

Terry Hollis read the letter and tossed it with laughter to
Phil Marvin, who sat cross-legged on the floor mending a
saddle, and Phil and the rest of the boys shook their heads
over it.

"What I can't make out," said Joe Pollard, voicing the
sentiments of the rest, "is how Bud Larrimer, that's as slow
as a plow horse with a gun, could ever find the guts to challenge Terry Hollis to a fair fight."

Kate Pollard rose anxiously with a suggestion. Today or
tomorrow at the latest she expected the arrival of Elizabeth
Cornish, and so far it had been easy to keep Terry at the
house. The gang was gorged with the loot of the Lewison
robbery, and Terry's appetite for excitement had been
cloyed by that event also. This strange challenge from the
older Larrimer was the fly in the ointment.

"It ain't hard to tell why he sent that challenge," she declared. "He has some sneaking plan up his sleeve, Dad. You
know Bud Larrimer. He hasn't the nerve to fight a boy.
How'll he ever manage to stand up to Terry unless he's got
hidden backing?"

She herself did not know how accurately she was hitting
off the situation; but she was drawing it as black as possible
to hold Terry from accepting the challenge. It was her father
who doubted her suggestion.

"It sounds queer," he said, "but the gents of these parts
don't make no ambushes while McGuire is around. He's a
clean shooter, is McGuire, and he don't stand for no shady
work with guns."

Again Kate went to the attack.

"But the sheriff would do anything to get Terry. You know
that. And maybe he isn't so particular about how it's done.
Dad, don't you let Terry make a step toward town! I *know*
something would happen! And even if they didn't ambush
him, he would be outlawed even if he won the fight. No matter how fair he may fight, they won't stand for two killings
in so short a time. You know that, Dad. They'd have a mob
out here to lynch him!"

"You're right, Kate," nodded her father. "Terry, you better stay put."

But Terry Hollis had risen and stretched himself to the full length of his height, and extended his long arms sleepily. Every muscle played smoothly up his arms and along his shoulders. He was fit for action from the top of his head to the soles of his feet.

"Partners," he announced gently, "no matter what Bud Larrimer has on his mind, I've got to go in and meet him. Maybe I can convince him without gun talk. I hope so. But it will have to be on the terms he wants. I'll saddle up and lope into town."

He started for the door. The other members of the Pollard gang looked at one another and shrugged their shoulders. Plainly the whole affair was a bad mess. If Terry shot Larrimer, he would certainly be followed by a lynching mob, because no self-respecting Western town could allow two members of its community to be dropped in quick succession by one man of an otherwise questionable past. No matter how fair the gunplay, just as Kate had said, the mob would rise. But on the other hand, how could Terry refuse to respond to such an invitation without compromising his reputation as a man without fear?

There was nothing to do but fight.

But Kate ran to her father. "Dad," she cried, "you got to stop him!"

He looked into her drawn face in astonishment.

"Look here, honey," he advised rather sternly. "Man-talk is man-talk, and man-ways are man-ways, and a girl like you can't understand. You keep out of this mess. It's bad enough without having your hand added."

She saw there was nothing to be gained in this direction. She turned to the rest of the men; they watched her with blank faces. Not a man there but would have done much for the sake of a single smile. But how could they help?

Desperately she ran to the door, jerked it open, and followed Terry to the stable. He had swung the saddle from its peg and slipped it over the back of El Sangre, and the great stallion turned to watch this perennially interesting operation.

"Terry," she said, "I want ten words with you."

"I know what you want to say," he answered gently. "You want to make me stay away from town today. To tell you the truth, Kate, I hate to go in. I hate it like the devil. But what can I do? I have no grudge against Larrimer. But if he wants to talk about his brother's death, why—good Lord, Kate, I have to go in and listen, don't I? I can't dodge that responsibility!"

"It's a trick, Terry. I swear it's a trick. I can feel it!"

She dropped her hand nervously on the heavy revolver which she wore strapped at her hip, and fingered the gold chasing. Without her gun, ever since early girlhood, she had felt that her toilet was not complete.

"It may be," he nodded thoughtfully. "And I appreciate the advice, Kate—but what would you have me do?"

"Terry," she said eagerly, "you know what this means. You've killed once. If you go into town today, it means either that you kill or get killed. And one thing is about as bad as the other."

Again he nodded. She was surprised that he would admit so much, but there were parts of his nature which, plainly, she had not yet reached to.

"What differences does it make, Kate?" His voice fell into a profound gloom. "What difference? I can't change myself. I'm what I am. It's in the blood. I was born to this. I can't help it. I know that I'll lose in the end. But while I live I'll be happy. A little while!"

She choked. But the sight of his drawing the cinches, the imminence of his departure, cleared her mind again.

"Give me two minutes," she begged.

"Not one," he answered. "Kate, you only make us both unhappy. Do you suppose I wouldn't change if I could?"

He came to her and took her hands.

"Honey, there are a thousand things I'd like to say to you, but being what I am, I have no right to say them to you— never, or to any other woman! I'm born to be what I am. I tell you, Kate, the woman who raised me, who was a mother to me, saw what I was going to be—and turned me out like a dog! And I don't blame her. She was right!"

She grasped at the straw of hope.

"Terry, that woman has changed her mind. You hear? She's lived heartbroken since she turned you out. And now she's coming for you to—to beg you to come back to her. Terry, that's how much she's given up hope in you!"

But he drew back, his face growing dark.

"You've been to see her, Kate? That's where you went when you were away those four days?"

She dared not answer. He was trembling with hurt pride and rage.

"You went to her—she thought I sent you—that I've grown ashamed of my own father, and that I want to beg her to take me back? Is that what she thinks?"

He struck his hand across his forehead and groaned.

"God! I'd rather die than have her think it for a minute. Kate, how could you do it? I'd have trusted you always to do the right thing and the proud thing—and here you've shamed me!"

He turned to the horse, and El Sangre stepped out of the stall and into a shaft of sunlight that burned on him like blood-red fire. And beside him young Terry Hollis, straight as a pine, and as strong—a glorious figure. It broke her heart to see him, knowing what was coming.

"Terry, if you ride down yonder, you're going to a dog's death! I swear you are, Terry!"

She stretched out her arms to him; but he turned to her with his hand on the pommel, and his face was like iron.

"I've made my choice. Will you stand aside, Kate?"

"You're set on going? Nothing will change you? But I tell you, *I'm* going to change you! I'm only a girl. And I can't stop you with a girl's weapons. I'll do it with a man's. Terry, take the saddle off that horse! And promise me you'll stay here till Elizabeth Cornish comes!"

"Elizabeth Cornish?" He laughed bitterly. "When she comes, I'll be a hundred miles away, and bound father off. That's final."

"You're wrong," she cried hysterically. "You're going to stay here. You may throw away your share in yourself. But *I* have a share that I won't throw away. Terry, for the last time!"

He shook his head.

She caught her breath with a sob. Someone was coming from the outside. She heard her father's deep-throated laughter. Whatever was done, she must do it quickly. And he must be stopped!

The hand on the gun butt jerked up—the long gun flashed in her hand.

"Kate!" cried Terry. "Good God, are you mad?"

"Yes," she sobbed. "Mad! Will you stay?"

"What infernal nonsense—"

The gun boomed hollowly in the narrow passage between mow and wall. El Sangre reared, a red flash in the sunlight, and landed far away in the shadow, trembling. But Terry Hollis had spun halfway around, swung by the heavy, tearing impact of the big slug, and then sank to the floor, where he sat clasping his torn thigh with both hands, his shoulder and head sagging against the wall.

Joe Pollard, rushing in with an outcry, found the gun lying sparkling in the sunshine, and his daughter, hysterical and weeping, holding the wounded man in her arms.

"What—in the name of—" he roared.

"Accident, Joe," gasped Terry. "Fooling with Kate's gun and trying a spin with it. It went off—drilled me clean through the leg!"

That night, very late, in Joe Pollard's house, Terry Hollis lay on the bed with a dim light reaching to him from the hooded lamp in the corner of the room. His arms were stretched out on each side and one hand held that of Kate, warm, soft, young, clasping his fingers feverishly and happily. And on the other side was the firm, cool pressure of the hand of Aunt Elizabeth.

His mind was in a haze. Vaguely he perceived the gleam of tears on the face of Elizabeth. And he had heard her say: "All the time I didn't know, Terry. I thought I was ashamed of the blood in you. But this girl opened my eyes. She told me the truth. The reason I took you in was because I loved that wild, fierce, gentle, terrible father of yours. If you have done a little of what he did, what does it matter? Nothing to me! Oh, Terry, nothing in the world to me! Except that Kate brought me to my senses in time—bless her —and now I have you back, dear boy!"

He remembered smiling faintly and happily at that. And he said before he slept: "It's a bit queer, isn't it, even two wise women can't show a man that he's a fool? It takes a bullet to turn the trick!"

But when he went to sleep, his head turned a little from Elizabeth toward Kate.

And the women raised their heads and looked at one another with filmy eyes. They both understood what that feeble gesture meant. It told much of the fine heart of Elizabeth—